The Merriman Chronicles

Book Eight

The Threat in the Atlantic

Copyright Information

The Merriman Chronicles - Book 8

The Threat in the Atlantic

Copyright © 2024 by Robin Burnage

With the exception of certain well known historical figures, the characters in this book have no relation or resemblance to any person living or dead.

All rights reserved. This book and all "The Merriman Chronicles" are works of fiction. No part of this book may be reproduced or used in any manner without written permission of the copyright owner except for the use of quotations in a book review.

First edition May 2024

Book cover painting by Colin M Baxter

Diagram of HMS Thunder by Colin M Baxter

ISBN: 9798875654435 (paperback)
ISBN: 9798323676408 (hardcover)

www.merriman-chronicles.com

Previous books in the series by Roger Burnage

James Abel Merriman (1768 – 1843)

A Certain Threat

The Threat in the West Indies

Merriman and the French Invasion

The Threat in the East

The Threat in the Baltic

The Threat in the Americas

The Threat in the Adriatic

Edward James Merriman (1853 - 1928)

The Fateful Voyage

Author's Note

This book helps me fulfil my late father's wishes - that I continue writing the series that sadly, he never got to finish.

The Merriman Chronicles follows members of the Merriman Family from the late 18th century through to the early 20th century. This particular novel picks up the story of Captain Sir James Abel Merriman after his returns to England from his mission in the Mediterranean (Book 7 – The Threat In The Adriatic).

This book is dedicated to my Dad, Roger Burnage.

I hope I do him proud.

Robin Burnage

Prologue

Ambush off the African Coast

The East Indiaman *Rochester* left Madras on the 5th of December 1810, laden with pepper, coffee, indigo and saltpetre. Due to favourable winds and a lack of incident, she rounded the Cape of Good Hope on the last day of January. Her captain, a twenty-year veteran by the name of Nibbs, had heard rumours of a French warship named the *Hercule* operating near the cape. Some were calling the captain of this ship the 'lone wolf'. Apparently, several Indiamen had already been taken off the isolated western coast and two frigates of the Royal Navy had been defeated.

Nibbs was therefore relieved when, on February the 3rd, the *Rochester* passed the mouth of the Orange River, some four hundred miles north of the cape. He had heard in the taverns of Madras port that the Frenchman had not attacked any vessels north of that point. Though his vessel was now skirting a nameless, desolate coast, he invited his senior officers to his cabin that night. Songs were sung, the cook roasted the last of the chickens and four bottles of port were consumed.

It was therefore with a slightly aching head that Captain Nibbs came on deck the following morning. The wind was a fifteen-knot southerly and the *Rochester*'s sails were full. She was relatively small for an Indiaman: only a hundred and forty feet long and thirty at the beam. Nodding to the bosun, who was viciously admonishing a sailor, Nibbs made his way to the stern, where he met his second in command, Halley – an American who'd been with him for six years.

'Morning, David. How do we fare?'

'Morning, sir. Well enough. I'll admit I was glad to see the dawn.'

'I'm sure. Now that we're past the Orange, we can allow some lights at night.'

'Very good, sir. We have some company to the south.'

Alarmed, Nibbs turned and looked out over the stern. He saw two vessels close together, at least five miles behind them, slightly closer to the shore.

'Must have caught up with us during the night,' added Halley. Lookout reports nothing to concern us. Merchant ships both.'

'Strength in numbers,' said Nibbs, relieved. 'I should have liked to do the same but there are not many of our size or speed. They were not spotted last evening?'

'No, sir.'

'Could they have come out of the river?'

'It's possible, sir.'

'I daresay they shall haul us in by day's end,' added Nibbs.

'As you always say, sir, it is only *our* progress that we must concern ourselves with.'

'Quite so.'

As well as her cargo, the *Rochester* was carrying sixteen passengers. The most vocal of them was a Dutch merchant named van der Linde who was travelling with his wife and four children. In the early weeks of the voyage, the children had been very ill but they now seemed to have settled down. A father of three himself, Nibbs didn't like to see the youngsters stuck down in their cabin of canvas walls and often invited them on deck.

Later that afternoon, while they looked out at the desolate coast with their mother, van der Linde approached Nibbs. The Dutchman did like to complain but his English was excellent.

'It is pleasant to have some other ships in sight, captain.'

The two merchant vessels were now only three miles behind them.

'It is, Mr. Van der Linde. We cannot yet see their colours but I hope at least one might be a British vessel. I may signal them.'

The Dutchman removed his sunhat and wiped his brow. 'For intelligence on this French wolf?'a

'Perhaps. Though I think we're out of danger in that regard. How are the children?'

'As well as can be, thank you. Three of the four have never set foot in Holland so they are excited to see their homeland. I worry about young Hendrik. A lover of the Arabian Nights. He suffers from an excess of imagination. Just now, for example, he told us that he could see three ships behind us, not two.'

Nibbs hadn't really been listening to the man but that caught his attention. There were after all no keener eyes than young eyes. He was already moving when the lookout gave a cry from above. The message was instantly passed on by the bosun:

'Another ship, captain! Hiding behind the others!'

Once at the stern with his officers, Nibbs soon realised that the third vessel was no longer trying to hide itself. The two merchantmen had reduced sail while the third vessel was shaking out reefs and setting upper topsails.

'My apologies, captain,' said Webb, the officer on duty, his face growing paler by the moment. 'I told the lookouts to keep an eye offshore.'

'Crafty bastard,' hissed the bosun. 'A ship of the line. We're done for.'

'Staying behind them all day?' added Webb, incredulous. 'I don't know how they managed it.'

'Fine seamanship,' murmured the captain. '*Very* fine seamanship.'

The dark bulk of what they all now assumed to be the *Hercule* soon pulled clear of the merchantmen. Before long, three tricolours were flying on the vessels to their south and

Nibbs knew his fate was sealed. Even so, he ordered the passengers below and that every scrap of sail be raised. Halley joined him at the stern with his spyglass. Around them, grim-faced sailors loudly cursed their luck. Nibbs didn't have the energy to censor them.

'One of the Bucentaure class,' observed Halley. 'Eighty guns. Almost a hundred and eighty feet at the keel. Seven hundred crew.'

When she was within a mile, the giant warship began firing her bow chasers. Laying one shot to larboard and the next to starboard, the French left their victims in no doubt about the accuracy of their gunnery. Nibbs had several cannons and two dozen muskets below (and enough men willing to shoot them) but there was no sense in resisting; certainly not with passengers aboard.

Halley caught his eye and shook his head. 'We were unfortunate, captain.'

'I honestly thought we were clear.'

Though there had been some unpleasant encounters with pirates over the years, Nibbs had always been careful and to be taken as a prize this late in his naval career was a bitter blow. No one aboard could truly know when – and if – they would return home.

'There's naught we can do now. Give the order: heave to and strike the colours.'

Nibbs had seldom felt so downhearted as when he saw the *Rochester*'s red ensign lowered. He could hear women crying below and men praying.

He sent a boy down for his best hat and coat, donning them as the *Hercule* pulled alongside. She was indeed an imposing vessel, powerful yet elegant and boasting two decks packed with heavy guns. Ranks of marines stood ahead of the sailors at the rail, muskets ready.

On the quarterdeck, a cabal of officers looked on, so relaxed that they might have been at a horse race. The captain was easily identified by his red trousers and blue coat, his bicorn hat edged by gold. He was immaculately turned out, a lean man with strong cheekbones and deep-set eyes that now perused the Indiaman as predator observed prey.

Nibbs approached the rail. He removed his hat and nodded politely. 'The lone wolf, I presume?'

It was not the captain who answered but a younger officer who spoke good English. 'May I introduce Captain Patrice Jourdan. And you, sir?'

'Captain Michael Nibbs.' He gestured towards his ship. 'And so you have another prize.'

The officer gestured to the two other merchant vessels. 'As you can see, we have taken three in less than a week. You are as wise as they were in not resisting.'

'Does the captain not speak for himself?'

'The captain does not speak the tongue of his sworn enemy. Even if you spoke French, I doubt he would be interested in conversing with you.'

'The Navy will not stand for this,' said Nibbs, angry at the affront. 'Ships will be sent!'

This caused some chuckling among the Frenchmen which became open laughter when Captain Jourdan uttered a line and walked away.

'What did he say?' demanded Nibbs.

'Let them come,' explained the officer, eyes gleaming. 'Let them come.'

Chapter One

A Ride Along the River

Captain Sir James Abel Merriman looked out at the leaden sky and the choppy water. On the near side of the river, a small fishing smack was coming in with the tide, lines tight, sails full, crew huddled low. Though the River Dee was not a particularly pleasant place to be in early March, Merriman rather wished he was still aboard *Thunder*, supervising the winter refit. Though his first lieutenant, Shrigley, was a man to be trusted, Merriman – as ever – could not help feeling that he was somehow missing out on something.

'I know what you're thinking,' said Helen, riding alongside him with one hand holding the hood of her cape.

Eyes narrowed against the wind, she nodded towards the water. 'You'd like to be out there, wouldn't you James? Even if it was with those poor fishermen in their little boat. You can't help yourself.'

Merriman offered his long-suffering wife a ready grin. 'I can't deny I am missing the sea, my love. Even though it has been a lovely few months with you and the children.'

'Months? It's been a mere five weeks. We still haven't caught up with Reverend Willis or the Blackburn. Oh, did you write that letter to the relatives of Mr. Clarke?'

'I did.' Said Merriman.

It had not been an easy task to locate the family of the resourceful spy who had given his life during Merriman's last mission in the Adriatic. But he had eventually done so, also assuring them that the Navy and the Treasury would offer some monetary recompense.

'And what of the Lord Stevenage fund?'

Merriman's horse started at the screech of a gull. He patted the animal's neck and it thankfully calmed down.

'Well, that will not be resolved quickly.'

Lord Stevenage, Merriman's late mentor and friend, had left him a considerable inheritance. Merriman's intention was to donate the majority of the money to the Marine Society, which supported young sailors. However, a distant cousin was now challenging the will, which had resulted in an extended legal wrangle.

Noting a nearby bed of reeds, he was reminded of a more immediate concern. 'What worries me is this issue of the wheat, Helen. Planting season will be here soon and our estate must do better.'

She sighed. 'James, as the old hands have told us, some years yields are better than others – or worse. There are limits to what we can do.'

'Of course. But the country is short enough of crops as it is. It's our responsibility to make sure this year is better than last.'

'I know.'

Just then, Helen's horse stumbled on the muddy path, threatening to toss her into a clump of gorse. Fortunately, she was a very able horsewomen and kept her balance – and dignity.

'Dear oh dear,' was the extent of her complaint. 'I am looking forward to spring already. The state of this path!'

'Well done,' said Merriman, proud of her skill. 'It reminds me of another unpleasant route – from London to Chester. Can it really be eighteen years?'

Helen's dark eyes smiled and she gave a little blush. 'It feels twice as long.'

'Because the children are growing up so quickly?'

'No.'

'Because I have a few grey hairs appearing?'

'No.'

They rode on in silence for a time, the horses' breath escaping as puffs of white mist in the chill air.

'Tell me, Helen.'

She at last answered him, her expression grave. 'Because of all the many times I have ridden here or along another such path alone. Or sat in front of a fire late at night. Or laid in bed. Always wondering where you are, what you are doing.'

'Most of the time I'll be reading a chart or eating bad food or listening to the oaths of a dozen jack tars.'

'Don't make light of it, James.'

'I'm not. I know you suffer twice as much as I do.' He reached across and took her gloved hand.

'Don't go get too amorous,' she replied. 'We have company.'

Merriman looked along the river path and saw another rider approaching. This man came to a halt as they neared him and removed his hat, nodding respectfully.

'Good day to you, Captain Merriman, and to you Mrs. Merriman.'

'Good day, Lieutenant Pike,' answered Helen. 'James, this is the former officer I told you about – we occasionally encounter each other out here by the river. I daresay you are off to call on Miss Sumner, Lieutenant?'

Pike grinned nervously as he brushed rainwater from his brow. 'Quite so, Mrs. Merriman.'

He was a slender man with a narrow face and a livid scar across one cheek. Merriman saw the wooden leg poking out beneath his long coat and recalled that he had left the service due to his injuries.

'An honour to meet you at last, captain,' added Pike. 'When your good lady wife and I last spoke, you were unleashing hell upon the French in the Balkans.'

'That seems a long time ago now,' replied Merriman honestly.

'My congratulations to you on your campaign,' continued the lieutenant, 'and how fares the *Thunder*?'

'Undergoing a refit at Portsmouth. I shall return there presently for sea trials.'

'I'll admit I am rather jealous,' said Pike. 'I am trying to adapt to the farming life but I find I'm not really suited to it – and I fear my father agrees.'

'I try myself but it does not come naturally. Wouldn't you agree, Helen?'

'I shall not comment.'

'Remarkable news regarding the king,' said Pike. 'Young George will rule as regent, so they say.'

Merriman was rather tired of discussing the subject. He felt only sympathy for the monarch who had ruled for his entire life, a man now brought low by what most referred to as mania.

'I am sure the Prince of Wales will rise to the occasion,' he said, feeling that he owed the regent his loyalty, despite his reputation for womanising and overspending.

'I agree, sir,' offered Pike.

'His majesty has suffered many blows,' said Helen. 'The loss of his daughter perhaps the worst of them. They say she was his favourite.'

The ensuing silence was broken by Pike: 'Did you read the latest on affairs in the Indian Ocean? Quite the victory for Commodore Rowley and Vice-Admiral Bertie.'

'Indeed, I did,' replied Merriman. 'There was talk of little else in Portsmouth before Christmas. Seventy vessels in the fleet that retook Mauritius, apparently.'

'No wonder the French didn't even attempt to resist. And naming it Isle de France – why the arrogance of Bonaparte never ceases to amaze!'

Helen said, 'When one has conquered much of Europe, an element of arrogance must be inevitable. I have long given up praying for Bonaparte's defeat. His desire for conflict and conquest seems never ending. Do you know,

Lieutenant Pike, we have been at war with France for almost as long as James and I have been married?'

'Somehow I have survived both war *and* matrimony,' ventured Merriman, drawing a chuckle from Pike and a fierce look from Helen.

As a cold gust of wind blew in off the Dee, Helen guided her horse around Lieutenant Pike's mount. 'It is a little too cold to tarry. Shall we head on, James?'

'Of course,' he said. 'Pleased to make your acquaintance, Pike.'

'Likewise, captain.'

'Ride swiftly, advised Helen. 'You should not keep Miss Sumner waiting.'

Thankfully, the wind eased off, and both Merriman and Helen were feeling rather warmer by the time they returned to Burton Manor. Located northwest of Chester, the house had originally been purchased by Merriman's father, funded by a combination of inheritance and prize money accrued as master of a frigate. Husband and wife handed their horses over to Hull, the groom, and walked briskly to the duck pond. It had been frozen for many weeks and the children were taking advantage of the thaw.

Eleven-year-old Robert was on the pontoon, assembling a fleet of wooden craft, while his sister, ten-year-old Mary-Anne looked on.

'That was a long ride!' declared the girl as her parents approached.

'Your father must build himself up,' replied Helen.

Merriman had sustained both a head wound and a broken arm during the Adriatic operation. It was only recently that the persistent headaches had receded, much to his relief.

'He might be out on the high seas again before long!' added Robert.

'Quite so,' replied Helen quietly.

Mary-Anne took her father's hand and beamed up at him. 'But not yet, Papa. You've not been back long.'

'Unfortunately, it's not my decision, poppet.'

Mary-Anne wrinkled her nose. 'Can you smell that? The apple pie is almost done! I'm off to the kitchen.'

'Apple pie, eh?' said Merriman. 'Cook's speciality. I'm looking forward to that.'

Though captains invariably ate better than their crew, Merriman had spent many a month living on navy rations and freshly-cooked food was always welcome.

'Come, Mama,' said Mary-Anne. 'Let's make sure we get the first piece.'

'We better wait until after dinner,' instructed Helen. 'But we shall go inside. It is cold if one is not moving.'

Mary-Anne didn't protest and they strode towards the house, arm in arm.

Merriman sat down on the pontoon, watching as Robert put the last of his vessels into the water. 'Ah. *Conflict* takes to the seas.'

'I wish I could make sails and rigging,' said Robert. 'Then she would really look like your first command.'

'Not an easy job.'

'Next time you come home, bring *Thunder*'s ropemaker with you, Papa. He could do it, I'm sure.'

'I reckon he could at that,' said Merriman.

Robert's fleet of four wooden vessels were connected by string. He held the end as they bobbed in the icy water: a convoy in miniature. The young man brushed away the fringe of the thick, black hair that marked him unmistakeably as Merriman's son. He then turned to his father.

'Papa, would you be able to collect me from school tomorrow?'

'That rather depends on my meetings here with the staff but I shall try.'

'Please do. Harry Salter simply will not believe that you met Admiral Lord Nelson. Will you put him straight?'

'Well, I wouldn't want to appear a braggart.'

'Why Salter is the biggest braggart of them all! His father is a captain of grenadiers and all we ever hear are tales of his adventures. Salter says he's killed more than a dozen Frenchies in his time.'

'An army man, eh? In that case, I shall see what I can do.'

'Papa, is it true that King George cried when he heard of Nelson's death?'

'So they say. And he was not the only man who cried at that news, Robert, I will tell you that.'

Once back inside the house, Merriman found his faithful ball of rags, which he used to exercise and strengthen his arm. It was Helen's father who had given it to him all those years ago, after operating on him. The old wound was now one of many and still gave him trouble in cold weather. Squeezing the ball, Merriman paced across the drawing room, mulling over his earlier conversation with Helen. Though they'd been interrupted, she had let her guard slip a little more than usual.

He had always known of the torment she endured while he was away – and she was hardly alone in that – but there had been so many, many years of it. Merriman wondered if the time was nearing when he might request a post on land, something in Portsmouth or London perhaps. Then he shivered at the prospect of being stuck behind a desk in some stuffy corner, telling old stories of war.

As he paused by a window and looked out at the bare orchard, his elderly steward – a man named Hopkins – entered the drawing room. In his bony hand was a letter, which he offered to Merriman.

'For you, sir. Came while you were out riding. I thought it best to keep it from Mrs. Merriman's eyes: I know how you don't like to worry her.'

'Very good, Hopkins,' said Merriman as he noted the postmark. 'Ah, yes – I see your point. From the Admiralty.'

Merriman had Hopkins fetch Helen from the kitchen. She was halfway through telling him that dinner was imminent when she saw the letter in his hand. To her credit, she hid her disappointment well.

'It had to come, I suppose.'

'The sea lanes are opening. The admirals will be issuing their orders.'

'What is the operation?'

'No detail. But Admiral Goodwin expects me in London. I don't suppose there will be time for me to return.' He took his wife's hands in his own. 'You could perhaps bring the children down to Portsmouth.'

'No, no. That would be too much for them,' said Helen. 'And for me.'

She placed her hand on his brow. 'The headaches. You were being truthful, James?'

'They've not troubled me for more than a week, my love. I feel fit as a fiddle.'

In fact, Merriman felt sluggish and dull, but this – he knew – was a result of late mornings and comfortable living. Once he was aboard *Thunder*, he'd begin to feel like himself again.

'And so, we lose you once more,' said Helen, now gazing at the fire.

'It will not always be like this,' he assured her. 'I know I cannot go on for ever.'

'It is my burden to bear,' said Helen. 'I would not deny you this. Nor would I deny England one of its best captains. You will write before you leave.'

This was not a question but an instruction.

'Of course.'

'Come then, James. Roast chicken and roast pork await. Not to mention the apple pie.'

Chapter Two

To London and Portsmouth

The next few days were dry, meaning a swift trip from Chester to London. Sleepy from the journey, Merriman instructed his driver to drop him several streets from the Admiralty, eager to clear his head. He told the man to continue to his inn with his bags and set off through Westminster wearing his dress coat, hat tucked under his arm.

Though he only walked a quarter-mile or so, he encountered pleading beggars, bellowing sergeants and a particularly vocal drayman trying to deliver kegs to a busy hostelry. Taking care to keep his newly-polished shoes clear of horse muck, Merriman exchanged greetings with a pair of young lieutenants and at last entered the cobbled courtyard of the Admiralty. He paused and looked up at the four large columns that marked the entrance. As ever, he was struck by memories of previous visits: briefings, promotions and many a conversation with Lord Stevenage and other men of great rank and influence.

He also thought of Sir Laurence Grahame, who he'd first encountered many years ago. Grahame had then been a field agent for the Treasury but had since risen to the top of that organization. Always busy with some scheme or intrigue, Merriman had heard nothing from him since receiving a letter after the Balkan operation.

Two young messenger boys shot past as he negotiated the steps and announced himself to the clerk on duty. He was presently led along the central corridor, past the famous Board Room, where the Lords Commissioners of the Admiralty met. Today devoid of admirals, it was occupied only by cleaning women. Merriman noted two of its most distinctive features: the fireplace which carried the arms of Charles II and the tall grandfather clock made by Langley Bradley, who'd also built the great clock of St. Paul's cathedral.

Merriman was almost relieved not to find himself in the imposing Board Room but he still felt a heady excitement as he was ushered into a dark-panelled office where Admiral Sir Henry Goodwin sat. Flanking him were his familiar white-haired servant and a young lieutenant with a tanned face and a sharp look in his eye.

'Ah, Merriman – good to see you.' Sir Henry stood and leaned across his desk.

'Sir Henry, likewise,' said Merriman as they shook hands.

'Off you go then, Kerr,' instructed the admiral, without looking at his servant. 'Fetch that new brandy.'

With a nod, Kerr departed.

'Please, sit,' said Sir Henry, a red-faced fellow whose broad face matched his portly frame. He was also one of the increasingly small minority who still wore a powdered wig.

'Well and rested, Merriman?'

'Indeed, sir.'

'And Harriet?'

Sir Henry had the reputation of a tough, intelligent officer. However, he was now well over seventy and had never been good with names.

'She's very well, sir.'

'Ah, damned rude of me.' Sir Henry turned and gestured to the young officer. 'Newcombe, Merriman; Merriman, Newcombe.'

The pair shook hands.

'Good day, Sir James.'

'Good day, Newcombe.'

'Sir Henry, might I enquire about Sir Laurence?'

'You may well enquire but I can offer no enlightenment. Concerned with affairs on the Iberian peninsula when last heard of.'

'Ah. Thank you, sir.'

Having spent recent weeks at home, Merriman was rather out of touch with current affairs. However, he had spoken to some fellow naval officers in Chester before setting off for London. There was talk of operations in the Adriatic, where two notable commanders – Captain William Hoste (who Merriman had fought alongside) and the French Captain Bernard Dubourdieu – were doing battle, as well as ongoing campaigns in the Indian Ocean and closer to home. As it turned out, Sir Henry had another matter on his mind.

'Now, I know I don't have to explain to you the importance of securing timber supplies. What do they say about how many are needed for a ship of the line?'

'Two or three thousand mature trees, I believe, Sir Henry.'

'Exactly. Our native supplies were used up decades ago and I'm ashamed to admit that, on occasion, we've had yards using untreated, uncured wood. Desperate. Ah, the brandy is here. Fine stuff this, Merriman.'

Sir Henry waited until Kerr had poured each of them a glass then took a long swig.

'Where was I? Yes – timber. In fact, we've done well to secure a reliable supply from Canada of late but we also rely on our imports of teak from India. Even more crucial is saltpetre which we need for gunpowder. Now, while our efforts in the Indian Ocean have largely seen off the French, another problem has arisen. Lieutenant Newcombe here has just returned from Cape Colony.'

Newcombe leaned forward in his chair. 'Sir James, have you heard of a French captain named Patrice Jourdan?'

'I believe I recall the name, though I couldn't tell you his ship.'

'His previous command was a 74 named *Tigre*. He fought at the Nile and the Basque Roads but it is in recent months that his name has become known – and feared – by every Indiaman captain between here and Calcutta. His ship, the *Hercule*, has taken no less than fourteen ships since last spring. It is an 80, one of the Bucentaure class. She has been located and engaged only once by our vessels and saw off a pair of frigates. One ship was so badly damaged that she barely made it back to port.'

Merriman listened carefully, taking in every detail as Newcombe continued:

'It seems that Jourdan is actually targeting vessels carrying teak and saltpetre.'

'The French have spies everywhere!' interjected Sir Henry. 'Even in the Indian ports. Go on, Newcombe.'

'Once taken as prizes, he sends them north to Spain or France. We believe he is being resupplied at sea but also using one or more bases on the West African coast. He has been known to employ all manner of tactics, including working with slavers and pirates. Simply put, he has turned that stretch of coast into his personal fiefdom. The costs can already be counted in the tens of thousands of pounds.'

'I see.' This was far from the first time that Merriman had found himself embroiled in an operation related to resources; hardly a surprise in a war that already seemed to have gone on forever.

Newcombe took a modest sip of brandy before continuing: 'Needless to say, our colleagues in Leadenhall Street are growing increasingly alarmed. I believe that is how the matter originally reached the cabinet.'

Merriman was not at all surprised by that. If any institution had reason to be concerned by this French raider, it was the East India Company.

Sir Henry took another glug of brandy before weighing in once more. 'The Lords Commissioners had originally allocated a pair of 74s under captains Wynn and Osborne but they are needed for the Adriatic campaign. When I heard that you were fully recovered, I enquired regarding the *Thunder*'s refit and learned that the majority of work is done.'

'That is true, sir, but I do not yet have a full complement of men, in fact-'

'Men can be found at short notice, Merriman. Especially by a captain of your repute. You will have ample time during your trip south to whip them into shape. The Cabinet have discussed the matter and agree that we cannot wait a moment longer. The Secretary of State and the First Lord concur. This is not a task that we would entrust to anyone but you have proved yourself over many a year.'

Merriman appreciated the compliment. He was less enamoured with orders that sounded more like a flip of a coin rather than a well-considered operation. The admirals were basically gambling that he could best this French captain, even though Jourdan possessed a larger ship and an evidently well-drilled crew.

Sir Henry lifted an envelope and pushed it across the desk.

'In the best tradition of the Navy, we give you your head and leave the tactics and methods to your own good judgement. Your orders are simple – take or sink the *Hercule*, whatever the cost.'

Though he said nothing, Merriman took exception to that last phrase. It was easy for the old admiral to say, less easy to do, especially for a man who had lost countless officers and crew under his command.

'Very well, sir.'

Sir Henry nodded to Newcombe.

'There is also this,' said the lieutenant, passing Merriman a thin folder containing a few sheets of paper. 'I have assembled all the intelligence we have on Jourdan and the *Hercule*. It is limited but I hope useful.'

'Thank you, lieutenant.'

'There is something else, Merriman,' said Sir Henry, leaning across the desk. 'This is not a man motivated purely by nationalist fervour or financial gain. Apparently, he seeks vengeance.'

'Sir?'

Newcombe spoke up once more: 'Jourdan comes from a well-known military family in Lyon. He had three older brothers. Two were army officers, one a naval man. All three have fallen at British hands. It is said that he will not rest until he has defeated every foe he faces and the war is won.'

Not for the first time, Merriman left the Admiralty building in something of a daze, absorbing all he'd heard about this marauding French captain and his ship. As if that wasn't enough to deal with, he would now have to hurriedly ensure that the *Thunder* and her crew were ready for a journey of at least six thousand miles and a possible battle with the *Hercule*. Merriman had spent enough years at sea to put his eventual goal to one side for the moment: first things first.

Reluctant to waste any time at all, he hailed one of the carriages waiting outside the Admiralty. Once at his inn, he ate a passable lunch then cancelled his overnight stay and made immediately for the southern coast. Fortunately, the rain stayed away and the increasingly solid roads allowed for good progress via poste-chaise. Staying overnight in the town of Guildford, he reached Portsmouth in late afternoon. Having sent a letter to his first lieutenant before departing Chester, Merriman expected *Thunder* to be in a reasonable state. She had left the yard some two weeks earlier and was now at anchor in Portsmouth harbour, along with numerous other naval vessels.

Standing alone with his bags, waiting for the harbour master to assign him a boat, Merriman heard a familiar youthful voice.

'Captain! Captain Merriman, sir!'

He turned and saw a slight figure approaching. Midshipman Eades was hastily doing up his tunic buttons as he neared Merriman. Under his arm was a leather case.

'Ah, young Eades.'

The midshipman saluted stiffly and glanced down at his captain's bags.

'Welcome back, sir. We'd heard from Lieutenant Shrigley that you were returning. I trust your family is well?'

'All well, yes. What are you doing here, Eades? Is our boat available? I'd rather not wait any longer.'

'Yes, sir.' Eades pointed along the quay towards where several small boats were moored. 'I came ashore with the bosun. I was sent to fetch some paper and a new log-'

'Is the bosun finished ashore?'

'I don't think so, sir. There was a delay with-'

'Then we shall take the boat now, Eades. They can return for the bosun later.'

'Yes, captain.'

Eades picked up the two largest of Merriman's travelling bags and slung them over his narrow shoulders. The captain took the third and the pair set off along the quay.

'A fine day, captain, the weather has-'

'Save your breath, young man. I know how heavy those bags are – you'll need it.'

Twenty minutes later, Merriman was sitting in the boat, enjoying the salty air and the breeze on his face. Eades sat beside him while two brawny sailors hauled on the oars. Neither were familiar to Merriman and Eades had informed him that there were no less than a hundred new men aboard. The captain was relieved to hear that none had been impressed. The presence of resentful men taken by force was an added complication that he did not currently need.

The boat rounded a frigate, where the officers on deck saluted, and Merriman caught his first sight of *Thunder* in over two months. She was the largest vessel currently at anchor in the harbour and the only ship of the line. Merriman felt a surge of pride that surprised him, considering his many years at sea and the mission he'd been given.

Now laden with hundreds of tons of food, water and other supplies, the seventy-four-gun vessel lay low in the water. Merriman fancied that he could already smell the paint of the glistening horizontal black lines that separated the gun decks. The gun ports were open for ventilation but only some of the cannons could be seen. Six topmen were up on the mizzen, making adjustments to a yard.

As the boat neared the ship, the sailors began to notice and the predictable whirl of activity ensued. By the time they came alongside, several dozen men and three officers had gathered to greet the returning captain. To the shrill sound of the pipe, the captain found himself once again aboard *Thunder*.

'Welcome back, sir,' said the sailing master, Tom Henderson, as steady and knowledgeable a sailor as Merriman had encountered.

'Good day, Tom.'

Merriman nodded to a few more familiar faces but did not see his first lieutenant, Alfred Shrigley, among them. Before he could ask about him, another lieutenant stepped forward: a dashing fellow with wavy blonde hair.

'Captain Sir James, please allow me to introduce myself. Lieutenant Matthew Smythe.'

'Ah, yes.'

Knowing he was in need of at least two lieutenants, Merriman had perused most of the enquiries that inevitably arrived once a naval ship was in port. Smythe had learned of the vacancies via the well-known Steel's List: a monthly booklet listing commissioned ships, their locations, officers, pay and so on. Both Merriman and Shrigley had read Smythe's letters of recommendation and he seemed a sound choice, with five years at sea on two frigates.

The pair shook hands.

'Pleased to meet you,' said Merriman.

Smythe then introduced the other new lieutenant, who was named Essex. He had been personally recommended to Merriman and Shrigley by the first lieutenant's cousin, who had served with him in the West Indies. Essex – a short, barrel-chested man with cropped hair – seemed quite reserved but greeted Merriman politely. The fourth of his lieutenants was Jones, the violin-playing officer who had been with *Thunder* for several years.

'Tell me, where is Alfred?'

'The first lieutenant is with his wife, sir,' explained Jones. 'He plans to return as swiftly as possible and asked me to pass on his sincere apologies. An urgent matter, as I understand it.'

Merriman was intent on leaving at the earliest opportunity but could not do so until he was up to speed on the condition of his ship and his men. No one would know more than Shrigley and his absence was a blow. Having said that, the man was very conscientious and would not have left without good reason.

'I shall depend on you for the moment, then, Jones.'

Smythe stepped forward. 'Sir, we have done all within our power to prepare the ship. We understand from Mr. Shrigley that we have our orders. Might I enquire-'

'All in good time, lieutenant. Have my bags taken below. I shall begin my inspection while we still have some light.'

Before the inspection began, Merriman went down to the great cabin, where he encountered both the marine guard stationed at his door and his long-serving attendant. As Peters began unpacking his belongings, Merriman looked around the cabin, which was illuminated by the orange glow of the setting sun coming in through the windows.

Hanging on the larboard wall were his three swords. One had been presented to him by the East India Company for his exploits in the Indian Ocean more than a decade earlier. The second was his dress sword, the third the heavy cutlass he used for close action. He was pleased to see his sideboard and wine cooler (the latter a present from his wife) well-polished. He complimented Peters on the state of the cabin and his sleeping quarters.

'Honestly, sir, it's a relief to have you back. While you were away, Lieutenant Shrigley insisted on sticking me with the purser. I've spent days hauling sacks and kegs. Might I ask if you'll be dining with the officers tonight? I'll need to speak to the cook if so.'

'No, no. Tomorrow perhaps. This evening, I am concerned only by the ship. As you have been busy with the purser, you will have seen much of what's gone on. Is there anything I should know about?'

Peters had been at Merriman's side for more years than he could remember. He could generally be relied upon to be frank about such things and – unlike the officers – did not have wide responsibilities that opened him up to personal criticism.

'Well, sir, the last of the women departed yesterday.'

'Their presence does not surprise me in the least. I'm glad none are aboard now.'

'Only a few dozen, sir, and most of them wives.'

'Or at least acting the role of wife well enough,' replied Merriman.

Peters grinned at that. 'The purser has been complaining about the meat, sir. He found some cheeks and shins in the last batch but I believe there are some new deliveries coming tomorrow. There was that fuss about the copper, of course, but it turned out well enough in the end, I believe.'

Shrigley had kept Merriman apprised of this matter. While in the yard, *Thunder*'s hull had been re-covered with copper, to protect it against both salt water and worm. Due to supply difficulties, this had taken a week longer than planned.

'And the new officers? Smythe and Essex?'

'Essex keeps himself to himself but the men say he's a hard worker. Smythe seems to be doing well. An enthusiastic fellow, sir. Likes a jape. They say he's fought at least three duels and he somehow managed to chat up Admiral Naughton's daughter without getting a telling off.'

'Is that right? And the new surgeon?'

'Mister Webster? I've not seen much of him but he's said to be very particular about ventilation and excess salt and so on. I believe Mister Shrigley might consider him a bit of a nuisance.'

'As insightful as ever, Peters.'

The servant nodded. 'Daresay you'd like a cup of coffee, sir? I've got some new in fresh.'

'Very good. Bring it to me. I shall start my inspection now – catch them off guard.'

Merriman reckoned that he was more friendly and open than many a captain but he kept his expression grim and his comments to a minimum as he toured the ship. Once aware that he was on the move, the lieutenants soon caught up and trailed along in his wake. There was in fact not enough time left in the day for a thorough examination of the ship but the returning captain wanted to show his face everywhere.

He moved from the ward room to the gun room and the bread room, then forward to the after hold, the main hold and the magazine. He then headed up, from the orlop deck through the gun decks and on to the bow. Requesting a lantern, he made a show of looking in dozens of corners for excess dirt, mess or other evidence of lubberly behaviour. Knowing how conscientious his first lieutenant was, Merriman was generally satisfied by what he found.

He reserved greetings only for those he'd known many years and aimed pointed questions at not only the lieutenants but his warrant officers: in particular the bosun, the gunner, the armourer and the carpenter. When told that *Thunder* might be departing within days, all were honest enough to disclose deficiencies. The only ones that caused Merriman real concern were a dearth of timber for replacement spars and a lack of cutlasses. The gunner, Mr. Hanscombe, was above all worried about the number of new men within his crews, though he was satisfied with matters of material. There were a few shortages of personnel across every department but Merriman was reassured to find that

Jones and Essex had a comprehensive list and were working hard to achieve a full complement. Merriman was realistic about such matters; it was a rare and fortunate captain who left port with every man he needed.

With his three lieutenants and warrant officers still accompanying him, he drank his second cup of coffee on deck as the last of the sun's light left the sky. For an hour, Merriman pressed the younger men on some of the issues raised by his inspection. There were yet more questions – mostly from Smythe – about their orders but Merriman disclosed little. Instead, he then asked each man in turn something about themselves: families, current events and so on. While some – like the forward Smythe and the friendly bosun Brockle – seemed to enjoy this, others – like the guarded Essex – seemed less comfortable. Though he believed that a captain must always remain a man apart, Merriman also thought it wise to engender friendship and loyalty amongst his officers. In the ensuing weeks and months, he would depend on every last one of them.

Chapter Three

Sir Laurence Grahame visits *Thunder*

In the morning, banks of grey cloud rolled in across the Solent, the rain veiling the land and most of the other ships. Merriman donned his oilskins and spent three hours on deck, consulting mainly with Henderson, Brockle and the bosun's mates. They freely admitted that the *Thunder* lacked experienced topmen, an area where superior skill and agility were a prerequisite. The lieutenants claimed that they'd exhausted their search and so Merriman instructed that some of the more suitable idlers – men not attached to either watch – be trained for the dangerous work up the masts and in the rigging. He was relieved to learn that the ship had her full issue of sails (including a complete spare set) though they were still awaiting a delivery of heavy blocks.

That morning, Merriman had been visited by Lieutenant Cary, leader of *Thunder*'s marine contingent. Cary, a powerfully-built champion boxer, requested that his men be taken ashore for some drilling. Knowing the quality of the man from the Adriatic mission, Merriman acceded immediately. He was also pleased to hear that – despite an outbreak of fever – Cary had under him almost a full complement of one hundred and ten marines. While dressing, Merriman had watched the first group of red-clad soldiers being rowed ashore. He took great comfort from having the capable Cary and the marine detachment at his disposal.

Having spent the morning on deck, Merriman headed below to inspect the guns, accompanied by the gunner, the armourer and the three lieutenants. All seemed nervous about the prospect of thorough drills but that was hardly a surprise given the length of time since *Thunder*'s long guns had been fired in anger. Again, they were awaiting material – in this case a ton of powder – but Merriman was pleased to see many eager fellows about the gun decks. He loitered with some old hands for a half-hour and heard of numerous births, marriages and deaths.

He was on his way back to his cabin when the gunner asked for his help in obtaining some *langridge*; a type of canister shot containing bolts, nails and any other type of scrap metal. It was known to be very effective at short range against personnel and Mr. Hanscombe thought it wise to have such an alternative available. Though he had not yet said a word to a soul aboard about the *Hercule*, Merriman agreed. The gunner asked for a note for the quartermaster in charge at the Portsmouth magazine. Mr. Hanscombe also informed the captain that, regretfully, there was currently a general shortage of bar and chain shot, which was particularly effective against enemy spars and rigging.

Merriman was in the middle of composing the note when there was a knock on his door. As Peters wasn't in evidence, he answered it himself and was soon face to face with a slender young man in civilian dress. Despite his youthful features, he was losing his hair, which was auburn in colour and very fine.

'Captain Merriman, sir, very pleased to make your acquaintance.'

Given his Welsh lilt and unmilitary bearing, Merriman was in no doubt that he was in the presence of his new surgeon.

'Mister Webster, is it?'

'Yes, indeed, captain. John Rhys Webster at your service.'

The surgeon held some bound papers in his hand which he now proffered to his superior. 'My letters.'

'Ah, yes. We must see that everything is in order in that regard. Do come in, Webster.'

Merriman retreated to his desk and sat down. 'If you'll allow me to just complete this note, I'll be with you. Do sit. I'm afraid my attendant has disappeared, otherwise I would offer you some coffee.'

'Oh, no coffee for me, captain – very bad for the nerves.'

'Not for mine.'

As he finished the note, Merriman was conscious of the surgeon examining his surroundings.

'Now I understand why it is called the *great* cabin.'

'And how is your accommodation, Mr. Webster? Have you spent much time at sea?'

'No, sir. Not much at all.'

'Might I ask then why you have joined the fleet?'

'I would very much like to see something of the world, sir. And I also wish to see the ideas of a physician I greatly admire put into action.'

Merriman put his pen and the completed note to one side.

'And who might that be?'

'Doctor William Turnbull, Fellow of the Medical Societies or London and Edinburgh. He wrote a volume entitled-'

'*The Naval Surgeon.*'

'You know it, captain?'

'I can't say I've read but I've heard of it. I gather it contains a list of ailments common to naval vessels and how best to treat them.'

'Amongst other things, sir. I have a copy with me and was privileged enough to hear Doctor Turnbull introduce it at Surgeon's Hall.'

Hearing Peters whistling outside the cabin, Merriman summoned him instantly and passed him the note. 'Have a boy take this to the magazine. I shall take some coffee and Doctor Webster will have…'

'Is there any fresh milk?'

Peters seemed rather taken aback by this request but retreated at speed and could soon be heard snapping at the boys, two of whom were currently working with the captain's clerk.

Merriman tutted at seeing a spot of ink on his white sleeve then leaned back in his chair. 'Given any opportunity, this ship's last physician, McBride, would order the strongest drink available. I take it you are not such an enthusiastic imbiber?'

'I have a strict rule of only one drink with dinner, captain. A physician must keep his wits about him, especially upon a ship of war.'

'I am glad to hear that. Now then – your papers.'

Webster placed them on the table and slid them across to Merriman. 'Three, as required, sir. From the Hall at Lincoln's Inn Fields, from the Surgeons' Company and from the Commissioners.'

Merriman briefly looked them over, recognising most of the signatures upon them.

'Doctor, I will depend on you. There will be bloody work and lots of it.'

'Sir, I was employed at the military hospital here in Portsmouth for three and a half years. We dealt with all manner of wounds and diseases.'

'Very good. But this will be different. You have your two surgeon's mates but you are to all intents and purposes alone. In my estimation, you have the most difficult task on the ship.'

Webster gulped anxiously as Merriman continued.

'That is why I will do all I can to assist you. Consider the door to this cabin always open to you. Despite your lack of interest in drink, I trust you will attend dinners with my other officers? I consider it essential that you all know and trust each other.'

'Of course, captain. While I have some of your valuable time, might I make some general points about health and hygiene aboard? During my week on *Thunder*, I have made several observations.'

'Please.'

Webster reached into the pocket of his coat and pulled out a piece of paper. 'Thank you, sir. Item one.'

'How many items are there, Mr. Webster?'

'I kept it to a minimum, sir. Just the seventeen.'

First Lieutenant Shrigley did not return on that day. Merriman had no set departure date in mind but didn't intend on tarrying longer than a week. Thankfully, the other lieutenants kept at their recruiting efforts and brought another dozen men aboard to fill various positions. Merriman would have invited all his officers to the great room to dine but did not wish to do so without Shrigley present. He had known the man for more than ten years and felt sure he would not be absent without good reason. Shrigley's home was near Winchester; if he did not appear the following day, Merriman would send someone to make enquiries.

Having occupied late afternoon by going over matters of finance with the purser and clerk, Merriman then spent half an hour with his midshipmen. As well as Eades and Hickey, there were two new arrivals now entered into *Thunder*'s muster book: a fifteen-year-old named Adkins and a thirteen-year-old named Chamier. Chamier's family hailed from Chester and his term aboard Merriman's ship had been arranged via Helen. Adkins had at least spent three months on a frigate while this was Chamier's first posting.

Knowing he might have limited time to engage with them later on, Merriman set the four a basic navigational task. Sitting in the great cabin, the youths silently copied down the instructions.

'How do you find the midshipmen's berth, young Chamier?'

Merriman knew his father was one of the richest men in Chester: his new surroundings must have been quite a shock.

'The hammock does take some getting used to, sir. And I fear Mama packed too many clothes.'

'Ah. You shall soon work out the essentials.'

Hickey then spoke up. 'I heard some of the idlers murmuring about Chamier's French name – so I put them right.'

Before Merriman could comment, there was a knock on the door.

'Come!'

It was Lieutenant Essex. 'A boat from the quay, sir. Visitor for you. A Mister Grahame.'

The Treasury agent came aboard in a hooded cloak to protect him from heavy rain. Even so, the familiar lean frame and hawkish face were unmistakeable. Despite his sodden condition, Grahame summoned a broad smile for his old friend. He was accompanied by a tough-looking marine – a bodyguard, no doubt.

'I was glad to learn that the *Thunder* was at anchor but – half way into that trip – I rather wished she was still in the yard.'

Merriman was already wondering about the purpose of this visit but he ushered Sir Laurence towards the hatch, leaving the marine in the care of Lieutenant Cary. Word travelled ahead of them and the midshipmen had made themselves scarce by the time they reached the great cabin.

Peters recognized him at once. 'A nice warm tot of brandy, perhaps, Sir Laurence?'

The new arrival answered after a coughing fit had passed. 'That would be most welcome, Peters.'

'You too, sir?'

'Go on then. If you're sure you wouldn't prefer claret, Laurence? The wine cooler is well stocked.'

'No, no. Brandy please,' he said, handing his coat to Peters. He put a hand to his stomach. 'Quite a chop out there. It has been a while since I was on the water and I wasn't feeling too well to start with.'

The pair sat down on the benches close to the windows, where two lanterns were alight.

'It is good to see you, *Sir* Laurence,' said Merriman.

'Likewise, *Sir* James. You know I still sometimes find it hard to believe that we two had the king's sword bounced on our shoulder.'

'As do I,' admitted Merriman.

'What a relief it was to learn that you had not yet departed.'

'You have communicated with Sir Henry?'

'Yes. I'm afraid it has all been very rushed.'

Again, Merriman was struck by that ominous feeling. He was truly glad to see his old friend but his sudden appearance invariably portended some intrigue and Merriman had enough on his plate. Grahame ran a finger down his angular nose and seemed to be about to speak just as Peters arrived with the brandy.

'The king,' they said, clinking their glasses together.

'How is Helen?' asked Grahame.

'Very well. She seemed to enjoy making a fuss of me over the winter.'

'And Robert? Mary-Anne?'

Grahame had never been one suited to idle talk and Merriman could not escape the feeling that he was preparing the ground in some way.

'Please, Laurence, I will gladly talk of other matters later – it has been too long. But I sense you are here on business.'

That lean face produced a thin smile. 'I am indeed, James. And it concerns another old friend.'

Merriman had some idea of who that might be; someone else he had heard little of in recent months. 'Moreau?'

'The one and same. As you will recall, he was quite enthusiastic about coming to work with me at the Treasury. More enthusiastic than some of my other colleagues, in fact. They seemed rather bemused by a Frenchman more dedicated to the overthrow of Napoleon than most Englishmen.'

Though it was warm in the cabin, Merriman felt a chill as he recalled Charles Moreau describing the death of his entire family during the revolution. A count himself, he had been away fighting in the American War of Independence when the ruling classes had been overthrown. Returning to his homeland, he discovered that even his young sister had faced the guillotine.

'Not long after he joined the Treasury, an opportunity presented itself. With his language abilities, Moreau can pass as a native in Italy and Spain – and Portugal. The army was desperate for information regarding movements on the peninsula. He first posed as a French military liaison, then as a Spanish arms dealer. His last assignment was gaining information on the armies of Marshal Massena, Prince of Essling. Massena is a favourite of Napoleon. His forces have been stretched thin but there are rumours of a planned counter-attack. Communication had been difficult and I had tasked him with nothing more specific than intelligence-gathering.'

A breeze rattled in through the great cabin's windows. Peters came in and took up one of the lanterns as he closed them.

Grahame continued: 'In typical Moreau fashion, he somehow obtained a report compiled by Massena's staff – alternative plans for a counter-attack. You will not be surprised to hear that Lieutenant General Wellesley is very keen on obtaining said plans. Unfortunately, overland routes have proved unworkable and it seems Moreau now has French agents on his tail.'

'I see.'

'We did, however, have a reserve plan, knowing that sea travel would be far easier by spring. We identified a spot south of Porto where – if able – he will wait for every day of March for a signal. I have the details here.'

Merriman took a long draft of his brandy and watched as Grahame unfolded the paper. He could barely bring himself to look at it. This was not because he didn't want to aid Moreau (and indeed the wider war); it was because he *had to*; he was obliged on account of loyalty and friendship.

Sir Laurence took up the second lantern, coughed several times, then shifted closer to Merriman. The paper featured a well-copied map and Grahame pointed out a village some thirty miles south of Porto. Below the map was a simple code to be issued by signal light. If Moreau was present, he would answer and expect to be collected from the shore.

'You're sure he's there?' asked Merriman.

'I'm sure he left for Porto. I can't be sure he arrived. But you know Moreau. Can you make it there by the last day of March, James?'

'I presume you know of our route from Sir Henry?'

For once, the Treasury man seemed hesitant. He glanced at Peters, who was presently topping up the glasses.

Merriman pointed towards the door. 'Peters, if you please.'

With a nod, the servant made himself scarce.

Grahame cleared his throat and put down the lamp. He leant his head back against the cabin wall.

'There have been some…tensions between the Admiralty and ourselves of late. Sir Henry and the other admirals were not receptive to a request from me that might compromise your mission. The most he would tell me is that you are heading south.'

Grahame glanced down at the paper still in his hand. 'James, I cannot insist – nor would I. God knows you've done enough for myself and the Treasury in the past. I may be able to secure another vessel.'

Though fully aware that he might regret his decision, Merriman found himself grasping the paper and taking it from his old friend.

'I will not leave Moreau alone in dangerous territory. If I can assist him, I will. But if he does not answer the signal, I cannot wait.'

Grahame opened his mouth to speak again but Merriman continued. 'Nor can I bring him back north. But those sea routes are busy. If we recover him, I will put him aboard a merchantman returning to England. Will that do?'

Grahame shook Merriman's hand. 'I am in your debt, James.'

'No – Moreau is in my debt. And by God I'll make sure he knows it!'

Once this matter was resolved, the old friends turned to shared memories of times good and bad. Despite further tots of brandy and a blanket supplied by Peters, the Treasury man's cough worsened and he began to shiver. Insisting that he take the blanket with him, Merriman had Lieutenant Jones escort him back to shore, having made arrangements regarding communications and the return of Charles Moreau.

It was now dark and the captain went up on deck, passing knots of men gambling and singing, which he did not mind to see at all; not while at anchor in home port. He also encountered Lieutenant Smythe and Lieutenant Cary, who were jousting with their swords, watched by many of the other officers. Seeing Merriman, they lowered their blades but he encouraged them to carry on. He knew how much he would be demanding of officers and crew; for now, they could enjoy a little leisure.

As he passed them, the purser came up from below and handed him a brief written note.

'Sorry, sir. Arrived a couple of hours ago but it got lost amidst the rest of the post. From Lieutenant Shrigley, sir. He will be with us tomorrow.'

'Ah. Very good.'

Up on the quarter deck, Henderson, the sailing master was smoking a pipe and contemplating the sky.

'Good evening, Tom.'

'Evening, sir. Settling back into life on *Thunder*?'

'I suppose so. Shrigley will be with us tomorrow.'

'Very glad to hear it, sir. Not many better officers in the fleet. I don't suppose we'll be able to keep hold of him much longer.'

'He is certainly ready for a command but – between you and me – we shall keep him as long as we can.'

As far as Merriman could gather, his ship now had most of the crucial equipment and supplies it needed and as near a full crew as it was likely to get.

Though the rain had stopped, a gusty wind was blowing in off the land. Merriman was not one to look for divine intervention but a northerly would suit them well.

'Wednesday today, isn't Tom?'

'That's right, sir.'

'As sailing master, it's as well you know before anyone else. We depart on Friday. We shall sail on the early morning tide.'

Chapter Four

The First Lieutenant Returns

As if eager for her next voyage to begin, *Thunder* tugged at her cables like a dog at its leash. Though he had initially felt oddly displaced back amongst his officers and crew, Merriman now shared his ship's apparent enthusiasm for the task in hand. As ever, there'd been so many demands upon him that he'd already spoken several times to all his lieutenants and warrant officers and visited most nooks of the ship.

Nothing, however, made him feel more at home than the return of Alfred Shrigley. As the first lieutenant boarded via the entry port, he was watched and welcomed by all the officers and much of the crew. Having seen him grow from youth to man to leader, the captain reckoned he knew him as well as his own children. Unfortunately, this meant that he could swiftly see that all was not well: Shrigley greeted Merriman and the other officers politely but said little in response to numerous enquiries. The captain therefore conducted him swiftly down to the great cabin.

'I stopped to pick up the latest intelligence reports, sir, but I understand Essex already has them. Then there are the quarter, watch and station bills. I had-'

'All in hand, Alfred. Come and sit.'

Merriman and Shrigley sat on the lockers near the open window. From outside came the intermittent hammering of a party fitting rudder gudgeons recently collected from Portsmouth's sprawling blacksmith's yard.

'Sir, please do not be kind to me.'

'Alfred?'

Below his head of curly brown hair, Shrigley's brow was furrowed. He was turning his fingers over one of his buttons which Merriman knew to be a sure sign of anxiety. He had observed it often in Shrigley's younger years; not much of late. The first lieutenant seemed to be about to speak but halted himself twice before actually doing so.

'What I...mean to say, Captain Merriman, is that I cannot discuss the issue that accounted for my absence without...it really is best that I don't.'

Shrigley briefly dabbed at his eyes.

'Understood,' said Merriman. 'Let us not do so then. I will merely say that I am glad to have you back aboard.'

Apparently relieved, Shrigley nodded and let out a long breath. 'Apologies again for my late return, sir. I understand that we're to depart tomorrow?'

'At dawn. I shall brief the officers before dinner tonight. Again, we face a long voyage and a difficult task: the commissioners have charged us with the defeat of a French captain who has been preying on Indiamen near the Cape of Good Hope.'

'Understood, sir.'

'We were also visited by Sir Laurence. Moreau has been spying for the Treasury in Portugal and we have been asked to extract him on our way south. Between you and I, he is in possession of crucial information that will assist Lieutenant-General Wellesley.'

Shrigley's eyes widened. 'Is that so? While at home, I was visited by my cousin Harry. He is a cavalryman under Lieutenant-General Payne and currently recovering from wounds sustained over there last year. Wellesley had the Portuguese and the Royal Engineers at work for months: dams, redoubts, fortifications.'

'Stopped the French,' observed Merriman.

'Saved the capital, so they say.'

'We will not tarry,' added the captain. 'Either we recover Moreau swiftly or we continue south.'

'The tropics again,' said Shrigley, shaking his head. 'We are as likely to lose men to illness as to French cannonballs.'

'Well, our new sawbones seems most conscientious.'

'And the books, sir? Are you satisfied with our recruitment efforts?'

'I am. We're still short of topmen but we have a caulker's mate and two more sailors arriving today. A few minor shortages to amend but otherwise we're in fair shape. The other lieutenants will bring you up to speed.'

'Very good, sir.' Shrigley stood.

'Alfred, consider the great cabin at your disposal. Even a ship of the line is a cramped space. If you need a little time alone...'

'Very kind, sir.'

Merriman watched the first lieutenant leave. He knew that Shrigley's wife had previously endured two miscarriages and he assumed this unspoken difficulty might be a third. When Peters reappeared, Merriman considered summoning the other officers, ordering them not to press Shrigley on such matters. But this was going too far; his first officer would have to negotiate this alone. Merriman admitted to himself that his concerns were not entirely selfless. All he could do was hope that Shrigley was able to put his worries aside – or at least deal with them – as the *Thunder* put to sea once more.

The captain was not surprised to find the last day at anchor a busy one. The purser and cook competed with each other as to who could be most outraged about a late delivery of fresh produce. It did eventually arrive on several wagons and both launch and tender made several trips to get the bread and beef and potatoes and greens aboard.

Because the two boats were busy, when one desperate tar jumped over the side (having decided that he did not wish to go to sea), he got some distance before being intercepted. Lieutenant Jones was forced to hail a nearby frigate and ask them to fetch the man. By the time the escapee was recovered, he was near-drowned and had only survived by holding onto a slender withy. Webster reckoned he would recover and – due to his condition – punishment was deferred. His messmates assured the captain that they would prevent a repetition of the episode, also remarking that he was 'in love with a red-headed prostitute'.

On that day, Mr. Webster also had to make a decision for the captain about a topman with a severe case of lockjaw. The surgeon seemed sure that the man was unlikely to recover while aboard and so he was to be sent ashore before departure. The keen Welshman also reminded Merriman that – due to the season and their location – there was only limited quantities of lemon and lime aboard. Despite repeated enquiries at Portsmouth's Victualling Office, supplies were desperately lacking. Merriman assured him that he would try to amend this when they reached warmer climes, though he stopped short of mentioning Portugal.

Due to various outstanding deliveries of men and material, Merriman did not order Peters and his assistant to start dinner until seven o'clock. An hour later, he sat at the table accompanied by lieutenants Shrigley, Jones, Smythe and Essex; Mr. Webster the surgeon, Mr. Rolfe the purser, Mr. Henderson the Master, and Lieutenant Cary, the only man clad in the red of the royal marines.

While waiting for the first course of soup, Merriman led a toast to the ailing king and his son, the regent, before at last telling the officers of his orders. This was greeted by a long silence, as those present took in the mission that would govern their lives in the ensuing weeks and months.

'We shall seize this *Hercule* as a prize, captain,' ventured Lieutenant Smythe eventually. 'I've not a single doubt.'

'That is the aim,' replied Merriman, recalling the days when he had felt such doubtless conviction.

'Those lanes must be kept clear,' added Mr. Henderson, in typically practical fashion. 'And the *Thunder*'s just the ship for the job.'

'Mr. Henderson has been telling us new fellows how fortunate we are to be sailing under your command, captain,' added Smythe. 'And a privilege it is.'

'Quite so, sir,' added the reserved Essex.

Merriman continued: 'Unfortunately, there is an added complication that I only learned of when Sir Laurence Grahame came aboard. Some of you will know the name of Charles Moreau – a Frenchman who has worked for both the Admiralty and the Treasury in the name of defeating Bonaparte. His latest assignment has taken him to Portugal and we've been asked to collect him from a remote spot south of Porto.'

Merriman could already see several alarmed expressions. 'Now that region is currently in allied hands but Moreau was being pursued by French agents, so we must be careful.'

Unsurprisingly, Lieutenant Cary took an interest in what might be an operation requiring marine assistance. 'Myself and my men are of course always keen to assist, sir.'

'Thank you, captain. Gentlemen, Moreau is an old friend but I would not risk the *Thunder* if this were anything less than a crucial mission. I cannot go into the details but the information in Moreau's possession is of great strategic value.'

A long pause followed until Lieutenant Jones spoke up. 'It is hard to imagine that old Boney was once a revolutionary and yet he has now made himself king of France and his brother king of Spain.'

'I daresay he aims to be king of the world,' ventured Webster.

'He shall never rule the waves!' countered Cary with a grin.

'Please,' added Merriman. 'Nothing to the men until we are safely in the Channel. The French do have their spies.'

'Poor young Chamier,' commented Lieutenant Jones, 'It is not easy to bear a French name and serve on an English ship.' Though junior to Shrigley in rank, Jones was actually five years older. He had once told Merriman that he had no desire to be promoted beyond second lieutenant as that was 'more than enough responsibility for him.'

'I do trust that you have your violin, with you, Mr. Jones?'

'Never leave port without it, sir.'

'Good. You new fellows are in for a treat.'

As for Shrigley, he had not yet said a word.

The bold Lieutenant Cary aimed a finger across the table. 'Mr. Webster, sir, you hail from the valleys. Do you sing?'

'It has been known, captain. Indeed, it has.'

The great cabin was already warm and Webster's face flushed pink.

'I should thank you for treating my man Taylor today,' added, Cary, catching Merriman's eye. 'One of my best, captain. Did himself a mischief with his bayonet while we were drilling. Mr. Webster sewed him up very nicely.'

Cary was known for his bravado and japing but Merriman noted how respectfully he treated the surgeon: like the captain, the marine would depend on the physician and his skills.

'Excellent,' said Merriman. 'Ah, at last – the soup. What do we have, Peters?'

'Pea, onion and clove, sir.'

All were clearly hungry because little was said until most of the bowls were clean. The talk turned swiftly to news of fellow officers on other ships, some of whom were now departing to the West Indies and the Adriatic. The officers also discussed the many foreigners within *Thunder*'s crew. As well as Scots, Irish and Welsh, there were Americans, Dutchmen, Swedes, Italians, one Russian and (of interest to Merriman), one Portuguese.

The main meal consisted of roast chicken, roast duck and a variety of vegetables that all knew they might not enjoy for some time. Peters and the cook received many compliments, especially when they also served up a fruit jelly for pudding. By that point, the officers had moved from wine onto port and conversation was flowing well. Smythe, Essex and Cary all had an interest in horse-racing and were soon relating their greatest wins. Merriman had little interest in such matters but he enjoyed the warm and amiable atmosphere. On these occasions, the great cabin almost seemed a different place.

Later, Mr. Webster disclosed his interest in poetry and Merriman invited him to make use of his small library, which consisted mainly of Shakespeare. Shrigley had often borrowed these tomes and Merriman tried to involve him in the conversation but he was evidently still preoccupied.

Two hours into the dinner, wine and rum seemed to loosen minds and tongues so that they at last turned to the task facing them.

'South it is then,' said Mr. Henderson, gazing down into his glass. 'More men to undergo the rituals of Neptune.'

'Myself included,' offered Lieutenant Essex sheepishly.

'I am keen to see the south of Africa,' added Smythe. 'So much unchartered territory: it is hard to imagine.'

'Disease is a greater barrier than any desert or mountain range,' said Webster. 'There are many ailments in that continent that a European simply cannot endure.'

'We will pass the slave ports, will we not?' asked Lieutenant Essex.

'That we will,' said Henderson.

'A friend of mine is a purser with the new Preventative Squadron,' added Rolfe, the purser. 'He claims there is no more dangerous duty. Many a disease as Mr Webster says and the slave ships will often fight. And the squadron only has a few vessels taken as prizes.'

'Seems a misuse of resources if you ask me,' observed Smythe.

'Our government has banned the trade,' replied Merriman, who very much agreed with the decision. 'And though we swear allegiance to the king, it is the government that gives us our orders.'

Despite Shrigley's continuing reticence, Merriman reckoned that this first dinner had achieved what he wanted it to. He would need clear heads about him in the morning and now was the moment to remind them all of their goal. In truth, at his age, he wasn't much given to excesses of enthusiasm – but sometimes the occasion demanded it. He raised his glass.

'On that note, let us make another toast. To the fair ship that will carry us to battle.'

'And to victory!' added Cary.

With a smile, Merriman continued. 'To the *Thunder*.'

All present raised their glasses. 'To the *Thunder*!'

In a light drizzle and perhaps ten knots of wind, the ship slipped her cables and was pulled clear of other moored vessels before Merriman gave the order that the sails be set. Down in the cable tier, the anchor cable was coiled by several men tasked with the duty as a punishment for an infraction the previous night: singing loudly even after the order to 'pipe down'.

"Topmen aloft!' ordered Master Henderson. 'Lie out and loose the fore top and main top!'

Due to the converted idlers now in the ranks, Merriman was not surprised to see a middling performance from the topmen. He did, however, note a young lad with remarkable speed and agility on the mainmast.

'Let fall and sheet home!'

As the topsails fell, this lad swiftly attended to his own section, then helped an older man.

'That young fellow knows his business.'

'Friar, sir,' remarked Brockle, the bosun, who was standing near the captain by the wheel. 'Only joined us in January but a very swift learner. Now more useful than men twice his age. Just fourteen.'

With the fo'c'sle party now cleaning off the muddy anchor, the sailors on deck began adjusting the sheets and braces.

Tom Henderson glanced up at the sails then hurried back to the captain. 'Wind's up, sir. I suggest we wait a moment on the great sails or we'll be a little fast for the first stretch. Few fishing boats heading out too.'

Merriman answered with a nod and turned to Shrigley, who stood with his hands clasped behind him. 'I recall leaving here on our first trip – to Malta.'

'Yes, sir. Seems a long time ago.'

'It does.'

Gripped by an anxiety that surprised him, Merriman had awoken early and used the time to consult the notes he'd made during that trip and the weeks before. Most concerned the sailing characteristics of the *Thunder*; how she coped with heavy seas, how much sail she could carry and so on.

'Did you sleep well, Alfred?'

'Well enough, sir.'

'I have set the midshipmen the task of navigating our way out of the Channel. Would you be so good as to supervise them?'

'Of course, sir.'

Merriman knew that his first lieutenant enjoyed navigation and he thought it wise to keep him busy. As Shrigley hailed Chamier and Adkins, the captain tucked his hands into his coat and wandered to the quarterdeck rail. *Thunder* passed a fishing boat with four men at the oars and two at the stern. The oarsmen had stopped rowing and the six men watched – awestruck – as the warship eased past them. Seeing the captain, they all waved; and one saluted.

Merriman returned the gesture, causing uproar and jubilation amongst the fishermen.

Chapter Five

The Thunder of Guns

His time ashore with his beloved family already seemed a distant memory as the captain settled once more into life aboard ship. At sunrise, the colours were raised and the sailors stowed their hammocks and set about daily tasks – cleaning the decks, coiling ropes, attending to sails – before taking their breakfast. At half past nine came divisions, when they were inspected by their officers. Two hours later came the order to 'clear decks and up spirits', when the first half of their daily grog was issued. Dinner followed soon afterward and – for the first three days – the crew of the *Thunder* spent the remaining hours on regular duties. At around four o'clock, the sailors received their second issue of grog. Just before sunset, the ship went to quarters and either Merriman or Shrigley inspected the men and the guns. At dusk, the lookouts were called down and six sailors placed around the ship for the nocturnal watch. The day concluded with the retrieval of hammocks and 'lights out'.

During those three days, the *Thunder* made reasonable progress, though the wind swung from northerly to westerly and most points in between. Keen to avoid any entanglements with French patrols, Shrigley and the midshipmen charted a course that kept them well offshore, passing west of Ushant and staying clear of the dangerous waters and ferocious tides off the Raz de Sein. Here, Merriman took the midshipmen aside and told them of a battle of 1798 in which Captain Alexander Hood had taken on a French captain by the name of Louis Lhéritier. Even the preoccupied Shrigley shook his head in disbelief when they realized that young Chamier had not even been born at the time.

Continuing south across the notoriously troublesome Bay of Biscay, they were assailed only by a two-hour line squall that passed as swiftly as it arrived: the results being a torn mizzen royal and some nasty rope burns for a pair of sailors. They had so far passed only merchantmen, though a French frigate had been sighted heading towards shore just before the squall. On the fifth morning, with the Spanish coast thirty miles to larboard, the wind dropped to around twelve knots. Merriman knew he had been fortunate with the conditions and – with five days of March remaining – judged himself to be ahead of schedule. This near to Spain and France, they might meet an enemy warship at any time and he wanted to take the opportunity for gunnery practice. With less than an hour of warning, the lieutenants went below to the gundecks.

At this stage, Merriman was more concerned with organisation and speed than accuracy. Now he would see how swiftly the long guns could be run out, primed, fired and reloaded. Every man in each crew would have to do his job, from the 'captain' who fired the piece, to the sponger who cleaned it out and the fireman who stood by with water, in case of accident.

Thunder's main gun deck boasted twenty-eight thirty-two pounders. The upper gun deck contained the same number of guns but these were the smaller eighteen-pounders. The quarter deck had fourteen nine-pounders, while the fo'c'sle was equipped with two carronades and two nine-pounders. On this day, Merriman had ordered a drill only with his main guns; the deck-mounted weapons could wait for another day.

Keen to see each section in isolated action, he first ordered three consecutive shots from the main gun deck, larboard side, which was overseen by First Lieutenant Shrigley. At Merriman's signal, Shrigley passed on the order. With his pocket-watch in his hand, the captain stood near the hatch, listening to the urgent shouts of the crews, then the sounds of the guns running out until finally they were fired. Though they were using up valuable powder and ammunition, he wanted the drill to be as close to battle conditions as possible.

By the time he stopped his watch on the last blast from the larboard side, Merriman was largely satisfied. Even so, he approached the hatch with a grim face as Shrigley looked up at him, surrounded by thick wreathes of smoke.

'They got slower as they went but that was passable.'
'Sir.'

Merriman was in fact a good deal happier than that but he could not show Shrigley favour or let any man aboard feel satisfied. As he knew from bitter experience, much would depend on their rate of fire.

As the older hand, Lieutenant Jones was placed in charge of the starboard guns on the main deck. His crews were a little slower – and one gun misfired – but again Merriman was not disappointed.

The problems arrived when the upper deck took its turn. Lieutenant Essex went first with the larboard side. Not only was his time a full half-minute behind the others, but the sound of the last shot soon gave way to agonised screams.

Merriman went down to investigate. Hurrying past dozens of men and through the thick, acrid smoke, he was relieved to see the surgeon, Webster, already approaching an injured man lying on his back, screaming.

'Let me through!' yelled the Welshman in his high, clear voice. 'Let me see!'

With some help from Essex, Webster was able to pull the man's hand away from his other hand, which was still smoking from a nasty burn. Webster dragged over the nearest fireman's bucket and emptied it over the hand. The man at least stopped screaming though he was soon biting his lip so hard that it bled.

'What happened here?' demanded Merriman.

'He fell against the barrel, sir,' explained the gun captain. 'Not sure why it was hot after so few shots.'

'Something's amiss,' agreed Merriman.

By now, the gunner, Mr. Hanscombe, had arrived on the scene. 'I'll look into it, sir.'

The two surgeon's mates had the man on his feet and were escorting him away.

Merriman remained on the upper deck to watch as Lieutenant Smythe's crews took their turn. Their time was respectable but – as Merriman and everyone else noted – one gun did not fire its second two shots. Arriving at the offending weapon, he found Smythe bellowing at the gun captain, a man Merriman did not recognize. The zealous Smythe had the sailor by his collar, his quiff of blonde hair dancing about.

'Useless dolt! What in the blazes are you playing at?'

The gun captain's fearful eyes shifted from Smythe to Merriman, who addressed Smythe first of all. 'All right, lieutenant. Unhand the man. Let us hear his explanation.'

'I am sorry, sirs,' said the sailor. 'We spilled the powder and didn't dare fire her.'

'Why didn't you tell me?' demanded Smythe.

'We thought we could tidy up in time for the third volley but…'

A lad of around sixteen came forward, still holding his bucket of powder. 'There's no "we" sir. It was me that dropped it.'

'This is why we drill,' said Merriman evenly. 'To avoid such mistakes in future. Let us see now…'

He cast his eyes around and spied the distinctive craggy face of an aged Scotsman named Muir. 'There's a man who's fired as many guns in battle as he has in drill. Muir, come here please.'

'Captain.'

'Your crew is up to speed?'

'I believe so, sir.'

'At next drill, you will oversee this crew – ensure that all goes well.'

'Aye aye, sir.'

Merriman turned to the officer. 'Lieutenant Smythe, this is only one of fourteen long guns in your section. Let us not forget that the others all fired successfully, though they will need to do so quicker in future.'

Smythe had at last calmed himself and now nodded respectfully. 'Yes, captain.'

Later in the day, it was the turn of the marines to practice firing their muskets. Lieutenant Cary and his second lieutenant, Harrison, summoned their troops in groups of ten, occupying an area on the quarterdeck cleared for the purpose. Though his officers were well turned out, Merriman knew they could not compete with the marines in terms of appearance. Maintaining their clothing and kit was an officer's best method of keeping the soldiers busy and Cary was known to be a true stickler. The gilt pommels of the officers' swords glinted in the afternoon sun amidst the scarlet tunics and white facings.

Despite some muttered complaints from both bosun and master, Merriman insisted that the drill go ahead. He enjoyed watching the marines using their muskets, and did not envy them their task on a moving vessel. Still, as Cary regularly reminded them, a marine was more likely to be firing from a ship than he was from dry land. Tough but fair, Cary also completed his own firing routine and – with hundreds of eyes upon him – did so more efficiently than the majority of his men.

Mr. Webster was currently on deck taking some air and also seemed interested in the marine drill.

'An impressive sight, eh?' said Merriman.

'Indeed captain, though I had not anticipated that the noise would continue beyond the firing of the long guns.'

Seeing the expression on the captain's face that greeted this comment, he added: 'Though I understand the necessity, of course. I'll admit I was surprised to see so many marines aboard.'

'We are allocated one each for every gun plus the officers.'

'Is that so?' Webster removed his sunhat and pointed towards the distant shore. 'Captain, might I remind you about our need for citrus fruit?'

'I am aware, Mr. Webster, and will attend to it when possible.'

'My thanks.' The surgeon then produced a scrap of paper from his waistcoat. 'I have here a list of sailors with intermittent fevers and catarrhal infections. Some are currently occupied on deck so they will at least receive sunlight and breezes. Others are in the bread room, magazine and so on. Might I have permission for them to be excused duties?'

'They can take their meals on deck and one additional hour. Is that sufficient?'

'For several days?'

'For as long as you consider it necessary.'

'Very well.' Webster grimaced. 'Captain, I remain dismayed by the excess of salt in the meat – far beyond that necessary for the preservative effect. However, we have enough fresh beef and pork so that the salted meat is not yet required. Could I also ask that you remind the officers to encourage the men to eat the sourkrout? It also provides a defence against scurvy. I gather that they dislike the smell but it really is important.'

'As long as you don't expect me to eat it, I shall indeed encourage others. By the way, I noted that the purser is limping. Rolfe is not one to make a fuss but perhaps you could examine him. I need him fit and well.'

'Yes, captain. Or should I say, "aye aye"?'
Webster grinned before replacing his sunhat and departing the quarterdeck.

Once at the larboard rail, Merriman removed his own hat and gazed out at the distant rocky cliffs of the north

Spanish coast. He hadn't been there long when Lieutenant Cary approached. His last set of troops had just concluded their drill.

'Satisfied, Cary?'

Though his nose had clearly been broken several times and he had little hair, the marine captain possessed a handsome, compelling face.

'Generally, sir. The men are glad to be on the move but I suspect some of them would like to see some action.'

'Yes, and I suspect none would like that more than you.'

That night, Merriman was awoken from a deep sleep by Lieutenant Jones. Sitting up, he saw the officer's fine features illuminated by a lantern's yellow light, framed in the doorway.

'Apologies for disturbing you, sir, but we have two vessels approaching from the south-west. Mister Henderson has had a look. Judging by the lights and close formation, he thinks they could be a French or Spanish patrol – frigates most likely.'

Merriman rubbed his tired eyes. 'Distance?'

'Three or four miles.'

'What's the time?'

'Middle watch. Just after three bells, sir.'

'Position?'

'Approximately thirty miles west of Fisterra point, sir.'

'When were they sighted?'

'About ten minutes ago.'

'Visibility good?'

'Yes, captain.'

'Then they can see us as well as we can see them.'

'Again, apologies, sir but I wasn't sure about beating to quarters. You have said before that there's not many a captain wants to fight at night.'

'Merriman had seldom felt so woolly-headed, so he ordered Jones to repeat the information and asked another question before giving him an answer.

'Is the wind steady?'

'Yes, sir. Very. Around twelve or fourteen knots.'

'If they change course, beat to quarters. That will be sufficient to wake me.'

'Aye aye, sir.'

With that, Jones gently shut the door and Merriman slumped back onto his pillow.

He was not disturbed again that night.

Chapter Six

The Sands of Sao Jacinto

'Looks peaceful from here, don't it, cap'n?'

'It does at that, Harris.'

The middle-aged sailor was one of Thunder's best helmsmen and was currently guiding the ship towards the Portuguese coast.

'Me nephew's on the peninsular somewhere, sir,' added Harris, making an adjustment to his blue scarf. 'Dragoon. I pray every night that he's safe. Me sister's only son, he is.'

'I hope he makes it home, Harris. Eades, how many miles south of Porto are we now?'

The midshipman was standing at the binnacle, poring over a chart pinned to a board. 'Twenty-five, sir.'

'Any sign of the tower, Alfred?'

Shrigley was at the rail, spyglass to his eye. The reference point provided on Grahame's map was a church tower but it was someway inland and behind the rolling, golden dunes that characterized this stretch of coast.

'No, sir. I'll consult with the lookouts.' As the first lieutenant departed, Merriman shook his head, wishing they'd had better luck that morning. At dawn, they passed through the approach lanes for Porto but encountered only a brig coming from the west that did not answer signals. Merriman had hoped they might come across a vessel of the Portuguese Navy that might offer material help. He thought it just as likely that they might encounter one of the many merchantmen commissioned by the Transport Board to keep the expeditionary army supplied. Now that they were off the isolated stretch of coast that Moreau had chosen for the extraction, such help was even less likely.

However, Shrigley returned with some good news. 'Sir, the tower is almost directly to our east. I can also make out Sao Jacinto – looks a tiny place.'

'Well done. Eades, you will determine our course and provide a bearing for Harris.'

'Aye aye, sir.'

The weather was already improving as they headed south and Merriman removed his hat once more as *Thunder* turned onto a close reach and sped towards the coast. When they were approximately a half-mile off the coast, he ordered that the great sails be furled.

The charts suggested that there was plenty of water here but Merriman had the midshipmen sound depth before the anchor was lowered. Once Shrigley reported that the cable was tight and the anchor well set, Merriman sent Lieutenant Essex to fetch the signal mirror. Moreau had suggested a simple series of five flashes on the hour, with mirror in the day and light at night. Due to the clement weather, the mirror did its job well and the first signal was made at noon. It was repeated at hourly intervals until dusk but no reply came.

At that point, Merriman approached the first lieutenant once more. 'I want at least three lookouts monitoring that shore. Please report any sighting to me.' He then lowered his voice. 'Doubtless the men will invent some wild tale regarding our presence here. Let it slip that we are merely collecting a Treasury agent.'

'Aye, aye, sir.'

Merriman dined alone on a meal of beef and potatoes followed by plum duff. His stomach felt tight and so he did not finish the heavy pudding, assuring Peters that this was no sleight on his cooking. He then despatched servants to collect two individuals.

The first was Cary.

'You'll excuse the lack of wine, captain. I think we should both keep clear heads on this particular night.'

'Not at all, sir. You have something for me?'

'I do. As you'll be aware, there has been no reply from Moreau. The sensible course of action is no doubt to sail onward but I feel duty-bound to at least investigate, especially as there are currently no enemy ships to trouble us. I intend to go ashore myself in the boat. I will take our Portuguese sailor with me for the purposes of translation. I was also thinking one of your sergeants and two marines to man the boat?'

'If you'll have me, I should be honoured to accompany you myself, Captain Merriman. I would hate to be aboard and think of you at risk ashore.'

Merriman knew it was risky for both of them to leave the ship together but he could hardly restrict Cary while going himself.

'Excellent. We shall depart at first light.'

A minute after Cary left, a petty officer arrived with *Thunder*'s sole Portuguese crewman. Felipe Oliviera was a sailmaker's mate who'd been recruited over the winter. Apparently awed at entering the great cabin, he took off his hat and bowed low. Merriman was leaning back against his desk, arms folded.

'I don't believe we've spoken.'

'No, captain. It's...privilege to serve with you.' Though heavily accented, Oliviera's English was clear. 'Please...please don't ask me to go ashore.'

It shouldn't have surprised Merriman that the sailor had put two and two together but he was shocked at the fearful look in his eyes.

'I'm afraid I need you, Oliviera. No one else aboard speaks your language fluently.'

'I know but...may I explain?'

'Go on.'

'My family was accused of working with the French. The rumour was false. Spread by a man from our village. He was jealous of my father, who came into some money. We all had to leave. I was lucky. I am a fisherman. My skill with rope got me a position on an American brig and then here on *Thunder*. My wife and children are safe in England. We do not wish to return to Portugal. Not until the war is over. Captain, it was so difficult to escape. Fighting everywhere. Death everywhere.'

'We are south of Porto. This area is in the hands of your government now.'

'Captain, the officials of the government have lists. Lists of names. Though it was never true, my name is on one of them. They think I am a traitor.'

Despite the dim light, Merriman could see that Oliviera's eyes were wet with tears.

'Calm yourself, man.'

'I am sorry.'

'I was planning to compensate you for this duty. An extra two weeks' pay.'

'Sir, it is not the money. Please spare me this.'

'You'll get the pay, Oliviera. And you are coming ashore. I don't plan to be there longer than a few hours.'

The Portuguese said nothing.

'You do wish to remain a part of this crew?'

'Yes, captain.'

'Good. I will also remind you how much English blood has been spilled in resisting the French on Portuguese soil.'

Oliviera remained silent so Merriman continued: You will obey this order and make no further complaint. I shall see you at the entry port at dawn.'

Merriman doubted himself right up until the moment he stood by the entry port himself. Oliveira was already there, clad in a fisherman's smock with a hat pulled over his eyes. As instructed, Cary and his two marines were also well disguised, though the officer had clearly borrowed some clothes from lower ranks. As for Merriman, he was wearing a dull set of grey trousers and a tatty overcoat located by Peters from somewhere. Beneath was his captain's coat, which he thought circumspect.

Landing in the territory of their allies, there was theoretically no reason why they shouldn't all be in uniform. But neither blue nor scarlet would blend in within a tiny Portuguese coastal town and any sighting would inevitably cause a fuss. Merriman was also troubled by the lack of response from Moreau and wished to approach with caution.

Cary used his lantern to illuminate a large sack. 'We've just swords and pistols, captain.'

'A sound choice, Cary,' replied Merriman. 'Hopefully, we won't need them.'

Shrigley approached, his brow furrowed. 'Captain, as I said, I am more than happy to go in your place. Moreau knows me well enough.'

'True but I accepted this unfortunate errand and I intend to see it through. *Thunder* is yours, Alfred. I will aim to return by this time tomorrow at the latest. If an enemy vessel is sighted, you are to push off immediately and give yourself some sea room. Barring mist or rain, we should be able to see you at all times so signal if necessary.'

'Aye aye, captain. Best of luck. And careful in the boat. We reckon there must be a bar between us and the beach. There's quite a chop.'

'Got two of my best oarsmen, captain,' retorted Cary.

'Very good.' Merriman clambered down the netting. The boat was jumping around but, with the help of a marine, he got himself to the stern and sat there with the silent Oliveria, who was clutching a satchel in his lap. Once they were all aboard, the boat was pushed off by a couple of long boathooks.

'May I, sir?' asked Cary.

'Your vessel, captain,' replied Merriman, who knew the marine had far more practice of landings than he did.

'Might I request that you take the helm?'

'Why of course.' Merriman could not recall the last time he had held a tiller and guided a vessel of any sort.

Even in the darkness, he could see that the two oarsmen were big fellows: the man who had helped him and another who was equally broad.

'Who do we have at the oars then?'

'Private Sheldon, captain.'

'Private Pasley,' added the second man.

Merriman stayed quiet while Cary, who was in the bow, directed he and the oarsmen. It was not easy for them to keep the boat straight upon the rolling waves and Merriman knew that getting ashore would be difficult. He thought it wise to introduce the fifth member of their party.

'If you don't know him, this fellow is Oliviera. He has his reasons for avoiding his homeland but here he is. His language skills will be most useful.'

The grim faced Portugeuse at least managed a nod, eyes narrowed against the salty spray.

The sun had now risen above the horizon, giving Merriman an alarming view of the cresting waves ahead. When the boat dropped down the rear of each wave, the stern threatened to turn and leave them side on – at risk of capsize – but Merriman did his best with the tiller and Sheldon and Pasley knew their work. Shrigley was clearly right about the sand bar because the waves became shorter and deeper for a time. The boat leaped up and dipped its bow repeatedly, leaving several inches of water at their feet. Without prompting, Oliveria grabbed a bucket and begin baling.

Once clear of the bar, they were within only a hundred feet of the shore and Cary directed them towards a spot where the waves seemed calmer. Even so, they twice came close to turning as they neared the beach. Thrown forward by a forceful wave, Merriman lost all control but this final surge was halted as the bow slid onto solid ground. Cary leaped out, closely followed by the two privates. Merriman had not even a chance to move as the brute strength of the three marines dragged the boat clear up the shore.

Having complimented the soldiers on their effort, Merriman followed them through the soft sand then turned to look back at his ship. The sea seemed almost tranquil and *Thunder* hardly seemed to be moving – a dark shape against the pale, yellow sky. Turning back, he saw the undulating dunes a hundred yards away.

'Shall we take the boat all the way in, sir?' asked Cary.

'Yes, I think so.'

Even though Oliviera leant a hand, the marines had to take a short break halfway to the dunes. Once there, they placed the boat on a slope amidst patches of high grass.

Lieutenant Cary now took out the sack in which their weapons had been placed.

'You men can stay here and mind the boat,' Merriman told Sheldon and Pasley.

'Sir, should we look around for any sign of Moreau?' asked Cary.

'I'm not sure it's worth the effort. If he was here, he would have made himself known. The town is just to the south. I hope to gain some intelligence there. Follow me.'

The yielding sand was not easy going and the dunes stretched back a remarkable distance. After a half-hour of walking, however, they reached a crest that allowed Merriman to make out the church tower and the cluster of low buildings that formed Sao Jacinto. Better still, he spied a clear path of well-trodden ground.

After perhaps a mile, they came to a timber building with fishing nets and baskets outside but it seemed unoccupied. Pressing on, they reached the outskirts of the town and met a raggedy young lad walking along with a dog in tow. He seemed very surprised to see them and tried to hurry past with head down. At an order from Merriman, Oliviera spoke to him. The boy was reluctant at first but considerably more enthusiastic when his countryman gave him a tiny silver coin. Oliveira questioned him for some time and then summarized for Merriman.

'He has seen or heard nothing of a Frenchman in the area. However, there is a guard tower south of the town, manned by a squad of soldiers and an officer. If anyone would know something, it's them.'

'All right. Let him go.'

The boy trotted off along the path, whistling happily while the dog barked.

'Guard tower, sir,' remarked Cary. 'This could get interesting.'

'Lieutenant, I have learned over the years that where Moreau is involved, matters are seldom *uninteresting*.'

Despite his tone, Merriman was concerned that they might find no trace of the spy in Sao Jacinto. If that was the case, the most likely explanation was that his enemy pursuers had caught up with him.

They passed two more wooden shacks but the only men they saw were in the surf, putting to sea in a small boat. They continued on until they reached the town itself, where houses of various sizes were constructed of stone, all topped by tiles of pale red. Faces in doorways and windows cast anxious looks towards the three newcomers but Merriman had spotted a promising location up ahead: a marketplace.

He estimated that the sun had been up for two hours and, considering the size of the town, the marketplace was busy: a dozen stalls arranged around a circular, white-painted well. Though the two Englishmen and one Portuguese attracted more suspicious glances, many of the locals were busy either buying or selling, and few of them did so quietly.

'That bread looks good,' said Merriman, pointing at a nearby stall. 'Buy us a couple of loaves, Oliviera, then some fish, then some herbs. These traders meet a lot of people; hear a lot of news. Make it clear that you'll pay for information if necessary. And, yes, I shall reimburse you for the local currency.'

The two captains waited while Oliviera visited no less than six stalls. An old women tried to engage them in conversation but soon gave up.

'Sir.' Cary nudged Merriman and nodded towards the largest building facing the marketplace, which looked like an inn. Three men came out with muskets over their shoulders. One was carrying a peaked hat; all three were wearing the blue coats of the Portuguese army. They turned to their right and followed a street that led inland.

'That's a relief.' Merriman felt sweat forming on his skin and he was beginning to question his tactics. By coming ashore in disguise, had he in fact made a dangerous incident more likely?

Oliviera soon returned, laden with bread and other bits of food.

'Anything?'

'Two of them said the same thing, sir. A week ago, a French spy was arrested here in the town. He is being held at the guard tower. It is a half-mile away.'

As they walked through the marketplace and picked up the path that led south, Merriman removed his smock to reveal his captain's coat, complete with epaulettes and gold buttons and edging.

'I think this situation calls for a straight-forward approach,' he said, also asking Cary to give him his sword. 'Hopefully, this officer is a respecter of rank and military comradeship.'

Soon, all three of them were walking with their hands raised to protect their eyes. A gusty wind had come up and was lifting the sand off the dunes to their right and casting it at them. To their left were some spindly trees and bushes separating the beach from a marshy lagoon. Thankfully, the path was easy to follow and there was not far to go.

Set between two dunes, the tower was made of stone blocks and around thirty feet high. On the western side was a drift of sand as high as a man. There were several square windows and from one of them came a cry.

The trio halted and Oliviera responded, his voice cracked by tension. The voice barked again and they heard more shouts from within. A frowning infantryman lurched out of the shadowy entrance, musket in hand, then came a second soldier, hand on the pommel of his sword. The third to emerge was an officer: a slight, brown-haired fellow who had lost two fingers on his right hand. Tucked into his belt was a pistol. Seeing Merriman's uniform and sword, his glare turned to a quizzical grin.

'You are English.'

'I am.'

'Lieutenant Rodrigo Duarte, at your service. What in God's name is a naval officer – a captain, no less – doing in our little town of Sao Jacinto?'

Merriman stepped forward and shook the man's hand. 'Captain James Merriman. I am pleased that you speak good English. I must ask you about an important matter.'

'I was honoured to serve alongside the Light Division during the Coa campaign. It improved my English quite considerably.' Duarte held up his mutilated hand. 'Less fortunately, I was injured on the last day of the battle – hence my current situation. Does this matter relate to the man I am currently holding in the tower?'

'It does indeed. His name is Charles Henri Moreau.'

'Yes. He told me that. He also told me that he is an English agent. I told him that I have never heard of any Frenchman working for the English.'

'May I talk to him?'

'You may, captain,' said Duarte. 'But please be aware that a magistrate and an army man are on the way from Coimbra to interrogate Moreau. There can be no question of releasing him. I simply do not have the authority. What is the expression? Ah yes – my hands are tied.'

Chapter Seven

Meeting Moreau

One side of the tower's ground floor was occupied by a staircase, the other by two small rooms. Though Lieutenant Duarte continued to be polite, he insisted that the Englishmen leave their weapons outside. As he took a ring of keys from his belt, the Portuguese tutted and caught Merriman's eye.

'I only arrived a few minutes ago. Somehow these idiots failed to spot your ship. Good patriots both but they have an alarming habit of sleeping on the job.'

Merriman was more concerned with Moreau; and how he might persuade Duarte to change his mind. He looked on as the officer unlocked the door and opened it wide.

Sitting in a dusty corner, one leg stretched out, the other propped up, was Moreau, the light from a tiny window illuminating the deep scar on his left cheek. He was barefoot, wearing only trousers and a flowing white shirt. Despite his condition, he smiled and wearily got to his feet, running a hand through his unkempt black hair.

'I was beginning to feel so hopeless that I prayed for a saviour. And here you are, James.'

The French agent staggered forward and fell into Merriman's arms, an unpleasant odour surrounding him. It took some time for him to recover himself.

'I had no idea if my communiques had reached Sir Laurence; or if he would send anyone. Then I imagined someone signalling me and receiving no response. Only *you* would go to such lengths.'

Moreau stepped back and gripped hand Merriman's tightly. 'My sincere thanks, mon capitaine.'

'Not at all, Charles. I am very relieved to see you. Are you well?'

'Considering the last few months, I suppose I am. Despite his intransigent attitude, Lieutenant Duarte here has at least watered and fed me, though I'll confess I cannot wait for my first glass of claret. Are we leaving immediately? You must also ensure that we recover my papers. I tried to hide them but these fellows were very thorough. I have tried time and again to convince them of my identity but to no avail.'

Merriman turned to Duarte. 'You have the papers? May I see them?'

'No, captain. It is only due to recognition of your rank and nationality that I have allowed you to speak with your friend.'

'You have examined them?'

'I have,' said Duarte, the two soldiers looking on from behind him. 'Most interesting. Please understand this from my perspective: we discovered a Frenchman acting suspiciously in the town and in possession of military documents. You can hardly blame me for assuming the worst.'

'A moment,' said Merriman to Moreau, before stepping back out of the room. 'You have been very frank, Lieutenant Duarte, so I shall follow suit. You will note that Moreau has the bearing of a nobleman – precisely what he is. Most of his family were murdered during the revolution, so you must believe me when I tell you that he has more reason to hate the armies of Bonaparte than either you or I. Those plans could make a crucial difference to the fate of this country and the wider war. They *must* be conveyed to England and then our commanders on the peninsula with all haste. I am sure you would not wish to be responsible for a military – and diplomatic – incident.'

'Indeed, I would not. Which is precisely what might occur if I hand over this man – and those plans – in error. Put simply, captain, it is a decision above my station, which is why I will await my superiors. Now, I think it is best all round if you depart.'

By now, Cary was bristling. 'Listen here, friend, our ship can destroy this tower in a matter of minutes. Or perhaps I should summon the hundred marines under my command?'

Merriman raised a hand and silenced the lieutenant but Duarte hadn't finished. He took the pistol from his belt and held it, rather shakily, in his left hand.

'Then you would be the ones responsible for the…incident, correct?'

Duarte approached the cell door.

'Vous êtes un crétin!' snapped Moreau. 'I have risked my life for your country. Have you no respect for your allies?'

The door clanged shut and was locked by Duarte, who then gestured towards the exterior. 'Good day, gentlemen.'

'Bloody fool!' hissed Cary as they walked away from the tower. 'In fact, I'd use a stronger word than that. Captain Merriman, please allow me to return to *Thunder* and-'

'A moment, Cary. Let us appraise this situation and assess our alternatives. A bribe might do it but – his blinkered attitude aside – Duarte doesn't seem the type. What about you, Oliviera – any bright ideas?'

The Portuguese had remained silent throughout the exchange at the tower and now morosely shook his head.

The trio trudged along the sandy path until they reached the marketplace once more. It was Merriman who saw the alarming sight on the far side of the square and he swiftly dragged Cary and Oliviera into cover: a stand of palm trees between two houses.

'What is it, sir?'

Cary's question was soon answered as they saw Pasley and Sheldon walking towards the tower, hands tied behind them. Sheldon had a black eye and one of the three soldiers they'd seen earlier was nursing an injured wrist. His two comrades were aiming their muskets at the Englishmen.

A few young lads trailed along behind the group until one of the soldiers barked at them.

'By god,' said Cary. 'Somehow our situation is even worse.'

Merriman wasn't so sure. 'Actually, I think it might have just improved.'

They had to move swiftly. At Merriman's instruction, Cary handed a pistol to each of them. The captain then led the way back out of Sao Jacinto, now following the muddy shore that edged the lagoon.

Cary drew level with him as they jogged southward. 'Sir, what do you intend?'

'No doubt Duarte will place our men in that cell with Moreau. That means the door will be open, which is our moment to strike. He also has only the two men there with him so I doubt anyone will be keeping watch. Hopefully, we can approach unseen. Duarte himself has only the one usable arm and you saw how clumsy he was with his gun and the keys. One of their men is injured, so it will be a case of three against four.'

Cary cast a cynical look over his shoulder. 'You're including Oliviera?'

Merriman couldn't really argue that point; the Portuguese looked like he'd never handled a firearm before and didn't wish to.

'We will depend on surprise. The tower is between two dunes so there is some cover. We must time it just right. Captain, I do not want a single shot fired. However, we must make it clear to them who is in charge. Your boxing experience might be a boon in this situation.'

'Understood, sir.'

Merriman had paced out the distance on their return and therefore had a rough estimate of when to leave the lagoon and turn westward towards the dunes. Ordering the others to wait at the bottom of a sandy hillock, he climbed to the top and looked down. By that point, he was somewhat out of breath. He couldn't deny there was a thrill to once again operating in the field but he also knew his true place was in the nautical realm.

It was not difficult to see the tower and he realised they had come a little too far. He could also see the returning patrol. The five of them were no more than two hundred paces away.

Then came a piece of luck: a cry from the top of the guard tower. It was answered by a wave from one of the troops. Merriman would gamble that the sentry was on his way down to join the other two. He quickly surveyed the ground to his right then scrambled back to Cary and Oliviera.

'They're close. Cary – fifty paces to the north is a gully between two dunes. That will get you quite close to the tower. Show yourselves when you think it best and I will appear at the same time from the beach side. Let us hope that surprise and the prospect of a crossfire deters any resistance.'

With that, Merriman primed his pistol and skirted around the base of the dune. He then had to negotiate a second and a third, exposing his position both times but hearing no shout from his opponents. He hurried to the tower and soon found himself wading through the drift on the seaward side. He paused and listened as the Portuguese soldiers arrived, also hearing the familiar voice of Duarte as he exited the tower.

Suddenly one of them gave a cry. Merriman rounded the tower – his shoes now full of sand – and was met by the sight of a standoff. One of the soldiers was aiming his musket at Cary and Oliviera who had halted twenty paces away, pistols aimed at the Portuguese. This man was swiftly reinforced by the two from the tower, while his compatriot kept an eye on their charges. The injured man looked on, still holding his wrist.

Merriman seized the moment. Quietly rounding the tower, he found himself no more than six feet from Duarte, who was standing at the door, bellowing at Cary.

'We have the advantage, Englishmen! Lay down your arms.'

Merriman cleared his throat, the pistol now aimed at Duarte's head.

'Not quite, lieutenant. You will instruct your men to lay down *their* arms. I have no desire to discharge this piece at you but – believe me – I will if I have to.'

Merriman later wondered if the Portuguese officer was as keen as him to prevent bloodshed, because Duarte paused only momentarily before issuing his orders. One of the men seemed to protest but he wasn't the one with a pistol two feet from his ear and Duarte repeated himself with some vigour. The four soldiers lay down their muskets, at which point Cary ran forward and pointed at the floor, gesturing for them to kneel down. Though Oliviera obeyed the instruction to gather their weapons, he had visibly blanched.

As it turned out, Duarte had not yet opened the cell but he took the keys from his belt and offered them to Merriman. Not wishing to anger the local men further, Merriman did not name Oliviera but ordered him to free Moreau. The harried ropemaker dropped the keys on the way inside but Merriman was relieved to soon hear the door open.

Cary was taking no chances; he had taken Oliviera's pistol and stood over the kneeling soldiers, a weapon in both hands.

'Moreau, are you out?' asked Merriman, keeping his focus on Duarte.

'I am!'

'Fetch the plans. Ensure that they are intact.'

'Of course.'

When two of the Portuguese soldiers began whispering, Cary darted forward and elbowed one in the back of the head. The second man thought he had a chance and made a grab for him but the experienced officer saw it coming and booted him in the side.

'Calm yourselves, lads,' he uttered. 'It will be a lot less painful.'

Duarte sighed and glanced down at his mutilated hand.

Perhaps two minutes after Merriman had sprung from behind the tower, Moreau emerged, carrying not only a satchel but a second bag. He was now wearing shoes and a smart black coat.

'May I assist?'

This was addressed to Cary who handed him a pistol.

'Put them inside,' ordered Merriman, watching as the pair ushered the soldiers into the cell. Once the four men were imprisoned, Moreau came out and addressed Duarte:

'This could all have been avoided, mon ami.'

'I am simply following orders and convention,' replied Duarte. 'Any officer would do the same.'

Still watching the soldiers, Cary reappeared and gestured for the officer to join them.

'For what it's worth, I believe you're right,' said Merriman. 'We will lock you in but give the keys to someone in the town – so that your injured man can be treated.'

'And by then, you will be long gone.' Duarte headed inside, head bowed, but halted in the doorway. 'You are evidently in a hurry, captain. Would you indulge a fellow officer and tell me why?'

Merriman lowered his pistol. 'I have orders to hunt and destroy a French warship.'

'On behalf of my country and army – I hope you blow it to pieces.'

* * *

Less than an hour later, *Thunder* was again heading south. The arrival of Moreau drew many curious looks but he was welcomed by those officers and crew who knew him.

As the last of the sails dropped from their yards, Merriman looked back at the guard tower, wondering how poor Duarte would explain himself to his superiors from Coimbra. He was at least relieved that no one on either side had been seriously harmed and that both the agent and the documents were secure.

In typical fashion, the Frenchman shunned an offer of food, instead demanding to see the latest additions to Merriman's wine cooler. The captain encouraged him to take any bottle he desired and they were soon both drinking a Bordeaux.

'My apologies, James. I am without doubt causing an unpleasant odour within the great cabin. After this glass, I will immediately attend to myself.'

'Why do you think I sat by the window?' countered Merriman with a grin.

'Very wise, mon ami. I must admit it was not pleasant to be locked in that tower knowing I could not respond to any signal, even if help came. Thank you for risking yourself and the *Thunder* on my behalf.'

'Not at all. Tell me, what's it like – inland? The war has raged for so long.'

'Chaos. Pure chaos. That man of yours, Oliviera, told me his sorry tale while the marines were preparing the boat. I have heard a hundred such stories. This fellow Wellesley, however, he may just turn the tide. I almost met the great man but my handler in Lisbon thought it ill-advised. James, I would very much like to stay aboard but the intelligence *must* travel north. What chance is there of finding me passage in that direction?'

'My plan is to cruise east to west until we intercept a likely candidate. With fair winds, you might reach the coast in a week or so. I'm sure Grahame has his ways of ensuring the information gets to Wellesley with all due haste.'

'By God I hope so. I would tell you the story of how I obtained the information but it would take me so long that I fear your nose would not survive.' Moreau stood up, drained his glass and made an appreciative noise. 'Ah. Mrs. Merriman has excellent taste in wine.'

That night, as *Thunder* began her east-west patrol, Merriman once again invited his senior officers to dinner. As expected, a refreshed Moreau regaled them with many tales of his adventures and Smythe questioned Cary about their successful foray ashore. Upon arriving in the great cabin, Lieutenant Jones had offered apologies on behalf of First Lieutenant Shrigley, who was apparently feeling unwell. With the others gripped by yet another narrative from Moreau, Merriman excused himself and made for the officers' accommodation.

Passing the midshipmen's quarters, he heard the youngsters excitedly discussing the day's events, no doubt wishing they were in the great cabin too. Merriman would invite them from time to time but there wasn't really enough space for them all. In the officers' cabin, a lone lantern was alight. Essex was on duty on deck, so Merriman knew Shrigley was alone.

'Alfred, might I disturb you?'

Shrigley stirred in his hammock. 'Captain?'

The first lieutenant was under a blanket and evidently in his sleeping attire, so Merriman swiftly put him at ease. 'Stay there, man. I'll not be here long. By God, I'd almost forgotten how poorly we treat you lieutenants – you've not much more room in here than the men.'

'My father said that's the main reason to obtain one's own command – the great cabin.'

'I wouldn't disagree. At present, Moreau is holding court with his many tales of adventure and espionage. Honestly, if it were anyone else, I wouldn't believe half of it.'

'I am sorry for my absence, captain. Some complaint of the gut.'

Merriman knew that for an excuse and did not address it.

'This issue that you wished not to discuss, Alfred. I didn't press you at the time but perhaps now we should do so. I am not one for expressions but Helen says "a problem shared, is a problem halved". Inaccurate probably but the sentiment is correct. I am your superior, I know, but also a friend, I trust?'

'Of course, sir.'

'I'll not force you though. Tell me to mind my own business if you wish and I'll let you sleep.'

Shrigley's face was barely illuminated by the lantern but Merriman suspected that suited them both well enough. The first lieutenant took in a long breath before speaking: 'Sir, you know that my wife and I have been unfortunate before. Two babies lost, both in the second half of Amelia's pregnancy. She is actually well past that stage, which is a cause for hope, but now of course I have left her.'

'As have many of your compatriots,' said Merriman. 'Brockle's wife is expecting, Rolfe's too. You know that I missed the birth of both my children.'

'Yes, sir, I know but...Amelia is so very frightened of it all. Nightmares, fits, fainting. Only my presence seemed to calm her. She has never been the strongest soul. Captain, I do love her so.'

Shrigley put a hand up to cover his face.

Merriman felt a lump form in his throat. He had only met Amelia on a couple of occasions; a delicate waif of a girl who had made a fine impression on both he and Helen.

He crossed to the first lieutenant and gripped his shoulder. 'Pray for her every night, Alfred. Write a letter every day if you wish. Sometimes it doesn't matter if the missives are not sent or received – it can help to unburden oneself. Does Amelia have help?'

'Her mother has moved in for the duration of my absence.'

'A capital idea. There is no reason to think you will not return to a healthy wife and a healthy child, is there?'

'Indeed not, sir.'
'Will you come and join us for a tot?'
'No thank you, sir. Next time?'
'I insist. Sleep well, Alfred.'
'Thank you, sir.'

Chapter Eight

Search for a Ship

Merriman had decided that they would patrol a stretch of water west of Lisbon and far to the east of the Azores. Any further south of this, they risked encountering French and Spanish vessels passing through the Straits. Searching this area, they might also encounter merchantmen arriving from the Americas. Any friendly vessel heading north along the Portuguese coast might be able to help them transport Moreau.

With lookouts atop every mast and at least two lieutenants on deck with their spyglasses, Merriman hoped it wouldn't take long to locate a likely candidate. One unidentified vessel sped inland at the first sight of the *Thunder*. The captain could have pursued but did not wish to waste hours running the vessel down, only to miss other opportunities. Around midday, an Irish brig was identified and hailed. The captain lowered his great sails and awaited the *Thunder*'s approach. Unfortunately, this man could not assist. He had endured terrible storms in the Indian Ocean and an outbreak of fever amongst his crew. He was down to just fourteen able men and would not countenance any destination other than Belfast.

The captain did, however, possess some intelligence and this was the first time Merriman heard Jourdan referred to as the "lone wolf". The Irish captain was grateful to have avoided the *Hercule* but, while resupplying on Tenerife, heard that yet another Indiaman had been taken as a prize by the French raider. At Moreau's suggestion, Merriman offered the Irishman a generous bounty to conduct him north (courtesy of the Treasury) but the man would not be swayed.

As the two ships parted, the older midshipmen told Chamier the story of how Admiral Lord Nelson lost his arm to Spanish fire while leading a landing party on Tenerife.

In late afternoon, the lookouts reported sails to the south-west. Desperate not to spend yet more hours simply waiting, Merriman ordered an impromptu gun drill. The fascinated Moreau, who stationed himself on the gun deck and emerged at the end of it stinking of smoke, with a broad smile on his face. Merriman was less amused. Shrigley's crew had again acquitted themselves well but were alone in this achievement. The exasperated Smythe had presided over another slow display. Essex and Jones's teams hadn't done much better. Merriman told the three lieutenants to speak to the gun crews one by one to better understand their encumbrances. Privately, he was beginning to wonder if he would have to punish men, officers, or both.

When the vessel was within four miles, all agreed that it was a French ship of the line, perhaps even a second or first rater. Merriman considered himself fortunate that the southerly wind offered him a straightforward escape route to the north. Despite its size, the enemy vessel had no chance of catching them before nightfall.

'You don't trust your gun crews to match theirs?' enquired Moreau when they were alone on the quarterdeck. Every scrap of sail was up and *Thunder* was charging north at eight knots.

'Not at all,' said Merriman, though it was perhaps a minor factor in his decision. 'But I do not have a roving commission. There is only *one* French warship I intend to engage and – unless something has radically changed – the *Hercule* could not be this far north.'

Two hours after nightfall, *Thunder* reversed her course and, at dawn, there was no trace of the enemy ship. There were, however, three sails coming up from the south. Two were fractionally closer together and so Merriman ordered a course towards the one nearer the coast, hoping that their luck would change.

Around four o'clock, he was at the binnacle with the midshipmen when the purser approached, looking rather sheepish. Rolfe was accompanied by the cook, who was rarely seen above decks.

'Begging your pardon, Captain Merriman,' said Rolfe. 'We've got a bit of a to-do down below. Mr. Webster is haranguing the men again.'

'Again?'

'About the sourkrout, sir. And the meat.'

'What about it?'

'He's insisting that every man takes some cabbage. And he's had cook leaving the meat in too long to get rid of the salt. The men don't like it.'

Merriman looked around to see if there was a lieutenant available but the only one on deck was Shrigley and he was at the bow, overseeing a repair to the bowsprit. It also occurred to him that Webster might need of a show of support.

'Right.' Already warm, Merriman removed his coat and led the way below. It wasn't difficult to work out where the dispute was taking place. The raised voices were echoing around the upper gun deck: Webster's melodious tones punctuated by the sailors' gruff complaints. The diminutive Welshman was surrounded by men young and old and holding up a plate of sourkrout. Merriman had to credit him with some courage; as a younger officer, he had often felt very intimidated passing through the packed lower decks.

At the sight of Merriman, the men quietened down and Webster turned.

'Ah, captain. I was just reminding the men of the importance of eating their portion of cabbage.'

'Quite so, Mr. Webster. Men, it is not the surgeon's fault that we failed to secure adequate supplies of citrus juice. In its absence, the cabbage can fulfil a similar function. Anyone here had scurvy? Want to be so weak you can barely stand? So weak you'll let down your messmates and your crewmates? Want your mouth to bleed? Your joints to ache like an old crone?'

'Mine already do, captain,' ventured the veteran Muir with a grin.

Merriman was practiced in the art of not succumbing to japes and so greeted this only with a thin smile.

'It is fortunate for you, Muir, that we have seen battle together; after that remark, a lesser man might find himself on no rations at all. Now, listen here all of you, and make sure the word spreads to the other watch. You will eat the cabbage and you will eat the meat – however much salt is in it. And if I hear of resistance, you can expect a reduction in your grog.'

Short of physical punishment, this was a sanction the sailors feared most of all and not a word was said.

'We'll consider the matter settled then,' added Merriman. 'Why look – this lad is eating his cabbage merrily enough.'

The agile young topman, Friar, was sitting in a corner and had his spoon halfway to his mouth. The cabbage fell off it when he was clapped around the head by an older fellow.

'Eating while the captain's speaking! Where are your manners?'

At the imprecations of his elders, Friar put his plate down, stood and bowed.

'Let the lad eat,' said Merriman. 'Friar, I've seen you fly up and down the rigging. Keep up the good work.'

'Thank you, sir,' said the young man, reddening.

Before departing, Merriman looked around and gestured to the surgeon. 'I'll also have you men know that we are *very* fortunate to have Mr. Webster aboard. A student of Doctor Turnbull, no less – a member of the college of surgeons and author of an excellent volume regarding matters of health in the navy. Would anyone here claim to have superior knowledge of medicine than Mr. Webster? No? I thought not.'

By the middle of the afternoon, the captain had begun to fear that he would lose another day to the search. Moreau seemed keen on consuming another bottle of Burgundy but – after they had spent several hours together – Merriman preferred to occupy himself by reading. In this case it was Julius Caesar. Concluding Act I, he was reminded of Laurence Grahame's love for Shakespeare. Imagining the Treasury man waiting for word in London only heightened his concern for the hours lost. Moreau was not certain when Massena's counter-attack might occur but it was generally considered to be a matter of weeks, not months. For Lieutenant-General Wellesley and the allied force, every hour might be crucial. Merriman even turned to prayer and it was answered shortly before nightfall.

The British merchantman *Joanna*, carrying a hold full of sugar, had departed Guiana thirty-one days earlier. The captain, a surprisingly young man named Georgeson, seemed immensely relieved that the warship bearing down on his vessel turned out to be friendly and was happy to help. His original destination was Bristol but when Merriman and Moreau told him that the Treasury would pay him two hundred pounds to divert to Plymouth, he jumped at the chance. With the light fading around the two drifting vessels, Merriman asked that the boat be hauled around to the entry port. While he was waiting, Moreau came up, bags at the ready. The Frenchman eyed the *Joanna*.

'You trust this captain?'

'As much as any we might encounter out here.'

Shrigley was close by. 'I've been watching those on deck, Charles. Only a few foreigners. Georgeson seems straightforward enough and the promise of two hundred pounds should keep him honest.'

'We told him you were Swiss,' added Merriman, 'to avoid another awkward situation.'

'Ah, very good.'

Shrigley took a sheathed cutlass from the armourer, Mr. Stones, and handed it to Moreau. 'We also thought you might feel comfortable with this at your side.'

The Frenchman took the weapon. 'Most kind.'

Moreau then took Merriman's hand. 'Sir James, my sincere thanks. I do not know how to repay you for rescuing me.'

'The only repayment I require is that the information be delivered. Best of luck, Charles. We shall meet again when I return to England.'

'Indeed, we shall. A night of wine and celebration at the home of Sir Laurence, perhaps? His wine cooler is even better stocked than yours!'

With an extravagant bow, Moreau slung the cutlass strap over his shoulder and descended into the boat. The bosun and three sailors rowed across the choppy water. As the boat returned, Merriman was pleased to see Georgeson greet Moreau himself and shake his new passenger's hand.

With the setting sun spilling orange light across the dark ocean, *Thunder* and *Joanna* parted.

* * *

Whether it was the will of God or the whims of the elements, their good weather-luck soon deserted them. Merriman knew that Atlantic gales were entirely expected for the season but that did not make them any easier to deal with. By dawn, the westerly was blowing thirty knots. With the wind abeam, *Thunder* was at least making good time but Merriman was so concerned about all the new crew and equipment that he remained on deck all morning.

By then, he had already ordered that the courses and topsails be clewed and reefed hard down. Lieutenants Jones and Essex had been despatched below to oversee the lashing of the guns to avoid instability and accidents. The galley fire had long been put out and anything vulnerable had been tied down. Hatches and gratings were covered. Above the sound of the wind and the slamming impacts of the hull, Merriman could make out the anguished cries of the three goats and four sheep yet to be slaughtered.

The captain had just thanked Peters for bringing up his sou'wester when a shout went up from the base of the mainmast. There, the bosun was pointing at the royal, one side of which had come loose, no doubt a result of motion and wind. Hand over his eyes to shield them from the spray, Merriman watched as two figures set off up the rigging. One was so small that it could only be young Friar. He was about to tell the bosun to not risk the youngster but Friar was already ahead of his compatriot. Despite his speed, there was a preternatural sureness – almost an elegance – to his movements.

'By god, that boy's a natural,' said Mr. Henderson.

'You worry about the ship,' Merriman told the master.

He reckoned the wind was now well past forty knots. Wind shrieked through the rigging and tore at the sails. So much spray was coming aboard that it ran in gushing torrents into the scuppers. He was glad to have the veteran Harris at the helm but at times even he needed assistance. Like Merriman, like them all, the sailor gazed narrow-eyed into the wind and gloom as *Thunder* charged southward.

Despite the strength of the wind and the commensurate pressure on sails, spars and lines, the captain saw – and heard – nothing to alarm him. In a way, he was glad to test the ship early on in the voyage. He did, however, realise that the months onshore had taken a personal toll. When he looked up and watched Friar and his companion working at almost a hundred feet in the air, he was nearly sick.

But by the time the topmen were back down on deck, the wind had lessened. Over the next hour, it dropped under thirty knots. Merriman was on the verge of going below when the accident occurred. At the time, he was talking to Eades and saw only the second part of it.

Harry Garland, one of the bosun's mates, seemed not to realise that the main hatch had been uncovered after the gale. Carrying a heavy block in that direction, he slipped on the slick deck. Merriman looked up in time to see him drop the block, make a despairing grab for the bosun, only to fall headfirst through the hatch.

'Eades, check on him!' ordered Merriman as Brockle hurried below. 'And for God's sake be careful. All of you!'

Merriman had witnessed such occurrences more times than he could remember; reckoned he'd seen at least half a dozen men die from falls, some from a great height. Along with the enemy and disease, such accidents accounted for a good many sailors.

When Eades returned, he was visibly pale. 'Fell badly, sir. Onto the corner of a grating where it was laid up. Bleeding from shoulder and chest. They've gone to fetch Mr. Webster, sir.'

Merriman ordered a nearby bosun's mate to put some sand on the deck to aid grip. He then dismissed Eades and stood beside Harris at the wheel for the next two hours. Only when the wind dropped significantly did Peters come up with a cup of coffee, which Merriman was in great need of.

'Anything on Garland?'

'Lost a lot of blood, sir,' said Peters, already leaving.

'Is that all?' demanded Merriman. 'How is he faring?'

Peters shrugged and went below.

After a time, Merriman realised he was being watched. Sitting between two adult topmen was young Friar. When Lieutenant Essex came back from the bow, the lad came over too, apparently to listen in.

'We think we can see Sagres Point, captain,' said Essex. 'Three points off the bow.'

'You *think*, lieutenant?'

Merriman felt on edge and knew he was taking it out on his subordinates.

'On the balance of probability, that's it, sir.'

'Tell Eades to make a note in the log.'

'Yes, sir.'

Merriman was actually satisfied to hear this. Sagres lay at the southern tip of Portugal, only one hundred and fifty miles west of the Straits of Gibraltar. They would have to be wary of enemy vessels in this well-used area but were at least leaving the Continent behind.

As Essex departed, Friar spoke up. 'Is Sagres Point important, captain? The lads were talking about it.'

'The ancients believed it to be the westernmost point of Europe, though in fact it's not. It is, however, the last of Europe we shall see for a while. The next land we spy will be Africa.'

The lad's eyes widened. 'Never thought I'd see Africa.'

'Leave the captain alone, son,' advised Harris.

'Concentrate on the helm, sailor.'

'Aye aye, sir.'

Merriman didn't mind the distraction from the foul weather and his foul mood. He'd often found that his children lightened his temperament and it seemed Friar might do the same.

'How did you like it up the mast earlier? You wouldn't catch me up there.'

'Not too bad, sir. I just look at what's in front of me. Not the sea. Not the sky. Not even the ship. Just the spars and the lines and the sails.'

'Is that right? Well, your technique clearly works.'

'Mr. Henderson says it's easier when you're young because you have no fear. I do have fear, sir, but I just try to ignore it. It was the same up the chimneys.'

'You were a sweep?'

'Yes, captain. That's where I learned my climbing. Better pay in the navy though.'

'I know you don't mind the cabbage but what about your mess-mates? Can't be easy – all older lads.'

'They're all right to me, sir.' Friar looked out to sea. 'You've been through the Straits many times, I suppose, captain.'

'I have, yes. Mr. Harris too, eh?'

Harris nodded. 'Aye, captain.'

Merriman sipped from his cup of coffee and continued: 'Do you know what the ancients called them, Friar? The Pillars of Hercules. Some of them thought that far out past them lay an island called Atlantis.'

'I've heard of it. Is it a real place?'

'No. A legend. But the ancients would have believed it because they hardly dared go far beyond the pillars. They thought the Atlantic was a sea without end. A place from which one would never return. It is said that three words were carved on the pillars. A warning.'

Despite the loud wind, Friar was hanging on every word.

Merriman enunciated the three words slowly: 'Nothing further beyond.'

Chapter Nine

First Sight of Africa

Reliable westerlies were common around the Azores and *Thunder* sailed south at a pleasing average of six knots for two days and nights. Unfortunately, the wind then backed to a southerly, forcing them to tack, slowing progress. After three days of this, the wind shifted back to west-south-west, allowing the ship to lay a course that eventually carried them towards the Moroccan coast.

On two occasions, conditions were clement enough for gun drills and slight improvements were noted. Both captain and first lieutenant found themselves rather frustrated by Essex, who was too taciturn and reserved to form a solid bond with his men. Smythe, however, was making clear progress. Though the sailors initially seemed wary of his brash persona, he seemed to be winning them over with his enthusiasm and had – generally – tamed his temper. However, Merriman soon had cause to reconsider this conclusion.

In a way, it was a situation of his making. There was seldom time for him and his officers to practice with their swords and so he asked Lieutenant Cary to lead a drill. Though the *Thunder* was heeling, she was steady enough and there was sufficient space on the quarterdeck. Aiming to spare himself and his officers too much of a crowd, Merriman made sure that the practice took place when most of the men were below, eating.

Along with Cary and Harrison, all four lieutenants attended. The marines had some wooden swords that they used for such occasions and Cary conducted a series of drills that focused first on defence. The uncompromising boxer did not spare his commanding officer criticism and – not for the first time – Merriman was reminded to improve his footwork. He did point out that he was the oldest present by at least a decade but was pleased when Cary later noted an improvement.

'Must we use these sticks?' complained Smythe as he tussled with Essex, who could barely keep pace.

Wiping sweat from his brow having just finished a bout with Cary, Merriman replied: 'After what happened to Garland, I'd like to avoid accidents for the time being.'

'How is the poor fellow?' asked Harrison, who was currently trading blows with Shrigley. Though he lacked muscle, the first lieutenant was light on his feet and an able swordsman.

'Not good,' he said, before parrying a straight thrust from the larger marine.

'A very deep wound, unfortunately,' added Merriman. 'Webster has done his best but there was a great deal of damage to bone and ligament. He is passing in and out of consciousness.'

'He might not be too popular with the men but that fellow knows his business,' said Cary. 'Especially considering his age.'

'Ha!' shouted Smythe as his latest telling blow knocked Essex's weapon clean out of his hand.

Essex said nothing as he went to recover it.

'I need more of a challenge. Cary?'

With the others looking on, these two set to it, the sharp crack of wood rising above the many other noises of the ship. Cary was both athletic and powerful but Smythe matched him; at least for the first few minutes.

'A moment.'

Smythe removed his coat, then threw it to young Eades, who was observing with Chamier and Hickey.

Smythe clearly preferred to take the front foot and was soon jabbing and swinging, sweat gleaming on his face below his blonde locks. Cary parried or avoided every blow and it soon became evident that he was simply allowing Smythe to wear himself out. Soon it was the marine who was attacking.

And when the tiring Smythe failed to parry a blow aimed at his stomach, he was struck by the blunt end. This knocked him off balance and Cary swiftly took advantage. Batting Smythe's weapon away, he placed the tip at his neck.

Spitting curses, Smythe knocked the weapon aside with his hand.

'Very well done, lieutenant,' said Cary politely.

'Indeed,' said Shrigley. 'Though I believe our marine commander has just taught you a lesson regarding the importance of endurance.'

'Once a boxer, always a boxer,' observed Lieutenant Jones.

With a sour look, Smythe retreated to the rail and leaned against it, breathing hard.

'Fortunate that the French marine wasn't so skilful.'

Smythe aimed a fierce look at Harrison.

'What's that?' asked Merriman.

Harrison continued: 'Captain, Lieutenant Smythe here has fought several duels. One was against a French marine officer in the West Indies. The story goes that he didn't sustain as much as a scratch but showed his opponent mercy and allowed him to live.'

Harrison delivered this with an arched eyebrow and so Merriman was not surprised by the response.

'*Story?*' snapped Smythe. 'What are you intimating, Harrison?'

'Nothing at all,' replied the marine. 'I simply relate what I heard. There is another rumour circulating: that you paid one of the sailors to claim knowledge of a second duel. I believe this one was with an American in Cork?'

Smythe seized his cutlass from atop a locker, his blue eyes unblinking. 'I shall give you a final chance to take that back!'

'Take what back?' retorted Harrison. 'I am merely reporting.'

'All right, Robert,' added Cary. 'That's enough.'

'Take it back,' demanded Smythe, now moving his hand to the hilt of his sheathed sword. 'Or I shall demand satisfaction.'

Harrison smirked. 'Very well – I shall be happy to keep the wooden sword. That will be sufficient to put you in your place.'

Merriman looked on, keeping his powder dry. He had seen such occurrences before, especially among proud fellows placed in close confinement for weeks on end. He had no intention of intervening unless the other senior officers could not prevail.

Sensible as ever, Shrigley stepped up beside Cary.

'Gentlemen, there is no need for satisfaction to be either sought or given. Let us leave the matter there.'

'I shall not,' spat Smythe from behind gritted teeth. 'This swine has openly insulted me.'

Now the raging Harrison looked for his sword, only to be blocked by Lieutenant Cary.

Merriman knew the time had come for him to weigh in.

'Smythe. Harrison.'

At the mention of their names, both men halted and turned towards him.

'I advise you to listen well, for I shall not repeat myself. Harrison, cease your provocations – now and for the remainder of this trip. Smythe, you were not directly insulted. Even if you were, I will not countenance duelling between my officers. Unless you can regain control of yourselves, you will not find another captain willing to have you aboard a vessel of His Majesty's Navy. I will personally see to it.'

There were other measures he could have used but Merriman knew the pair of them were fiercely ambitious, covetous of promotion and prizes. He had it in his power to ruin their careers and they knew it.

Cary fixed his first officer with a steely stare. 'Best find some words for Captain Merriman.'

'My apologies, captain. And to you, Smythe.'

'My apologies, captain. May I be dismissed?'

'You may.'

With a final glare at Harrison, Smythe stormed away towards the foredeck.

That evening, Merriman was alone in the great cabin, halfway through Act II of *Julius Caesar* when there was a knock on his door. As it was the third knock in less than an hour, he sighed. The first visitor had been the purser, who'd informed him that the bottom half of three tubs of pork had been found to be rotten. The second visitor had been the armourer who – as requested – had detailed the repairs made to two misfiring guns. The third visitor was the surgeon's mate and he carried ill tidings: Garland had just died.

Dismissing the man, Merriman spied Shrigley coming towards him.

'You heard, sir?'

'I did.'

'His mess-mates are putting him in his hammock now. Webster said it was only a matter of time with all the blood lost. Brockle told me he was always very sure-footed. It can happen to any of us, I suppose.'

'I'm afraid it can. He was with us in the Adriatic, yes?'

'He was sir. Brockle already has a suggestion for a new mate. I took the liberty of-'

'Yes, yes, of course.'

'I'll make the arrangements for tomorrow. Eleven o'clock, sir?'

'Conditions permitting, yes. I'm hoping the lookouts spy the coast tomorrow. I've a feeling our best chance of picking up intelligence is to stay close to land. What of our warring officers?'

'Seems to have calmed down, sir. Smythe has been regaling us with *very* detailed versions of both duels.'

'Is that so? This rumour of him paying a man to spread favourable tales. Is it credible?'

'Honestly, sir - I've no idea.'

Holding his Bible reminded Merriman that he had not yet conducted a ceremony of any kind. Without a chaplain on board, the duty fell to him. He had so far been more occupied with gun drills but told Shrigley to remind him to gather the men on the following Sunday. While not particularly devout himself, he respected those who were and knew from experience that such occasions helped bring the crew together.

Those not required to man the sails gathered at the after-hatchway the following morning. Garland's body had already been placed there by his mess-mates, two cannonballs in his hammock to carry him down and the Union Flag covering him.

Removing his hat, Merriman looked out at the hundreds crammed into the rear of the ship. After two readings on the matter of death, he added a few words of his own, using information gathered by Shrigley.

'Yesterday, John Owen Garland of Derby departed this life. One of six, he leaves behind a wife, Mary, and son, Arthur. He was thirty-one years of age and had spent thirteen of those at sea. He had sailed on the *Winchester*, the *Duke of Argyle* and the *Pennington* to name only a few. He had been with us onboard *Thunder* for two years. Remembered fondly by all those here present as a fine sailor and friend.'

He turned to his right, and the four mess-mates manning the grating on which the dead man lay. 'We now commit his body to the deep.'

Merriman watched young Chamier and some of the other sailors cringe at the sound of the corpse striking the water. The *Thunder* left the dead man in her wake, apparently as indifferent as the waves and the wind.

'Before we separate, I have one more thing left to say. Poor Garland lost his life due to an accident. It might not be written down but I have another standing order for every last one of you: take care. Be it on deck or below, in a gale or a calm, in the day or the night – look out for yourselves and your mates. Dismissed.'

Barely a minute later, a cry went up from the foremast and word swiftly reached him.

'Land sighted, captain. Africa.'

Merriman ordered that *Thunder* be taken in close so that they could better establish their precise position. Along with the midshipmen, Lieutenant Jones made good use of spyglass, compass and chart to establish that they were off Cape Cantin in the north of Morocco. Merriman took up his own spyglass and examined the pale brown cliffs of the African coast.

He then joined Jones and pored over the chart. *Thunder* was currently three hundred miles north of the Canary Islands. Bearing in mind the fact that the Irish captain had gathered some intelligence regarding the *Hercule* on Tenerife, Merriman considered exploring the area. However, that would mean losing several days and he would still be very far from where the French raider had previously struck. If they could reach the Cape Verde islands in good time, he would be happier with their progress. The islands were a Portuguese possession and another place where he could resupply and possibly gain intelligence.

'Sir?' asked Lieutenant Jones.

'As long as the wind remains in our favour, we shall aim to pass the Canaries to the east and continue on to the Cape Verdes.'

First Lieutenant Shrigley had just come on deck and joined the others at the binnacle. It was a bright, cloudless day and he shielded his eyes as the approached. Merriman could tell that the man was feeling better: on the early part of the journey the buttons of his coat appeared dull and greasy. Now they were polished and gleaming.

'Very good, sir.' Jones took up his dividers and made some calculations. 'Around eight hundred miles.'

'A week or so,' said Merriman before turning his attention to Shrigley. 'The Cape Verdes, I think.'

'Very good, captain.' Shrigley looked out at the coast for a moment. 'Remember that fellow in the officer's club, Jones?'

'I do indeed,' said Jones.

Shrigley addressed Merriman: 'Sir, he was a member of something called the Association for Discovering the…'

'No,' interrupted Jones. 'It was the Association for the Promotion of Discovering Africa.'

'The *Interior* Parts of Africa,' corrected Shrigley.

'That's it,' said Jones. 'Quite a mouthful.'

'I believe I've heard of it,' said Merriman.

Shrigley continued: 'Sir, this fellow was bemoaning the fact that the war has interrupted European exploration of the continent. He himself is a post captain but I do believe he'd rather be out there, exploring.'

'One can see the attraction,' added Jones. 'Imagine entering virgin territory, encountering sights and peoples and animals that no white man has ever seen before.' He gestured to the map and the featureless area east of Morocco. 'The Great Desert of Zaara. They say it's nothing but a sea of sand.'

'I want to see a camel!' exclaimed young Adkins, who was listening in. When the officers frowned at him, he blushed and pretended to examine the map.

'At least we know the desert is there to the north,' said Merriman. 'We know almost nothing of the central and southern interior.'

'This fellow claimed that we know less of the African continent than the Romans and Greeks,' added Shrigley. 'He seemed to think it was something of a disgrace that British ships sail around the entire world but we know so little of the Dark Continent.'

'They all want to find Timbuktu,' said Jones. 'The city of gold. That Scotsman did at least find the Niger river a couple of years back. I read his book. What was his name?'

'Park,' said Shrigley. 'Mungo Park.'

Merriman was just as fascinated by all this as the other officers but he brought the conversation to a quick close.

'Gentlemen, the foretopgallant is in need of attention and those idlers are living up to their name. Please see to it.'

Chapter Ten

Cape Verde Islands to Freetown

Eight days later, on the fourteenth of April, the *Thunder* dropped anchor off Praia, capital of t he Cape Verde Islands. Merriman had spent the previous hour on deck; like the officers and men he was keen to see land after so many days at sea.

In the distance sat the high mountains that dominated the north of Santiago, the largest island of the archipelago. On this morning, the lower reaches were wreathed by haze and mist, the peaks stark in the blue sky. Closer were the rolling lush hills that surrounded the capital. Along the coast from Praia were numerous wide, sandy beaches with a smattering of high palms. The town itself consisted of a few dozen white-washed houses with thatched roofs. There were two merchant ships anchored, one of which was taking on supplies.

At the first sight of the British warship, small boats – some with sails, others with only oars – had converged on them. Each contained two, three or four of the locals, many of whom wore only long, sleeveless tunics. They seemed very friendly but caused a hazard until Mr. Brockle bellowed at them to move away.

Once the anchor was set, however, they were allowed to come close. Mr. Rolfe and Mr. Webster had already recruited Oliviera to translate and he swiftly explained that they would take as many oranges, limes and lemons as the locals could supply. Word of this quickly spread. Those already selling fruit negotiated with the purser while others frantically made their way ashore to stock up and return.

Merriman did not intend on tarrying any longer than was necessary but sent Lieutenants Jones and Smythe ashore with four marines to watch over them. The officers had orders to learn what they could about Jourdan and the *Hercule.*

When they returned in mid-afternoon, the lieutenants had to wait for the last of the small boats to deliver its cargo. Dozens of crewmen had been tasked with hauling up the bags, barrels and boxes crammed full of colourful fresh fruit. It was rather early in the year but certain types were in season, including some small but tasty oranges. The day was a warm one and Merriman sat with Shrigley and Essex, eating the oranges while the purser and clerk frantically tried to keep track of their purchases and pay their suppliers. Meanwhile, the purser's mates had to find somewhere for all the new produce. With the captain's permission, Webster had already placed a barrel of the oranges by the scuttlebutt and the sailors had been told they could take one each.

One of the ship's boys caused some laughter by juggling three of the oranges while singing, 'no more sourkrout for me!'

Shrigley then departed to assist the busy purser, giving Merriman a rare chance to speak to Mr. Essex.

'I haven't heard much about your family. You're from Lancashire, correct?'

'Yes, sir. Near Oldham.'

'You haven't much of an accent.'

'I've not lived there since I was thirteen, sir. My father says I've lost the local dialect completely – being around what he calls Southern toffs.'

'Ah. A nautical family?'

'Miners mostly.'

'You didn't fancy that trade? This is hardly less dangerous.'

'I had a distant cousin who had served with the navy, sir. My father was badly injured when I was ten and can no longer work. My mother cares for him and my sister's earnings don't go very far.'

'Injured in the mine?'

'Yes. An explosion. Can't use his legs but says he was lucky – lost five friends in the blast.'

'I see. So, you are the breadwinner?'

'Yes, sir. I send most of my earnings back to Oldham. Always have.'

'That must make things difficult at times.'

'At times, sir. But I'm proud to do it. Father insists on taking me to the local inn every night when I'm home. He is proud, I suppose.'

'And so he should be.'

Merriman was then approached by one of the petty officers, who was accompanied by a Scottish sailor who he recognized as a member of the veteran Muir's gun crew.

'Begging your pardon, sir,' said the petty officer. 'Archibald here asks if there might be a possibility of visiting that church. I don't suppose we'll come across another one anytime soon and some of the men would greatly appreciate being able to attend a service.'

Merriman hadn't actually noticed the church but now saw that it was set on a plateau some way above the town, the tower and cross quite clear.

'Were we here longer I would of course allow it.'

'Understood, sir.'

'However,' said Merriman. 'I have been remiss of late. Perhaps if you and some others would like to choose a psalm or two, you can read them next Sunday.'

'Much appreciated, cap'n,' answered Archibald in his Highland brogue.

The deck was so busy that only when Smythe and Jones reached the quarterdeck did Merriman realise they were not alone. Trailing along behind them was a weatherbeaten fellow with scabs upon his nose and cheeks. He was walking awkwardly and seemed in pain but he removed his hat and nodded politely when he neared the captain.

Jones spoke up. 'Sir, this is Ernest Trent, sailmaker from an Indiaman called the *Rochester*. He was until recently abed in the town's hospital. We were directed to see him by a British merchant who thought we might be interested to hear his tale.' Jones gestured to Trent, who did not look entirely steady.

Merriman grabbed a nearby box and turned it upside down. 'A seat perhaps, Mr. Trent.'

'Thank you kindly, captain,' said the sailmaker, grimacing as he sat.

Merriman now noted that his hands were also scabbed and scarred. 'If I am not very much mistaken, you have spent some time on the open sea.'

'I have, captain. I must say it is pleasant to hear English voices again. I have felt quite alone in that hospital.'

At Jones' prompting, Trent began his testimony. 'February 4th, sir. My ship – the *Rochester* – became the latest victim of the lone wolf. I...' Trent paused, grimaced and made fists of his hands. 'By god, I hope you...'

'Come, sir,' said Jones. 'Please tell the captain what you told us.'

'We were taken without a shot being fired,' said Trent, his expression still sour. 'Though if we'd known what we were in for, we would have fought 'til our last breath. The *Hercule* had already taken two other merchantmen that week so were thinly stretched for prize crews. We were disarmed and eight Frenchies were put aboard. Five marines and three sailors. We were to make for Gijon. We headed north and for a time all was peaceful. But the marines were led by a corporal named Durand. He seemed to think that he had taken not only the ship but all our possessions as prizes. He robbed our sea-chests and there was naught we could do about it. Captain Nibbs is – was – not one to fight but Durand went too far. He took a locket that contained a picture of the captain's wife. When he refused to return it, the captain grabbed one of the marine's cutlasses and stuck him.'

Trent shook his head. 'Honestly, for all his talk of us playing along and staying alive, I think Nibbs realised he should have put up a fight from the start. Not of one us wanted to end up in a French prison hulk.'

'Please continue your account,' said Jones.

'The marines attacked.' Beneath his sun-bleached eyebrows, Trent's eyes were bloodshot. 'They killed the captain and eight of the men. They threw the bodies over the side. The passengers stayed out of it. The four of us that surrendered were put in the boat and cast adrift. They left us barely enough for a few days. We were in it for *nineteen*. Wouldn't have made it if not for a couple of flying fish sent by the Lord. Fortunately, the Frenchmen had put me in charge of navigation and so I'd a recent look at the charts. I knew these islands were our best chance. We washed up on Maio two weeks ago. By then, the bosun, Charters, had died. It was just me, the cook and a lad.'

'They're still in the hospital, captain,' explained Smythe. 'So parched that they cannot yet speak.'

'You've had quite an ordeal, Trent,' said Merriman. 'And I commend you for your courage and fortitude. What can you tell us about the *Hercule* and her captain?'

'Sir, you'll understand that we had our own concerns at the time but two of our men had served and I'll tell you all I remember. I'm not all that knowledgeable about military affairs myself but Fellows reckoned she had at *least* eighty guns.'

'Some of the other Bucentaures have such modifications,' remarked Shrigley.

'And this Jourdan is a sly bastard,' added Trent. 'We ourselves were tricked; the French captain hid his vessel behind the two other merchantmen so he could get close. Only then did he fly his tricolour.'

'And what of the man himself?'

'I only glimpsed him before we were put to work. A sharp face, almost like a man who's been ill. Eyes sort of sunken and dark.'

'Anything else, Trent?'

'Some of the lads had a bit of French and we picked up some titbits once we headed north with that accursed prize crew. The marines were happy about their share but didn't like being split up from their mates. Sounded like Jourdan replaced his prize crew sailors with able men from the ships he nabbed. I wouldn't have worked for that swine but I suppose some would.'

'Might have no choice,' said Jones.

'Marines are harder to replace,' added Trent, 'so his contingent was down to about half its original, so they said. Sort of a victim of his own success.'

'Anything else at all, Trent?' said Merriman. 'Think carefully now.'

'They've been operating off the south of Africa for quite a time, sir. We heard them talk of several ports – places we would never have risked. Novo Redondo, Bengo, even the slave ports. Hope that was of use, cap'n.'

'Yes, Trent,' said Merriman, considering all he had heard. 'Most useful indeed.'

Less than an hour later, powered only by a weak westerly that barely filled her sails, *Thunder* raised anchor and continued south. All things considered; Merriman reckoned the stop to have been more than worthwhile. Mr Webster now seemed the happiest man aboard and, with the two surgeon's mates and other conscripts, immediately set about distributing the citrus juice in time for the afternoon meal.

The wind fell away to almost nothing overnight and, by dawn, they had made barely thirty miles. Merriman decided to use the opportunity for another full gun drill. This was the first occasion in which all the long guns functioned well and there were thankfully no more accidents. The times were still too slow for the captain's liking but he now felt confident to move onto accuracy drills when the next chance came.

In the afternoon the wind veered to the north, white cloud rolled in and the breeze picked up to fifteen knots and remained steady for several days. Still keen to gather information where possible, Merriman wished to keep *Thunder* in sight of the coast. He was, however, careful to steer clear of Dakar, the French possession and slave port.

Eighty miles south of Dakar, they passed the broad mouth of the river Gambia. Though the blue water was here full of silt, one of the lookouts claimed to have seen a crocodile.

'Wouldn't know a bloody crocodile if he saw one,' remarked Henderson, the sailing master.

'They say crocodiles feasted on the dead at the Battle of the Nile,' added the helmsman.

Though the cloud had come in, it was a warm day. A canopy had been put up at dawn and the officers were gathered under it in their shirt sleeves, gazing out at the river.

'That's where Mungo Park began his expedition,' said Shrigley, examining the verdant jungle that seemed to begin at the shore and roll on endlessly into the interior. They had seen a few small local boats but no ships at all.

'One of his servants was taken by a crocodile,' added the first lieutenant, 'there was a picture of it in the book.'

'Nasty way to go,' said young Eades.

Hickey shook his head. 'Shark would be worse.'

* * * *

There were two reasons to give the Bissagos Islands a wide berth. The first was the dangerous shoals to the south, the second was the reputation of the islanders themselves, who had resisted all attempts at invasion by European powers and given the Portuguese a very bloody nose three centuries earlier.

The captain and his officers daily consulted not only their charts but the nautical almanac which – as well as the usual celestial and navigational information – had been fortified by Lieutenant Shrigley with various reports and accounts obtained by the Admiralty over the years. Though information on the African coast was patchy, this proved invaluable to Merriman as they charted their way south.

Passing lands known to be occupied by the Jaloff people, then the Feloops and Foolahs, they eventually reached the coast off Freetown. Retaken by the British only three years earlier, it now served as the base of the West Africa Squadron. On the morning that they passed the port, Merriman was in two minds about making a stop. Mr. Webster had reminded him of the danger of disease in this area; then again, the Squadron might have some information about the *Hercule*, though they were operating in an area thousands of miles north of the Cape of Good Hope.

In the end, no decision was necessary. An unusual easterly brought a vessel out from Freetown as *Thunder* approached. Despite their location, it seemed that the dangers of the area had caused fear among officers and crew; Merriman only saw this tension recede when the lookouts reported that the vessel was also flying the red ensign.

The ship was found to be the *Arrow* and she looked to be a converted whaler, boasting at least a dozen cannons on her gun deck. She drew close and lowered her sails, the two ships rolling in a light swell. The captain was a white-haired man who was seen to put on both coat and hat before addressing Merriman.

'A sight for sore eyes!' he declared with a gritty rasp. 'Captain Bartholomew Lukin at your service. And you, sir?'

'Captain Sir James Merriman. Sir, I know you – were you not first lieutenant of the *Calcutta*? It would have been in, what, ninety-one?'

'Merriman, by God! The last time I saw you, you were little more than a snivelling lad. I'd heard you'd done well and now I see it's true.'

Lukin spoke to his officers before turning back to Merriman.

'*Thunder,* is it? Damn fine name for a damn fine ship!'

'Much appreciated, sir. I presume you've come out of Freetown. Are you part of the Squadron?'

'Part? We are *half.* There are only the two of us down here and a damnably difficult job they've given us. On that subject, may I ask for your assistance? We've had word of a big slaver heading up the coast from Lagos. A ship-of-the-line would make the task considerably easier.'

Aware that virtually the entirety of both crews was listening in, Merriman had no desire to continue the conversation in public. 'Captain, won't you join me for a tot so that we can catch up and exchange news? I will send a boat across.'

Merriman gave the order and headed down to the great cabin so that he might change out of his damp shirt. While Peters brought him a new one, Mr. Webster came to his door.

'Yes, doctor?'

'Sir, it might take only one visitor to bring fever or another ailment onto *Thunder.*'

'I am fully aware of that, but he is a former shipmate. I can hardly sail on past without at least showing a fellow captain some hospitality.'

His tone clearly alarmed the Welshman, who apologised and made himself scarce.

It seemed to take an age for Lukin to come across and he looked very slow on his feet as he entered the cabin, escorted by Lieutenant Shrigley.

'You must excuse my tardiness, James,' said Lukin. 'Sixty-four this year.'

'Is that so? Most admirable, Bartholomew.'

As the pair shook hands, Merriman wondered what on Earth had persuaded the aged captain to take on this most onerous and perilous duty.

Lukin ran a hand through his curly white hair and looked about him. 'If we had more time, I should greatly like to see more of this fine vessel. If I'm not mistaken, she's new or close to it.'

'Recently refitted,' said Merriman, pouring them both some rum as they sat near the window. 'Now, we could spend an age on the past but I'm afraid we must concern ourselves with present and future. Tell me, does the Squadron have any information regarding a French ship named *Hercule*? The captain, Jourdan, has been picking off prizes north of the Cape of Good Hope with some abandon.'

Lukin downed some rum and wiped his dry lips. '*Hercule* – we've heard of her, yes, but no sightings as I recall. As you can imagine, the slavers give us quite enough to contend with. You have been tasked with stopping this Jourdan?'

'I have.'

'No roving commission then?'

'I'm afraid not.'

'I myself have only a letter of marque,' replied Lukin. 'It often seems that we are to carry out this odd duty with one hand tied behind our backs. *Arrow* is weatherly enough but I've neither enough men nor enough guns. Now listen, James, this vessel we're after is Spanish – the *Isabella*. She is regularly spotted in the Gulf of Guinea. We have it on good authority that she is sure to appear off the Ivory Coast some time in the next week. We cannot take her alone.'

Merriman sighed, having expected to face such a dilemma. Though his orders were specific, he had already diverted his ship for another purpose: rescuing Moreau. That was undoubtedly of more military significance but he felt great sympathy for his former compatriot and his difficult mission.

'There would of course be a share of prize money,' added Lukin.

'Bartholomew, I wish I could be of assistance but we simply cannot spare the time. We still have very far to go to reach the *Hercule*'s hunting grounds.'

Lukin leaned forward. 'Could you give me three days? By God, with these guns of yours pointed at her, those Spaniards won't even put up a fight.'

Merriman said nothing but then Lukin clapped a hand on his knee and downed the rest of his rum. 'Ah, what am I saying? This is not your mission. Forgive the desperation of an old man.'

'Not at all.'

Lukin leaned back once more and regarded his glass. 'At the beginning I did not wish this mission to be mine. Wilberforce, Clarkson and their like – I'll admit I did not understand their case. To me it was a trade like any other. That was before I came down here.'

'You must have seen slave ships before,' replied Merriman.

'Only at sea. I'd never been onboard one.' Lukin seemed to shiver. 'I took the first of my three slavers last year. One man – I shall not call him a captain – decided that he would rather lose his human cargo over the side then see them taken by us. Chained together they were – in groups of a dozen or so. Over they went, one after the other. The shouts and the screams chilled the very soul but it's the eyes I shall never forget.'

'By God.'

'The bastard didn't stop until one of my sharp shooters put a ball through his arm. Then we boarded. They wouldn't tell us how many had been in the hold but we worked it out from the books. Near six hundred. A hundred of them died at sea and he rid himself of two hundred more right in front of us. There was barely enough food for them but we got them back ashore. Would have been nice to send them home but most were from deep in the interior – didn't even know how to get there.'

Merriman just shook his head.

'At least they're safe enough in Freetown,' continued Lukin. 'You know it was founded by slaves – with the help of Granville Sharp.'

'With that name, is an appropriate place for the squadron to reside. Bartholomew, I am truly sorry not to be able to help. However, I do have the ear of Admiral Sir Henry Goodwin. When I'm back in England, I will make him fully aware of just how under-equipped you are for this task. I cannot guarantee it will reach the commissioners but I will do my best. Now, listen, the *Thunder* is well-stocked. What can I give you and your ship?'

Chapter Eleven

A Broadside for the Slavers

After parting from Captain Lukin and the *Arrow*, *Thunder* ploughed her way south once more before abruptly dropping into a wind-hole. With the sea as calm as a millpond and none of the sails stirring, the warship wasn't even making a knot. Merriman and his officers could see from the clouds and the distant sea conditions that there was a bit of wind elsewhere; not one of them could recall such a singular event. However, a sailmaker's mate named Miles – the oldest man aboard at sixty-six – remarked that he had encountered such conditions in the nearby Bight of Benin several decades earlier.

Though First Lieutenant Shrigley made the suggestion, Merriman had already decided that they would run out the guns. On this occasion, he had the launch deploy a twenty-foot-high floating target that the carpenters knocked together while the gun crews readied themselves. In this case, individual crews were to be tested. With the target placed at a range of two hundred feet, the drills began, with the officers gathered on the quarterdeck.

There was a predictable variance in quality, with most cannonballs whistling away into the distance. Every direct hit was greeted with a 'huzzah!' from their compatriots. Three hours into the drill, there had been sufficient direct strikes for the target to be in need of repair.

Merriman paid several trips to the gundecks and – liaising closely with the officers – worked with individual teams. Old Muir had done a fine job of improving the struggling crew and by sunset, every gun had fired at least four times. Most had made significant improvements and

Merriman ordered an extra ration of grog for successful captains and their crews. The most accurate crew of all manned a gun that they called Lightning, in honour of their ship's name and their reloading speed. Led by another experienced hand, Butcher, they managed two direct hits and a near miss from their four attempts.

As night fell, Merriman considering putting the boat and launch out and having the ship towed clear of the windhole. However, having concluded dinner with the great cabin still reeking of smoke, he sensed movement and looked out of the window to see a slim trail of wake. Moments later, an enthusiastic Chamier rushed down to report that there was a breath of breeze and that *Thunder* was on the move again. Greatly relieved, a weary Merriman fell asleep with his *Julius Caesar* in his hands.

He was roused before dawn by Midshipman Eades, who apologised profusely for disturbing him.

'Eades, you need not apologize – I am quite accustomed to being woken, you know.'

'Sorry, cap...er, I'm here at the request of Lieutenant Essex, sir. We can hear cannon fire to the east. A sea battle of some kind.'

Five minutes later, Merriman was on deck. The sun was as yet nothing more than a faint orange bloom to the east. To the north-east, more blooms of colour could be seen: the blasts of long guns. Seconds later, the reports rolled across the water to the *Thunder*.

Essex was at the rail, spyglass in his hand.

'How far would you say, lieutenant?' asked Merriman, still buttoning up his coat in the chill air.

'Around five miles, sir.'

'Can we lay a direct course?' asked Merriman, without looking at the sails.

'Yes, sir. Near a run. We've at least fifteen knots of wind.'

'We shall bring her around then.'

'Aye aye, sir.'

More crew were summoned on deck and up came Bosun Brockle and Master Henderson to oversee the change of course and change of sail as *Thunder* ran before the wind. Merriman couldn't help wondering – and hoping – that they might have encountered the *Hercule,* though he knew they were probably too far north. He had no wish to subject himself to a tense wait so headed downstairs for some coffee and a light breakfast.

Upon learning that they were now within two miles of a pair of vessels exchanging fire, Merriman ordered Shrigley to clear for action. At the brisk sound of the marine's drum, the captain made his way through both gundecks to ensure all was ready. While there, he encountered Lieutenant Cary, who seemed as eager as usual. The marine officer swiftly swallowed the piece of biscuit hanging out of his mouth.

'Morning, sir. Judging by the intermittent fire, those are not warships.'

'I agree.'

'You'd prefer my men with their crews, I suppose.'

'Please. Though a few sharp-shooters wouldn't go amiss.'

Cary had his musket in his hands. 'Ready if you need us, captain.'

'Very good.'

Merriman made way for a dashing powder-monkey and his precious load, took his hat from the ever-dutiful Peters, and headed up on deck.

He was greeted by an excited Lieutenant Smythe. 'Sir, it's the *Arrow*. Captain Lukin. He's in close action with what looks like the slave ship.'

'What? You're sure?'

'We imagine he must have picked up a fair wind further inshore while we were stuck in that hole.'

'Possible, I suppose.' Merriman followed Smythe forward, to where Shrigley was already stationed at the foremast, spyglass in hand. He instantly handed it to the captain.

'Mile and a quarter perhaps, sir. Sounds like neither of them have more than a dozen guns firing. Might take a while to settle it.'

Merriman saw that both vessels were sailing south, wind on their beam.

'The *Arrow*'s nearer to us, sir.'

'Yes, that's her all right. Ensign's clear enough.'

'We have the weather-gauge and the weather luck, captain,' exclaimed Smythe. 'Seven knots at the last count. We'll be on them in a quarter-hour.'

Merriman looked forward, at the bowsprit dipping as *Thunder* leaped towards the warring craft. Though he'd elected not to commit days to assisting Lukin, the elements had conspired to place his ship here. And he found himself bristling at the sheer greed of the slave ship and its captain, who would rather see more life lost than give up the profits of his illegal trade. More than that, he was concerned for the ageing Lukin and his ill-equipped vessel.

Retreating to the quarterdeck, he sent Shrigley down to take charge of the guns and stationed himself close to the helmsman.

'Aim for the stern of the *Arrow*, Harris.'

'Aye aye, sir.'

The two ships were still reaching south on parallel tracks.

'What do you suggest, Smythe?'

The lieutenant seemed surprised by the question but answered swiftly enough.

'Assuming the slaver flees, run him down and fire warning shots, sir.'

'Is a warning shot sufficient? He is already engaged in combat with a ship of His Majesty's Navy.'

'I believe Captain Lukin would like to take the prize intact, sir.'

'True. Ah, look there – Lukin's going for his stern.'

The *Arrow* had slowed and was now turning to larboard, presumably to target the enemy's rudder. However, the Spanish vessel had anticipated the move – or perhaps seen the *Thunder* – and the captain answered with his own more pronounced turn toward the coast. Merriman could make out men scrambling around aboard the slaver and he spied two puffs of smoke from deck guns mounted on her stern.

Thunder was now so close that all heard the impacts on the *Arrow* and the cry that went up. Whatever had happened, it so affected officers and crew that they did not change course with the still-turning slaver. In fact, within seconds, some of the sails could be seen flapping. The enemy vessel, meanwhile, was heading eastward with full sails.

'Range, Smythe?'

'I should say three hundred yards, sir.'

'I agree. Hickey, tell the lieutenant to fire all the larboard main guns on my order. Range three hundred yards.'

Midshipman Hickey repeated the orders in his high, clear voice.

'Helm, two points to starboard – put us directly behind him.'

'Aye, captain,' answered Harris.

'Mister Henderson, we will turn to starboard so the wind is abeam. Please attend to the sails.'

'Aye aye, captain.'

Henderson passed on orders to ensure that all went smoothly at mizzen, main and foremast. 'Ready, captain.'

'Helm to starboard.'

The sailors were ready with their sheets but it was the guns that concerned Merriman. Their target was narrow but he hoped the sheer volume of fire would dissuade the Spaniard from continuing his pointless resistance. *Thunder* was upwind and a far larger ship: they would catch her in minutes.

Thankfully, *Arrow* had by now at least also turned north to stay well out of the way.

'Fire!'

Only seconds after Hickey repeated the order, the fourteen twenty-eight pounders of the larboard main deck boomed. The majority of the shots whizzed past the slaver but at least two struck home: one putting a hole in a topgallant, the other slamming into the stern with a splintering crack.

Merriman knew the gunners would be reloading and that the upper deck teams were ready if he needed them.

Midshipman Eades was at the stern, watching the ship of the West Africa Squadron.

'What's going on there, Eades?'

'Sails filling again, sir, but many men gathered at the stern.'

Merriman could not help feeling that only injury or the death of her captain could account for *Arrow*'s failure. He prayed that poor old Lukin had not been killed.

'The slaver is easing her sails and heaving to, sir,' said Smythe, looking ahead. 'Lowering their colours.'

Despite the surrender, Merriman remained wary. He kept the *Thunder* upwind of the slaver, which they now found was indeed the *Isabella* Lukin had mentioned. Merriman also had Cary place twenty men with muskets on the foredeck. He then told the lieutenant to take another twenty marines across in the launch and seize control of the stationary ship.

'There are really slaves in there?' mused young Chamier as Merriman crossed the quarterdeck to the larboard rail. The *Arrow* now came alongside, some of her royals flapping. Merriman was met by the disconcerting sight of Captain Lukin covered almost head to waist in blood. And yet he was standing up and appeared in fair condition.

'My thanks, captain,' said Lukin, his voice shaky, 'and my apologies for our slowness. My...'

He turned and gestured to a body close by, covered by a white sheet already stained red. 'My first officer. That shot from their stern chaser damn near took his head off.'

'I am sorry.'

'Why do these bastards fight so hard!' uttered one of Lukin's other officers, fists clenched.

Another was kneeling by the first officer's body, eyes gleaming with tears.

Merriman understood entirely. It was common enough for men to be injured in battle but such a grisly occurrence to a senior officer could often paralyse a crew.

As the ever-curious Chamier trotted across the quarterdeck to investigate, Shrigley barred his way. 'You don't need to see that, lad. Go and complete the log.'

'Aye, sir.'

Lukin cleared his throat and began doling out orders; swiftly sending an officer and his own small detachment of marines to join Cary's men on the *Isabella*. Not long after they reached the slaver, Cary returned with the ship's captain. The experienced marine took the man by the collar and ushered him across the quarterdeck to where Merriman and his officers stood. By now lines had been secured and the two British warships lay side by side in the water.

'Name of Studenty, sir,' said Cary, face grim.

'Estudiante,' corrected the captain, an overweight fellow with a greying beard. He was well dressed and wore several gaudy rings and a pocket watch.

'Happy with your handiwork?' demanded one of Lukin's officers. The Spaniard looked at the bloodied body and replied in his clear but heavily-accented English. 'Bad luck. It could easily have been one of *my* men.'

Merriman bristled at this and Cary could not control himself. Keeping one hand on the man's collar, he used his right arm to elbow Estudiante across the face. Evidently not lacking courage, the Spaniard tried to strike back, only to receive another blow into his gut, which doubled him over.

Merriman said nothing when Cary glanced at him with a faintly apologetic look. 'Sorry, sir. Hand slipped.'

'Twice?' asked Shrigley.

Cary shrugged.

Estudiante straightened up, speaking only when he had composed himself. 'We have sailed for months. Risked pirates. Disease. Paid good money for those slaves. Why should I just give up?'

'Because that trade is now illegal,' said Lukin.

'Only by *English* law. I am *Spanish* and we are a long, long way from England. Though you think the opposite, your country does not own the oceans.' The captain spat onto the deck. 'English law means nothing here.' He looked around at the officers. 'By God, the arrogance of it. Five years ago, men like you were making money off slaves just as we do. More, in fact. You are no better than I.'

'Not men like us, captain,' replied Merriman.

'What happens now?' asked the Spaniard.

'You and your vessel will be taken to Freetown,' said Lukin. 'And from there the courts will decide. How many slaves do you have aboard?'

'Four hundred or so.'

Some of Lukin's officers glanced at each and nodded.

'What is it?' asked Estudiante.

'We receive a small payment for every slave landed,' said one of the men, with a smug grin. 'Your efforts are much appreciated.'

'It is as I said,' replied the Spaniard, shaking his head in disbelief. 'You are no better than us.'

* * * *

While she'd been under way, the access ports of the *Isabella* had been closed. When they were opened, the smell from the hold was so terrible that – even on the open sea – it spread swiftly to the *Thunder*. Assisted by Cary's marines, Lukin's men had taken Captain Estudiante and his officers onboard *Arrow*. The crew were mainly Spanish and a couple of them took exception to the English intervention: they too were placed under lock and key. The remainder – twelve men in total – seemed compliant enough. They would now be governed by Lukin's prize crew of a second lieutenant, four sailors and six marines. Merriman felt great sympathy for the young officer, who seemed somewhat overawed by the task in hand. He emerged from the hold with a handkerchief over his mouth, immediately ordering that some of the slaves be freed and allowed on deck. These turned out to be several invalids who could barely move, two pregnant women and four women with infants.

The sight of this was too much for Alfred Shrigley, who excused himself and went below.

'By God,' said Lieutenant Jones, 'those poor souls.'

'The Spaniard made a fair point though,' added Lieutenant Essex. 'We profited from the trade for centuries, as have most in positions of power: many Africans included.'

'It is usually they who bring the slaves from the interior,' added Tom Henderson. 'Most are prisoners of war.'

'Not them,' said Jones, nodding towards the *Isabella*.

Though they had been unchained, the two female slaves were still manacled at ankle and wrist. One held her babe to her thin breast and gazed out at the warship, a hand veiling her eyes from the sun.

'What must she be thinking?' said Jones. The musician had always struck Merriman as a thoughtful fellow and he had taken the time to also express his sympathies to Lukin. The captain was now watching as his crewman attended to the body of his unfortunate first lieutenant.

'We must be thankful for small mercies,' said Merriman, though he was affected by the sight as much as the less experienced men. 'They will be in Freetown before long.'

'That wind-hole,' said Jones with an ironic half-smile. 'Without it, we would have been a hundred miles further south. The Spaniard would have got clean away.'

'It is shameful,' said Merriman after a long moment of reflection. 'Any officer of the navy who has spent a few years at sea will have seen such a vessel, myself included. We knew of the trade in all its terrible detail. Yet we did nothing. It took better men than us to see the error of our ways. I wonder that we dare call ourselves Christians.'

'We cannot right every wrong though, sir,' said Essex. 'And we are in the middle of a war. Some would say that it is folly to try and right the world's ills.'

Merriman nodded, though he did not agree.

Jones was still gazing at the slaves. 'What did Wilberforce say? "You may choose to look the other way but you can never say again that you did not know." That man is not only good but wise.'

Essex spoke up again: 'Apparently, he now spends his time trying to persuade the Yankees to follow our lead.'

Hailed by Lukin, Merriman crossed to the rail and spoke to his fellow captain.

'Bartholomew?'

'James, I should say we are in reasonable shape. This westerly will do us well enough and I'm keen to get under way.'

Lukin ran his fingers through his snow-white hair and glanced anxiously at the *Isabella*. There, the young lieutenant was overseeing operations at the ship's mainmast.

'I do worry for Simkins but we shall stay close by. My sincere thanks, James. There will be a share of the prize for you and the *Thunder* – I'll see to it.'

'Do not concern yourself with that. I am just glad we could help. I meant what I said about Admiral Goodwin and I do hope the Squadron receives some more assistance.'

Lukin cast an approving eye over *Thunder* once more. 'You have a fine ship and crew there, James. Farewell.'

A quarter-hour later, the ships parted for the second time. Shrigley returned on deck and Merriman made no mention of his temporary absence.

'*Isabella*,' said the first lieutenant after a time. 'Pretty name. Ugly trade.'

Chapter Twelve

The Besieged Fort

Two days later came the Sunday on which Merriman carried out his first service. For an hour, the deck became "the church", complete with benches for the officers and prayer books for those who could read. As was the case on most ships, a few made themselves scarce, usually due to them being Jews, Roman Catholics or of other faiths. Merriman made no issue of this, hopefully ensuring that those individuals would not be persecuted for their difference. He encouraged Archibald and his devout comrades to make their readings and a prayer was said for their fellow sailors aboard the *Arrow*. Mr. Webster proved himself to be a fine singer when the time came for hymns and Merriman was keen to see almost all the sailors joining in.

After a conference with his lieutenants, the captain had concluded that they were better off sticking to the coast than striking directly south-east for the Cape itself. They might reach the southern tip of Africa in around twenty days but with much less chance of gaining intelligence regarding the *Hercule*.

Four days after the encounter with *Arrow* and *Isabella*, *Thunder* reached the territory commonly known as the Grain Coast or the Pepper Coast, due to the prized seed that formed the spice named the Grain of Paradise. Two days after that, the identification of known landmarks confirmed that they were now off the Ivory Coast.

Though miles from land, they found that the strong westerlies deserted them and progress was slow. Merriman resisted the temptation to seek stronger breezes offshore because he wanted to at least pass the settlement of Assinie, one of the few colonies in the area still in French hands. They knew now that *Hercule* was in the habit of visiting numerous ports and – though still north of their hunting ground – this was surely worth a visit.

However, the elements stymied his attempt. As they approached Assinie, the wind backed to a stiff northerly. Merriman did not wish to give up the weather-gauge to any enemy vessel he might find in the harbour and so *Thunder* reached past. It was an exceptionally clear day, however, and the harbour was clearly visible from the cross trees. No large ships were seen.

They then came to the territory known as the Gold Coast. While guiding the midshipmen through another navigational exercise on deck, Merriman was asked by Hickey if they might encounter any ships carrying gold. The young man seemed to think that any share, however small, would greatly impress his family and friends back in England.

'Unfortunately, this coast is more known for the slave trade these days,' answered the captain. 'Though the Portuguese originally settled it to acquire gold. They traded with the locals, exchanging guns, knives, mirrors and such like. We've a few settlements there now, and I hope we might learn something.'

The following morning, they encountered a British brig that had just cast off from the colony of Fort James. From the captain, they learned that the fort was in a dire situation: the small British post had become embroiled in a dispute between local tribes and besieged. Their enemies had withdrawn for now but it was thought that another attack might come at any time.

Aboard the brig were a number of civilians that seemed highly relieved to be leaving Fort James. One of them was the daughter of the governor and she made a tearful appeal to Merriman to lend whatever assistance he could. Her companions confirmed that the defenders of the fort were desperately short of powder and ammunition.

Before making a decision on the matter, the captain asked if anything was known of the *Hercule*. No one aboard had even heard of the French warship – or Jourdan. With a final appeal from the governor's daughter, the brig continued west.

Merriman called Lieutenant Cary and Lieutenant Shrigley to the great cabin. When they entered, he had been pacing up and down for several minutes, tugging on his ear as he mulled the decision.

'Another distraction from our main task,' he said. 'But hardly one we can ignore.'

Predictably, Lieutenant Cary was eager to assist. 'Sir, allow me to take a small shore party and assess the situation. I can ask what the governor needs and see if it is feasible.'

'Alfred, the powder?'

'At present, we are well-stocked, sir. Nine tons at least. But I daresay we will continue regular drilling and there's no telling how long we'll be looking for the *Hercule*. It could be months. Down here there are very limited alternatives for resupply.'

'Ammunition?'

The folk on the brig said the fort had eighteen-pounders. But only six of them so a little will go a long way. We can spare some, if necessary.'

'Necessity can be a rather subjective concept,' said Merriman. 'If he has been besieged, I daresay the governor will take every grain of powder we can give him. Then again, we may eventually need every grain ourselves. Alfred, would you like some time off the ship?'

'I would, captain, thank you. However, I believe Mr. Webster will be concerned by-'

'The danger of disease,' interrupted Merriman. 'The daughter and her associates claimed there was little within the fort but they would say that, wouldn't they?'

Shrigley nodded. 'We can approach in the boat, find an officer and hope for an honest conversation. In the event that we're satisfied, we can go ashore.'

'Very good. I would not ask you to do so in the dark so we shall take the ship in now and set you on your way. Let us ensure that the correct flags are visible – I wouldn't want the guns turned on us.'

The fort itself was a great cube of pale stone built upon low cliffs. Below was a mix of rocky outcrops and sandy beach and nothing approaching a harbour or shelter of any kind; only a few small boats were spotted close to the cliffs. Fortunately, the sea was calm and a steady south-westerly allowed them to ease their way in. Two hundred yards off the coast, the midshipmen reported that *Thunder* was in eighty feet of water and the main anchor was dropped. Waiting to ensure it was well set, Merriman then ordered Cary and Shrigley ashore in the last of the light.

He was just settling down to dinner when his marine sentry knocked on the door.

'Some of the petty officers to you see you, sir.'

Merriman had his cutlery in his hand but a visit from these men as a group was a rarity so he told them to, 'enter but be quick'.

'Begging your pardon for disturbing you, cap'n, said Able Seaman Lee, the oldest of them. 'But as we're at anchor for the first time for a while, and the weather's fair-like, we wondered if we could have a sing song on deck. We've got a couple of fiddlers and I think the lads would enjoy it.'

'You mean the hymns on Sundays weren't sufficient?'

'Er…' Lee glanced warily back at his fellows, who looked equally ill-at-ease.

Merriman chuckled. 'Merely a jest, Lee. Have at it but not for too long: some on the other watch will be sleeping. Do notify Lieutenant Jones: if there's some music to be played, he will wish to be part of it.'

Even before Merriman had finished his salted ham and potatoes, the music began. As the petty officers had suggested, there was no way of knowing when they might be at anchor again and it had been a trying few weeks since their departure. Merriman thought it an ideal opportunity for the men to enjoy themselves.

After Peters came to collect his empty plate, he leaned back in his chair and sipped at some claret. The merriment above sounded strangely distant. He took his wine with him and went to sit on the lockers by the window. The African coast east of Fort James was no more than an undulating black line, with not a single light.

He imagined the scene back at Burton Manor. Only four days of April remained. Helen would be taking charge in the garden, ensuring that the climbing roses were well tied and overseeing the sowing of herbs and wild flowers. Robert and Mary-Anne would be enjoying the longer evenings; some time to play outside after school and dinner. No doubt *Conflict* and Robert's other toy boats had made several voyages across the duck pond and perhaps even farther afield. Many was the time Merriman had tried to describe and explain the naval life to his son but he suspected it was a task beyond any man. How could anyone relate the vast emptiness of the seas? The endless, mysterious coasts of this Dark Continent? The vagaries of happenstance that had allowed the *Thunder* to assist the *Arrow*; that had seen a hapless officer cut down in such bloody fashion? On several occasions, he had discussed with other officers if they wanted their sons to follow in their watery footsteps. Merriman still was not sure.

He had just given Peters his empty glass when he heard the shout from above that confirmed the return of the boat. Donning his coat, he went up on deck. The fiddles were scratching a jolly tune and the sailors were singing a shanty with such enthusiasm that he momentarily considered joining in. By the time he reached the entry port, Shrigley was already aboard. Cary was still in the boat below, holding a lantern.

'For you, sir,' said the first lieutenant, handing him an envelope. 'When we got there, a marine corporal was about to come out in his own boat. I asked him about illness and he also says there is little, though he admitted that is usually not the case. Apparently, they've been trapped in the fort for so long that there hasn't been much travel or mixing so I suppose it makes sense. All is peaceful for now but they expect hostilities to resume and are indeed in great need of powder. I tried to discuss specifics but he wouldn't be drawn, claiming it was a matter for our superiors. When he reported our arrival, the governor sent this note down.'

'Thank you, Mr. Brockle,' said Merriman as the bosun brought over a lantern for him to read by. The note was very brief; it was an extremely diplomatic and polite invitation to dinner, signed by one Geoffrey Howard Northcote, Lieutenant-Governor of Fort James.

'An invitation to dinner,' he told Shrigley. 'A shame I have just eaten.'

'No doubt he wishes to press you personally,' said the first lieutenant. 'Happy to go in your place, sir.'

Merriman looked towards the shore. The angular outline of the fort was made clear by a number of burning torches. He had rarely set foot on African soil and felt immensely curious about this remote outpost of British rule and its inhabitants.

'Let us both go. Mr. Brockle, please fetch Mr. Stones so that we may be precise about matters of powder and ammunition.'

Merriman approached the entry port. 'Cary, we have an invitation to dinner. Will you escort me to the shore?'

'With pleasure, captain.'

Just then, Lieutenant Jones arrived, violin in hand.

'Ah, there you are, Jones,' said Merriman before gesturing to the deck. 'I shall have to ask you to cease playing. *Thunder* is yours for the evening.'

The corporal from the fort mentioned by Shrigley was named Portswood and he could not have been more compliant. He and his men helped the marines drag the boat up the shore and secure it. Two of Cary's marines and two local soldiers were posted to watch the little vessel while Merriman and the remainder were escorted to the fort. They followed a sharply sloping path up the cliff to the base of the great structure. About halfway up, they came to a gateway guarded by four marines. The soldiers cheerily greeted Cary and his men, declaring that it was more than two years since they'd seen fellow soldiers clad in red.

Just past the gate, Portswood led the party to the right, through a tall passageway protected by a studded iron door. Merriman now found himself between the high rampart to his right, and a square, white-washed building of several floors to his left. Unlike the imposing bulk of the walls, this was in typical colonial style, with windows bordered by short pillars above ornate black rails.

Portswood pointed at the rampart. 'Half the guns used to face out from there. Hell of a job to move them all to the northern wall.'

'I can imagine,' answered Merriman.

They reached the central doorway of the building and trooped inside, leaving the marines outside with their compatriots. Just as Merriman removed his hat, an African man in English dress appeared from a small room. With a smile, he took the hats of all three officers and gestured along the corridor.

Once there, Merriman was met by a most curious scene. Two figures were leaning over a table, examining a map. One was a lean fellow in the white breeches and gold-embroidered blue tunic of a lieutenant-governor. The other was a broad African man clad in a thick, multicoloured robe that reached down to his ankles and his shoes of cloth. Hearing the interlopers, the pair turned around.

'Ah, you must be Captain Merriman.'

'Pleased to make your acquaintance, Governor Northcote.'

As the pair shook hands, Merriman noted the man's bushy white eyebrows and keen, dark eyes. He then introduced

Cary and Shrigley before Northcote gestured to his companion.

'Chief Odapagyan. A great ally of ours in this area.' The chief seemed a friendly sort and shook the hands of the Englishmen with some enthusiasm. He summoned a functionary from an adjoining room and each of the trio was furnished with a miniature tribal mask.

'Those are made of polished shell,' remarked Northcote. 'Quite valuable. Now, as I am entertaining three sailors, I shall not offer you rum. Will brandy do? I'm afraid we're running short of everything.'

'Of course,' said Merriman. 'And I believe we have quite a supply of rum aboard, so I shall send some ashore with the powder.'

Northcote smiled at this but then led the way through to a dining room. 'Business later, perhaps, captain? Shall we eat first? Our cook passed away last year but we have a local fellow who suits us very well. My daughter even taught him how to make a few English cakes, would you believe?'

In the dining room, they encountered another marine, this man a sergeant, who had apparently just arrived. Wiping sweat from his brow, he introduced himself but seemed rather uncomfortable.

'Sergeant Sumner is the highest-ranking officer remaining with the garrison,' explained Northcote as they sat down. 'I have tried to promote him but he steadfastly refuses. An excellent man. He has been here almost as long as I have.'

'And how long is that, sir?' asked Shrigley as two servants – one African, one English – filled their glasses.

'Twelve years,' answered Northcote. 'And I'm afraid to say this has been the worst of them all.'

Before he could continue, there came the sound of many people entering the residence beyond the dining room. Merriman heard the voices of men, women and children and what sounded like French and Dutch.

'Forgive the noise,' said Northcote. 'When the latest hostilities broke out, I felt obliged to open the fort to some of our merchant friends and other allies in the area. It is rather cramped but we make the best of it. Some of the families refuse to separate but I was relieved to get Emma away on that brig.'

The servants then returned and began to fill bowls from a steaming cauldron. 'This is a favourite of both mine and Chief Odapagyan. Fish stew with kenkey – a type of dumpling. I do hope you enjoy it.'

As they began eating, Cary spoke up. 'Governor, what's the cause of these hostilities?'

'It all goes back several years, and in truth there is not one single cause. Politics here is as complicated here as it is back home. The chief here is part of a confederation known as the Fante. They fell out with another group of tribes, the Ashanti. Some say it is because the Fante granted refuge to Ashanti men accused of grave robbing but that is disputed. The truth is that both tribes have opposed us at various times but in recent years the Ashanti allied with the Dutch and the Fante with ourselves. There is open conflict to the north between them and a victory over the winter allowed the Ashanti to strike us here. Chief Odapagyan's men fought bravely alongside our own and, largely thanks to him, we have now pushed the Ashanti away from the coast – in this area at least. But they send raiding parties regularly and scouts to monitor us. We are fortunate that they do not know the true extent of our weakness.'

'You were besieged for some time then?' asked Merriman. Though he hadn't much of an appetite, the local dumplings were satisfying and tasty.

'For six long weeks at one stage. With the Ashanti on the loose there was no possibility of resupply from another fort. Winnebah is only thirty miles away but I've not seen my old friend Governor Deans for damn near two years.' Northcote sighed. 'The Ashanti are formidable warriors. Around a hundred years ago a leader named Osei Tutu developed a highly organised and disciplined army. They could teach us a few things, I tell you.'

'And you expect to be attacked again?' asked Merriman. 'Do your enemy have long guns?'

'No but by cutting off our access to the surrounding land, they can starve us. If our cannons are functioning, we can at least keep them at distance and help cover the chief when battles flare up. Sergeant Sumner knows the area like the back of his hand and even speaks some of the local lingo.'

'I speak English!' declared Chief Odapagyan.

'Fortunate for us,' replied Shrigley with a smile.

'You like food?' asked the chief.

'Very tasty,' answered Cary, the others signalling their agreement.

'I saw your ship,' continued the chief in his sonorous voice. 'Beautiful ship. I have some gold. If I have more, I buy a ship like that.'

Shrigley put down his spoon and leaned across the table. 'Chief, have you heard of Timbuktu? The city of gold?'

'I have heard, yes.'

'Do you know where it is?'

'Yes.'

Now all the others were interested.

'North of here,' answered the chief.

'How far?' pressed Shrigley, eyes wide.

'Very, far,' said the chief before downing a large piece of dumpling. 'Yes. Very, very far.'

* * * *

Once dinner had concluded, Governor Northcote led his visitors through the residence and out to the north side of the fort. Down at ground level, a squad of marines was gathered and they instantly sprung to attention and put on their hats when their sergeant and the officers appeared.

Corporal Portswood was with them and Northcote introduced another few notables who had been with him for many years. Though they put on a good show, Merriman saw clear signs of wear. Some of the uniforms were missing buttons and braid and their weapons appeared well-used and tired.

Chief Odapagyan was very keen to introduce his personal bodyguard, who had accompanied him on his trip to the fort. All four were very tall men armed with fearsome spears. Unlike the chief, they wore pale knee-length tunics and their chests and arms were striped with white markings. Northcote explained that, though the chief had previously sought refuge at the fort, the Fante were now in a reasonably strong position. They currently dominated the southern side of a stream that separated the warring tribes and their European allies. Apparently, the Dutch contingent among the Ashanti was down to a few opportunistic arms traders and mercenaries.

Northcote did not pass up the opportunity to show them the meagre contents of the fort's magazine, which was comprised of two well-protected kegs of powder and a small pyramid of cannonballs. Their armoury was at least equipped with two dozen muskets and twice that number of blades. Alongside these weapons were some native bows, spears, swords and javelins. Sergeant Sumner retrieved a small arrow and pointed at the tip. 'The Ashanti often use poison. We've lost at least half a dozen men that way.'

'This isn't *all* your men, surely?' asked Lieutenant Cary.

'Most,' admitted Sumner. 'I have another eight currently stationed down near the river.'

'We shall go up to the rampart,' announced the governor, 'but before that, I believe the chief wishes to be on his way. He has already stayed longer than planned in order to meet you gentlemen.'

Though clearly disappointed that he would not have a chance to go aboard *Thunder*, Chief Odapagyan bade them all farewell in his cheerful manner. Shrigley made a point of thanking him for his gifts and the five locals departed via another reinforced gate.

'Follow me,' said Governor Northcote, leading the visitors up narrow, steep steps to the rampart. As they neared the top, he spoke over his shoulder to Merriman. 'I daresay it seems strange to you, captain: me dining with an African chief.'

'Perhaps a little.'

'Affairs here have always been muddied by trickery and betrayal on all sides but my dealings with that fellow have been straightforward and honest. I suppose we rather depend on each other.'

They reached the rampart and made way for the others coming up behind them.

Northcote continued: 'You know, the Ashanti and the Fante are not so different to we British and the French. I rather agree with what Kant has to say on the matter: "War itself requires no particular motivation but appears to be ingrained in human nature." Hard to disagree, eh?'

'Indeed. Governor, it is to your credit that you stay on here in such circumstances. Is there any great benefit to the Crown by maintaining possession of Fort James?'

'Well, it was originally established as a trading post and, at times, trade has been most profitable, especially in slaves. In recent years, gold and ivory have been taken out to merchantmen moored where your ship is now. Strategically, it is of limited value. I have actually put the case for abandoning it but my superiors do not agree. Now, look here.'

Northcote led the visitors past two sentries and the long guns that faced the interior. In the distance, a line of lights could be seen.

'The river?' suggested Cary.

'Quite so, captain,' replied Northcote. 'The Ashanti keep those torches aflame on the far bank from dusk until dawn. I imagine they do not wish us to forget they are there.'

The officers stood in a row, gazing out at the night, and Merriman shivered at the thought of joining one of Sumner's patrols, facing native warriors on their own ground.

A few minutes later, some of the other inhabitants of the fort came up to join them. One of these men was a Danish trader and he was in possession of a case of cigars which he generously doled out. Two of the others were British and one was Swiss. As the new arrivals fell into discussion with Sumner, Cary and Shrigley, Governor Northcote led Merriman along the rampart and paused beside one of his few cannons.

'An apt location for this discussion, I suppose. Captain, I cannot help but feel like a beggar with his hand outstretched. And now that I've heard of your mission, I feel even more embarrassed about asking – but you have seen our situation. And you now know that I cannot claim any great strategic or economic significance for Fort James. However, I am convinced that we will not survive another siege without more powder and ammunition. If we cannot defend ourselves, the Ashanti will eventually get inside. I still have almost two hundred people in my charge, some twenty women. The Ashanti will show us no mercy.'

'Understood, governor,' said Merriman, who had already made up his mind. 'I had originally planned to send a quarter ton of powder and a ton of shot. I suppose your invitation to dinner has been effective because I will double that. A half ton of powder and two tons of shot.'

Even in the darkness, Northcote's broad smile was clear. He reached out and gripped Merriman's hand. 'My sincere thanks, captain. That will make the world of difference to us here.'

'It will require quite a few trips with the boat and the launch and careful handling. We must hope that conditions remain clement. I will have the operation begin at dawn.'

'Again, I thank you.'

The pair returned to the others and Merriman accepted the offer of a cigar from the Danish trader.

'I don't suppose you encourage smoking aboard ship,' remarked Northcote.

'Certainly not below deck,' replied Merriman, drawing in his first inhalation of smoke, which was more pleasing than he had expected.

Not long afterward, he was approached by an unusually excitable Lieutenant Shrigley, who was accompanied by the Swiss gentleman.

'Sir, Monsieur Lascelles here has some information for us. He came here in January from Porto Novo, during a lull in the fighting. While there, he stayed at an inn and spoke to another merchant who had arrived from the island of Sao Tome – what we call Saint Thomas. This fellow mentioned that he'd recently seen a French ship-of-the-line taking on stores there and apparently it wasn't the first time. Judging by the intelligence reports I read over the winter, it's unlikely there would have been any other French warships in the area. Odds are it was the *Hercule*.'

Chapter Thirteen

South-East to Sao Tome

*Beware, beware, the Bight of Benin,
For few come out, where many went in.*

So went the lines familiar to the sailors of the Royal Navy. The island of Sao Tome was five hundred miles south-east, which meant that *Thunder* would bypass the Bight, where disease had accounted for innumerable sailors over the years. Merriman knew he might have cause to return there but this was as solid a lead as they'd encountered and he intended to follow it up. The island was isolated; over a hundred miles off the coast of Gabon and therefore a desirable location for resupply. It was still some way north of Jourdan's usual hunting grounds but if he had been there before, he might return.

Departing Fort James took far longer than anticipated. They used both launch and boat but delivery of the powder and shot required no less than eight trips. The wind was from the west but had become gusty and unpredictable. Two kegs were lost when the boat was almost tipped by a rogue wave and one of the marines twisted his ankle badly while landing. Corporal Portswood and his men were of great assistance at least; and Governor Northcote came down to the beach himself to wave *Thunder* off. By then it was early afternoon and Merriman was relieved to at last get away.

He knew that, in all likelihood, he would never hear of Fort James and its inhabitants ever again but – as with Captain Lukin – he'd been glad to help his fellow Britons.

With the wind on her beam and every scrap of sail up, *Thunder* made good progress south, monitored at every step by First Lieutenant Shrigley and the midshipmen. Though they were all at different stages, the youngsters were making progress. As ever, the use of the sextant and the astronomical tables proved the most challenging.

With every passing day, the temperature seemed to increase, though the weather remained unpredictable, with occasional cloudbursts and squalls. The officers removed coats and hats when they could and all were grateful for the shade provided by sails and canopy.

The superstitious aboard – which was in fact most of the sailors – were pleased by the visit of dolphins. The elegant creatures could easily outpace *Thunder* but enjoyed leaping by the bow. Mr. Webster had overcome some early seasickness and was quite thrilled by the sight. He seemed less enamoured by the prospect of meeting Neptune when they crossed the equator just south of Sao Tome. As with Lieutenant Essex and many others first-timers, he would have to endure the ceremony as a "rite of passage".

When the wind dropped on the third day from Fort James, the captain ordered another gun drill and was pleased to see improvements in accuracy across both decks. Butcher and the crew manning Lightning continued to lead the way, which was a clear source of pride to Lieutenant Essex. At the suggestion of Master Henderson, the following morning was spent on tacking drills. Due to clement weather, they'd enjoyed few opportunities to practice and Merriman knew as well as Henderson how crucial the manoeuvre might be in combat. After ten repetitions (five for each watch), the time for a full tack was reduced from eight minutes to six. Despite the improvement, this was still not good enough for the captain.

A day later, came another encounter with a sea creature. Merriman was below inspecting the magazine when a loud impact reverberated through the ship from the bow. It was so strong a contact that he could tell that the vessel had been virtually halted. The *Thunder* had been flying along well and Merriman could not imagine what had happened. Meeting Shrigley on the upper gun deck, he flew up top, narrowly avoiding two sailors carrying a boiling cauldron of water.

'Mr. Brockle?'

The bosun was on his way back from the bow, his expression anxious. 'Whale, sir. Not too big.'

Merriman reached the rail in time to see the motionless, bleeding body of the creature slide past the ship. He had no idea of the type but it possessed dark, shiny skin, some parts encrusted with barnacles.

'Thirty-footer, at least,' remarked Shrigley.

'We shall heave to,' ordered Merriman. 'Mr. Brockle, take a carpenter with you and inspect the bow. Alfred, you will check the interior – also with one of the carpenters.'

'Aye aye, sir.'

While he waited on the quarterdeck for their reports, Merriman watched as a man was dragged up through the hatch by three others. A fourth fellow was following with a bucket on a line. The last man out was a petty officer who approached the captain.

'Sir, if I might explain.'

'Go ahead.'

'That there is Slaven and his mess-mates have had enough of him. The filthy swine will not wash. Lice were found in his hammock and the lads have no desire to find them in theirs.'

'Then let us allow them to proceed.'

Slaven was held in place by two of his mess-mates and deprived of his clothing. The other two then forcibly scrubbed at him with water and soap. His cursing later became active resistance but a heavy slap from one of the larger men dissuaded him from persisting. This was no isolated incident and, as far as Merriman was concerned, an entirely justified form of rough justice.

Only a few days earlier, he had lambasted two men whose pony tails had grown too long. He had merely to point out that he'd once seen a man's hair caught in a block: the hapless sailor had been hauled ten feet off the deck and was fortunate not to break his neck.

On the larboard side of *Thunder*, two dozen sailors with their trousers rolled up were hard at work scrubbing the decks. Young Friar the topman was taking his turn, pushing a holystone up and down with some vigour. Though working hard, the curious youngster observed as Brockle returned from the brow, his legs dripping water.

'Lost a bit of paint, sir, but nothing buckled or out of alignment.'

A minute later, Shrigley made a similar report and they got under way once more.

* * *

Six days after leaving the Gold Coast, *Thunder* reached Sao Tome. The lookouts had sighted the island at dawn and the warship neared the coast in mid-afternoon. Along with Essex and Smythe, Merriman had moved up to the bow. Essex had a chart in his hand and Smythe was studying the almanac notes.

'Odd that *Hercule* would stop here,' said Essex. 'A Portuguese possession.'

'Not necessarily,' said Merriman. 'With a ship of the line, a captain has more than enough might to ensure cooperation.'

Smythe then spoke up: 'Also, the Portuguese transferred their seat of power to the settlement of San Antonio on the neighbouring island of Principe some fifty years ago. Due to persistent pirate attacks.'

'Then there is likely to be even less of a military presence here,' said Merriman. He checked the chart once more and saw that the capital was situated on the north-east corner of the island, which was no more than twenty miles across at its widest.

'We shall proceed cautiously around the coast. And we must be ready to open fire at once – in the unlikely event that we encounter the *Hercule*. We shall clear for action.'

With the wind on the beam, *Thunder* rounded the coast of Sao Tome with guns at the ready. At the fo'c'sle, even the two nine-pounders and the pair of carronades were manned. Smythe was stationed at the mainmast, to relay anything spotted by the lookouts.

Near the centre of the island, huge crags of rock rose up from lush, green forest. Two of these towering formations were topped by horizontal plateaus that seemed almost to reach the clouds. Much of the coast was also rocky and many small outcrops made the shore even more hazardous. There was so far no sign of humanity at all; the land was covered by high palms, some so close to the shore that they hung out over the water.

'How far to the capital?' asked Merriman. 'The old capital, that is.'

Eades was now at the binnacle, studying the only chart they had.

'Around six miles, sir.'

As they moved into the lee of the island, *Thunder* slowed to three knots. The only sounds that reached them were the cries of birds, though even these could not be seen. They passed a small bay and a long wooden pontoon that had fallen into disrepair. At the landward end of it were several equally neglected buildings and a wide patch of level land.

'Those fields were cultivated,' observed Mr. Webster, who was with Merriman and Shrigley on the quarterdeck. 'Though not for some time.'

'The main trade used to be slaves,' remarked Shrigley. 'These days it's cocoa and coffee – though clearly not here at the moment.'

Thunder eventually rounded a promontory, providing a view of a short but deep bay: a perfect natural harbour. Here was much more development, with dozens of buildings lining the coast. A banner was flying from the largest of them, which was eventually identified by a lookout as the flag of Portugal. That was no surprise; what was a surprise was the complete lack of other vessels, large or small.

'They may have moved the capital but surely trade wouldn't have died off entirely,' said Merriman.

'Hardly, sir,' replied Shrigley. 'And if *Hercule* took on supplies here, there must be some still present.'

'Curious.' Merriman scoured the coast with his own spyglass. He could not see a single boat on the water nor a person on the shore. The closest they came to spying any activity was a donkey wandering along the beach. There was also a thin trail of smoke rising from a settlement some distance from what looked like the main port.

Lieutenant Smythe returned from the mainmast with a request. 'Permission to take the launch in, captain? Find out what we can.'

Merriman considered this. He certainly would not put the *Thunder* in the bay; this would leave him with no sea room if any danger appeared. It was a good two miles to the shore but that needn't take long in the launch and the sea was calm.

'Very well, Lieutenant – it's certainly your turn. Please liaise with Lieutenant Cary regarding a marine detachment. I shall keep *Thunder* on the move. Do ensure that you have your signal flags with you so that we may communicate if necessary.'

'Aye aye, sir.' With a broad grin, Smythe headed for the hatch.

'Oh, and Lieutenant,' added Merriman.

'Sir?'

'Do proceed with caution.'

Lieutenant Cary paired Smythe with his former enemy Second Lieutenant Harrison but also sent his most experienced sergeant along with eight men. With *Thunder* reaching back and forth across the mouth of the bay, Merriman kept one eye on the launch, one eye to the south: unable to avoid the feeling that danger of some kind was near.

Midshipman Hickey had taken Smythe's position at the mainmast and he had some intriguing information for the captain.

'Sir, lookout reports a pirate flag – on land!'

'What?'

Hickey joined the captain at the rail. 'Sir, you see the tower of rock in the far distance? Lookout reports that the flag is flying from a building roughly in line with it.'

Raising his spyglass, Merriman noted that Smythe and the launch were now close to a long stone quay. Following Hickey's directions, he eventually saw the flag, which was on a pole between two of the larger buildings. In the slight breeze, it was difficult to make out the detail.

'Can't see it well.'

'Lookout seemed sure, sir. Skull and crossbones.'

'What's that?' Mr. Webster hurried over, an anxious look on his face. 'The skull and crossbones, did you say?'

'That's what the lookout reports,' confirmed Hickey.

Merriman lowered his spyglass.

'Doesn't make any sense,' remarked Shrigley.

'Actually, it may make *complete* sense,' countered the surgeon. 'The smoke – it's coming from that building at the near end of the bay. If you look closely, there is an inlet separating it from the rest of the settlement. An ideal situation for a lazaretto; to divide the healthy from the diseased.'

'Or the dead,' said Merriman. 'Bodies – they're burning bodies.'

Webster nodded.

'But what about the flag?' asked Hickey.

133

Merriman answered: 'Long before it was taken up by pirates, the symbol denoted disease.'

'Quite so,' confirmed Webster. 'Often plague. Captain, please recall the launch.'

'I will indeed, Mr. Webster. By God, I can't believe I didn't see it for myself.'

Shrigley had his spyglass up. 'Sir, they're pulling alongside now.'

'No time for flags,' said Merriman. 'Fire a nine-pounder to get their attention!'

Shrigley and Essex took charge of this personally and soon a blast went up that echoed into the bay. The shore party halted and saw the signal flag put up to order their return. In no time at all, they were rowing away from the port towards *Thunder*.

'A narrow escape,' said Merriman, clapping the blushing surgeon on the shoulder. 'Well done, Mr. Webster. Very well done indeed.'

Unfortunately for Webster, the following day brought a less welcome occasion. It was known that the equator passed through the land mass of Sao Tome so, once *Thunder* was clear, Shrigley reminded Merriman that it was time to introduce the debutants to King Neptune. There were in total fifty-one who had never crossed the equator, including Webster, Essex, Chamier and nine of the marines. Along with the men, they were in turn dunked in a water-filled sail suspended over the gundeck. From there, they faced King Neptune himself, a role fulfilled by Bosun Brockle.

He sported long hair, a beard made from rope and a cloak decorated with pictures of starfish, octopi, whales and fish. Someone had found some green weed to decorate his hair and beard and he carried a trident adapted from a boathook. King Neptune of course had to be accompanied by his wife and there was Bosun's Mate Nicholls, apparently proud of the homemade dress that exposed his remarkably hairy legs.

Once they'd been pulled from the water, each man had to kneel in front of the king to undergo his punishment, which involved being covered with a foul-smelling sludge composed of more weed scraped from the hull, bilge water and stale milk. Those who dared protest were made to climb the mizzen mast and the whole affair lasted some two hours.

Merriman observed most of it and concluded the ceremony by requesting a tot of rum for King Neptune and his crew, plus all his victims. With that, one of the marines ventured a rousing, 'Three cheers for Captain Merriman!'

The rest of the crew joined in and Merriman answered by raising his hat before going below to eat a much-delayed luncheon.

Chapter Fourteen

Enemies Engaged

With the Bight of Benin and the Gulf of Guinea now in her wake, *Thunder* passed the territories of Gabon and Loango. After what they'd seen at Sao Tome, Merriman had elected not to go ashore unless their advance southward proved fruitless. Pacing the deck, three nights after they'd left the island, he found himself gazing at the dark horizon, gripped by a certainty that his enemy was close.

He felt sure something would happen soon but, though there were a number of busy ports on this stretch of coast, they saw no vessels for a day and a half. As midday approached, Merriman was on deck in his shirt sleeves, preparing to observe the recording of noon with the midshipmen when there was a call from above.

'Deck there!'

As his lieutenants were busy, Merriman advanced to the mainmast.

'Sails on the horizon!' added the lookout. 'Two points off the larboard bow. Hull down and heading our way.'

Thunder had faced southerlies for two days, zig-zagging across the wind. Since dawn, she had sailed twenty miles west-south west, away from the coast, then tacked back onto an east-south-east to take advantage of strengthening winds. This put her on a long route towards the land before geography and wind demanded another offshore tack to gain sea room.

Coming up from the south, this vessel must have passed through the *Hercule*'s hunting grounds and Merriman therefore elected to intercept it, preferably before nightfall. Seven bells of the afternoon watch had recently sounded so he knew he had about three hours of good light. He also knew that a first sighting from his hawk-eyed lookouts meant a rough distance of sixteen miles. At the last log reading, *Thunder*'s speed had been six knots. Merriman concluded that, if the current speed were maintained, they would intercept the vessel in daylight.

The captain ran his hands through his salt-encrusted hair and looked around. Despite the report from above, few of the men were moving. The yards were straight, the lines taut, the decks pristine from a thorough going over with the holy-stones. Merriman looked higher: the sails were trimmed to perfection, balanced fore and aft, with Master Henderson instructing the crew to ease the spanker on occasion and keep the *Thunder*'s speed up. Apart from the hiss of water past the hull and the creaking of timbers, there was little noise. Then he saw the expectant eyes of the midshipmen, the questioning gaze of Bosun Brockle.

There had been more gun drills – plus plenty of tacking of late – and Merriman reckoned his crew had progressed well since departing Portsmouth several weeks ago. But they had not yet seen serious action and were in need of more practice. Whatever vessel those sails belonged to, he decided to treat it as if it were the *Hercule*.

Lieutenant Shrigley had obviously been notified of the sighting because he now joined Merriman and the midshipmen at the mainmast.

'Sir?'

'Let us assume that it is an enemy vessel. We shall beat to quarters. Clear for action but keep the sails as they are.'

'Aye aye, sir.'

Shrigley bellowed a repetition of the orders.

Merriman slowly withdrew to the quarterdeck as the marine drummer appeared, hastily fastening his jacket and throwing the loop of his drum over his shoulder. 'Heart of Oak' was soon rippling through the air and sailors boiled out from below decks like angry ants. Even though they must have known the vessel was distant, their eyes displayed the grit and intent that Merriman sought. Not all of course – two men were admonished for slowness by Brockle – but Merriman was generally pleased by what he saw.

From below came the sounds of the partitions being put away and the guns being unleashed. Upon the deck, the carronades and nine-pounders were also readied. Buckets of sand and water were brought out by a team of idlers. Other crewman scrambled to raise the netting that would protect the deck from debris while others collected the goats, sheep and chickens that had been out getting some air. Lastly, a crew tasked with washing clothes in tubs on the foredeck emptied the water over the side and headed below, each burdened by sodden garments.

Once the main hatch was clear of sailors, Lieutenant Cary came up on deck with Second Lieutenant Harrison. While the majority of the marines were down on the gundecks with their crews, forty more were available should Merriman need them.

'Sir?'

'Nothing urgent for now, Cary. As long as your sharpshooters are ready if required.'

'Just give the word, sir.'

'Pretty damned quick, captain,' was Brockle's view when he joined Merriman on the quarterdeck.

'More than respectable,' said Merriman as Master Henderson also joined them, having hastily ceased smoking his pipe.

Next to arrive were Lieutenant Shrigley and Lieutenant Smythe. His usual conscientious self, Shrigley checked that Merriman did not yet want his officers on the gundecks; the captain confirmed this. As for Smythe, he seemed desperate for action. Wide-eyed and restless, he occupied himself by oiling his cutlass.

An hour later, Merriman took up his spyglass. He could just make out the new ship. 'Two points to larboard, if you please.'

Henderson passed this order on to the helmsman. Today it was not Harris at the wheel but a brawny younger fellow named Calder. The wheel squeaked as the sailor moved it with his large, calloused hands.

'How far off the coast are we, Hickey?'

The midshipman made an unconvincing sound, then moved towards the binnacle.

'You've no need of instrument or chart,' instructed Merriman. 'We have been sailing along this stretch for days: give me your best guess.'

'Er...eight miles, sir.'

'I shall not ask you, Chamier – you were just at the chart. Eades?'

'I should say ten, sir.'

'Adkins?'

'Ten and a half.'

Shrigley tutted and Merriman shook his head. 'Dear oh dear. None of us can estimate half miles at this distance. I should say Hickey was not far off. Alfred?'

'I concur, sir.'

'Now, Adkins, we are closing on this vessel. What must we be wary of?'

'Getting too close to the coast, sir. Losing sea room.'

'Yes. And?'

'Williwaws, sir, and other winds that can come off the land.'

'Quite so. Now what else must we consider? Hickey?'

'The ship has the weather-gauge, sir. We are beating, which puts us at a disadvantage in manoeuvring and gunnery.'

'Also true.'

'If I may, sir.' Shrigley had been looking through his own spyglass for some time. 'She seems to be matching our speed. We're closing quickly.'

'How long before we're in range?'

Shrigley glanced at his pocket watch before replying. 'I should say just over an hour, sir.'

Before Merriman could utter a word, another shout when up, this time from the foremast lookout. The news swiftly reached the quarterdeck.

Three ships were now visible. The ship dead ahead was being pursued by another and a third was reaching out from the coast.

A quarter-hour later came another report: smoke and fire had been seen by the lookouts; the pursuing ship was firing upon its target. What had been a relatively straightforward situation had become rather complex and it was all unfolding in fading light. Merriman could not yet know if he had one legitimate target, two, three – or none at all.

Not one of the four vessels changed course. The two ships to the south were, respectively, three and four miles distant. The ship approaching from the south-east was perhaps five miles away. Desperate to know more about this unfolding situation, Merriman was soon informed that several large, multi-coloured flags had been identified upon the masts of both pursuing vessels. They appeared to be frigates of some variety. Their prey was a British merchantman that was being rapidly gained on.

'It appears that we may encounter pirates yet,' said Shrigley.

'Barbary pirates?' asked Smythe. 'Why they're no match for us.'

'Historically that was the way of things,' answered Merriman. 'But there are some rather modern types who sail ships like our own and continue the activities of their ancient forebears. The Moroccans have signed treaties of friendship with America and some other nations so I doubt these two originate from there.'

'What about this fellow Amidon?' said Shrigley. 'He is Algerian – known to have taken dozens of ships for prizes.'

Merriman knew the name. Though he had still to consider *Thunder*'s main mission, he was also duty-bound to protect the British vessel and he did welcome the chance to test his crew. Even facing two ships, the odds were in his favour.

'Perhaps we shall take Amidon's ship for a prize,' said Smythe, his pale eyes glinting at the prospect.

Merriman was now at the rail, observing the two closest ships. He saw small puffs of smoke from the stern of the British vessel and more from the bow of the pirate. Much smaller than *Thunder*, the enemy frigates had only one gun deck and perhaps around thirty or forty guns. This was not the first time Merriman had faced Barbary pirates and he was confident that *Thunder* still had the advantage. But he would need to play this carefully.

'We shall make our intentions plain. Run up signal flags and communicate to the merchantman that we will run astern of her and attack the enemy. If they stick to their task, we shall strike one or both enemy vessels with a broadside. If necessary, we will tack back to the west and attack again. Smythe, Essex, please attend the gundecks. Alfred, you can remain with me.'

As the two officers hurried below, Merriman noted young Chamier, who was crouching by the binnacle, his face pale, clearly gripped by nerves. Instead of embarrassing the boy any further, he nodded to Lieutenant Jones – who had just arrived – and subtly pointed to the struggling midshipman. In moments, the kindly Jones had Chamier back on his feet, though the boy then anxiously clutched his stomach.

By now the signal flags were flying, though no immediate answer came from the British vessel. *Thunder* would be level with her within minutes and so Merriman knew the time had come to change course and cut across her stern to defend her from the pirates.

'Get ready to ease sail,' he told Tom Henderson. 'We will reach across at due east.'

Merriman felt a breeze on his neck. He turned and looked out to sea. Far to the west, low, dark clouds had gathered. Despite the gloom, he could see also white horses in the distance. Henderson saw him glance up at the sails.

'Still southerly for now, sir, but I think it's veering to the west. Getting blustery too if those clouds are anything to go by.'

'You're right, Tom. Which means we must resolve this swiftly.'

Shrigley had been examining the merchantman, which could be seen clearly. 'Name of *Stalwart*, sir. Hundred and twenty or longer, I should say. She's lying fairly low: a fat prize indeed.'

'Still no flag raised in answer?'

'Afraid not, sir.'

'Bring her around.'

By the time Calder began to turn the wheel, the sailors were ready to adjust their sails. As *Thunder* turned to the east, aiming for the wake of the *Stalwart*, Merriman at last put on his jacket, which Peters had just brought up from below. The experienced servant briefly perused the situation, shook his head and returned to the hatch.

Henderson spoke up. 'You expect to receive fire, sir?'

'I do.'

'Shall we furl mainsail and forecourse?'

'Very good, Tom.'

Sheets and braces had been frantically adjusted to swing the yards around for the new heading and *Thunder* built to what Merriman estimated to be six knots. The pirate to the east was on a reach too and seemingly unperturbed by the aggressive move. The first ship was still aiming at the *Stalwart*'s stern, perhaps now only a mile from *Thunder*.

The captain seemed to think that by presenting only his bow, he need not fear a broadside.

'He is clearly not to be deterred,' remarked Merriman, 'so we shall proceed.'

Hickey had been stationed at the hatch to pass on orders and Merriman now told the starboard crews on both decks to ready their guns.

'Still nothing from the *Stalwart*?' he asked.

'No, sir,' confirmed Shrigley. 'I count at least a dozen pieces but they seem to be running.'

'What a poorly named ship.' Merriman leaned against the starboard rail and peered down at the guns. All twenty-eight had been run out.

'Dead astern of the *Stalwart*,' said Shrigley as they passed through the freighter's wake.

The first pursuer was perhaps a quarter-mile away now, bounding on, great flags of red, green and yellow flying from all three masts. Her pitch-soaked hull glistened in the evening light and Merriman could make out patches of moving colour as her crew busied themselves. She had still not changed course.

'Mr. Hickey. Range at time of firing will be four hundred yards. One minute or less.'

As Hickey relayed the information, Lieutenant Jones reported on the eastward vessel.

'He's come on to the wind, sir, south-east towards his mate.'

'Very sensible.'

Still more than a mile distant, the second vessel hove into view off the starboard bow, clearly aiming to support its compatriot. Merriman noted the same arrangement of flags high on the masts. The pirates were clearly not afraid of a fight.

The first ship was now almost directly on the beam.

'Starboard battery, fire!'

The reports of the twenty-eight long guns came ten seconds later and lasted a similar amount of time.

'Incoming!' yelled Shrigley as the pirate's bow chasers sent up smoke.

Merriman had been in enough battles to not concern himself with pride and he went down on one knee and ducked his head. But the balls from the bow-chasers sliced through only sail: in this case the mizzen topgallant.

By the time he peered over the rail, Merriman knew that *Thunder* had inflicted considerably more damage. A red flag fluttered downward as the pirate's top foremast splintered and crashed down through the rigging. A low thud went up and some great block or other object struck the deck. Several men were then seen to fall from the foremast.

The damage, he knew, would affect the accuracy of the inevitable enemy response. His stern was exposed but *Thunder* was still doing six knots. Merriman considered a momentary change of course but knew it was also important to see – and gauge – the accuracy and volume of the pirate's fire.

'Incoming!' yelled Shrigley again. 'All hands down!'

Within a few seconds, Merriman was smiling.

'Someone got their elevation wrong,' remarked Tom Henderson. 'Every last one dropped short.'

'I'd say they're more concerned by their foremast,' added Jones.

Standing tall once more, Merriman watched as more of the rigging and gear tumbled down and the pirate vessel slowed.

The second ship may well have seen this for the captain had altered course and was coming straight for *Thunder*, two points off her starboard bow.

'Three hundred yards, sir,' stated Shrigley.

'Bold,' said Merriman. 'Very bold.'

Adkins was at the rail and frowning.

'He knows we can't bring the larboard battery to bear,' explained Merriman. 'He thinks he can fire before we have time to reload the starboard battery.'

Shrigley said, 'It may be close.'

'Deck guns, prepare to fire!' ordered Merriman. The crews had already loaded the small guns and now primed them too.

The pirate's bow shifted another two points to the north. The vessels would pass close to one another and exchange broadsides. Merriman would have preferred to keep his distance but the wind was veering to the west and the light was fading. If he was to save the English merchantman and resolve this battle, he would have to do so now. He could only hope that the *Thunder*'s thick hulls would save his crew from the pirate's guns.

'This man must have a death-wish,' observed Jones.

'One hundred yards bow to bow,' announced Shrigley.

Merriman called out to Adkins. 'Are they ready to fire?'

Shortly afterwards came the reply. 'Main deck ready, sir. Upper deck, most guns ready.'

'Very good,' said Merriman, trying to remain calm. 'We have time.'

'Fifty yards,' reported Shrigley. 'By god man, get down!'

This was addressed to a sailor on the mainmast, who was heading up the rigging for some unknown reason.

Merriman saw now that the two vessels would pass within a few boat lengths of each other. He saw dozens of dark, bearded faces clad in colourful clothes; one proud fellow standing with a hand on the mainmast, a great cutlass at his belt. These were Barbary pirates; and as fearless as their reputation.

'Twenty yards,' said Shrigley.

There was little practical need to give the order. The officers down below looking out of the gun ports would see the enemy ship pass by.

But Merriman gave it as *Thunder*'s bow drew level with the enemy ship. The pirate captain must have been a little anxious because he was a tad premature and his first shots missed.

'Fire!' cried Merriman before ducking down alongside Shrigley and Jones.

The barrage from *Thunder* was loud but short. Merriman did not get a chance to appraise the accuracy of their fire because his own vessel was struck several times.

Cries went up near the mainmast and from below. Hearing a splintering crack, he looked up to see that the lower yardarm of the mizzen had been struck and was hanging down. The haphazard fire from the pirates continued and the unfortunate mizzen was hit again. This must have been a direct strike because the top half began to shudder and shake. The wind in the topsails did the rest, hauling it to larboard and dragging yards of rigging and rope with it. No men were up there but those below had to take cover. The falling debris was too heavy for the netting and sliced easily through it.

Unfortunate sailors manning one of the quarterdeck guns were caught, throwing their arms up as gear heavy and light rained down on them. The captain and his two lieutenants sprang forward just as an errant block thumped into the deck. A section of netting whipped down across Merriman's ankles and he almost collided with Jones.

'Assess the damage, you two.' Turning to his right, he saw instantly that the exchange of broadsides had been worthwhile.

The pirate vessel was in a wretched state. Smoke was still rising from numerous impacts. Agonized cries rang out across the water. Dozens of pieces of wreckage littered the sea behind her. The starboard side was badly marked by the impacts of cannon balls and at least six guns were out of commission. Though none of the masts were in danger, several sails had been holed. The bowsprit had also been blasted away and two men lay limply over the rail nearby, blood seeping from their bodies into the water. Merriman could see more casualties on the quarterdeck.

Hearing a whimpering from behind him, he saw young Adkins down on his backside and examining a nasty wound to his shin. He saw the captain watching him.

'Just a splinter, sir.'

'Someone will help you momentarily, lad. Hold fast.'

Jones had been forward to the hatch and now hurried back.

'A couple of strikes into the gun ports, sir. Several casualties.'

Merriman grimaced and looked back at where the mizzen topgallant mast and topmast had come down. Sailors had gathered there and were now helping their fellows. He looked up; all the mizzen sails were hanging loose and of no use.

'Alfred?'

'That there's the worst of it, sir. One hit to the foremast but only a glancing blow. Will we come around?'

Merriman glanced over the taffrail. To the north, the merchantman was continuing on its way, as if oblivious to the deadly battle fought for its sake.

With its foremast down, the first pirate ship wasn't in a much better state than the second.

'That rather depends on our enemy's willingness to fight. I would hope we have done enough to deter them from that course of action.'

'Sir, I…'

This came from Calder, the helmsman. As he turned towards Merriman, his hand was already on his head and when he took it away, his palm was slick with blood. His eyes were bulging, his mouth set in an unsmiling grin. He sank to his knees and toppled silently forwards on his face.

Chapter Fifteen

The Headland

Nothing could be done for the unfortunate helmsman. It was discovered that a bolt blasted off the mizzen had penetrated his skull. Calder breathed his last on the deck and – along with another fatality and three more injured – was taken below. Adkins had gone with them, while the other midshipmen supervised the clearing work on the quarterdeck.

Considering they had only two usable masts, wearing sail in only six minutes seemed to Merriman a good result. The wind had now fully veered to the west. He had therefore briefly ordered a northward course to gain some distance and a better angle on his foes, then turned *Thunder* back to the south west.

The pirate vessels were still struggling north, only a quarter-mile apart. They clearly imagined that this proximity might afford them some form of strength but Merriman found himself angered by the loss of his men and had just been informed that three more had perished on the gundecks. Seeing they were facing a ship of the line, these accursed pirates should have taken the hint and run while they had the chance.

Thunder was making perhaps four knots back towards them and Merriman was determined to strike again before the dark closed in. The sun had already dropped below the horizon, making it hard to assess just how black the clouds to the west were.

Shrigley was with Brockle and a dozen men, attending to the launch, which had come loose from its mountings during the wearing manoeuvre. Jones had been sent below to report on the damage and now returned, his face clammy with sweat. Merriman kept his eyes on the two Barbary ships as the lieutenant spoke.

'Damage to two guns, sir. One from enemy fire, one from a misfire. A bucket of powder ignited which caused a small blast on the upper deck near the bow. It was put out quickly but two men were badly burned and did not survive. It's…a nasty scene, sir.'

'Understood.'

'That's not all, sir. Lieutenant Smythe was close by.'

'He's hurt?'

'No, sir, but…he is not himself. He refuses to move.'

Merriman wasn't entirely sure what Jones meant but there was no time for such distractions. The wind had risen to at least twenty-five knots and had shifted again to be almost on the nose. He had lost the weather-gauge utterly and would now have to tack towards his foes. *Thunder* was beginning to rise and fall in the increasing swell.

One of the men working on the launch slipped and fell. Shrigley helped him up then went to Merriman.

'Sir, we'll struggle to lay accurate fire in this.'

'It won't need to be particularly accurate.'

'Sir, that's a fierce westerly now and we're barely five miles off the shore. A shore we don't know.'

'Calm yourself, Alfred. I am well aware of our situation.'

In the event, the pirates made the decision for him. Though neither was making maximum speed, they clearly had no interest in another engagement and were reaching away to the north. Given their condition, Merriman reckoned it inconceivable that they would catch the *Stalwart*. At least the loss of men and mast had been in a good cause.

'Let us gain what sea room we can.' Merriman turned to Harris, who had replaced poor Calder at the helm. 'South it is. Wear sail and lay as close to the wind as you can.'

Any light left in the sky was swiftly obscured by the dense black cloud blown eastward by the gale. The wind rose to thirty knots, howling through the rigging and tearing two of the topgallants. A middling but persistent rain began to fall. Merriman stood at the wheel with Harris, half an eye on the fifty or so men still labouring on the quarterdeck. The mizzen had snapped about twenty feet from the deck. Brockle and the carpenters had a replacement ready but it had not yet been brought up. Merriman decided to spare them their discussions and summoned the bosun.

'You've no chance of raising it in this. Concentrate on clearing the remaining mess below. Anything large can be lashed down. In the meantime, plan a repair that can be carried out immediately when this weather passes.'

'Aye aye, sir.'

Merriman had stationed Lieutenant Jones at the larboard rail and now met him there.

'Well, we're certainly making good progress south, sir.'

'And some way east, unfortunately.'

Though *Thunder* was laying a west-south-westerly course, Merriman knew that the powerful winds were simultaneously pushing her towards the coast.

'Yes, sir. It's hard to make out the land but I'd guess we're roughly parallel for the moment. Five miles off, six if we're lucky. Charts show no shoals. We must hope the wind eases off; or changes direction.'

'Indeed. Or this could be long, unpleasant night. You have the watch, Jones.'

Not knowing when he might have another chance, Merriman crouched low and crabbed across the slippery, sloping deck to the hatch, then made his way downward. A young sailor carrying a bunched section of sail over his shoulder descended behind him and helpfully grabbed the captain's arm when he tripped on the penultimate step.

'Thank you.'

'Sir,' said the sailor, touching his cap before heading forward.

'Another lantern here!' shouted Merriman. 'Can't see a bloody thing.'

'Aye aye, sir', answered a nearby marine, before hurrying away.

Merriman brushed rainwater off the arms of his sou'wester and headed astern, hoping to find Lieutenant Smythe in the wardroom. But the only man present there was the gunner, who was changing his shirt.

'Captain?'

'Hanscombe, do you know where Smythe is?'

'Still on the gundeck, I believe, sir. They haven't been able to move him.'

With a sigh, Merriman hung his sou'wester from the nearest hook, retraced his steps and made his way to the main deck, where dozens of sailors and marines were still occupied with lashing the guns and safely storing ammunition. *Thunder* was rising and dipping now as the sea-state worsened, making their work all the harder. Merriman resisted the temptation to hold his nose as it was assailed by the odours of vomit, blood, smoke and burned flesh.

Lieutenant Essex was walking along the larboard side holding a lantern, inspecting the guns.

'Essex!'

'Yes, sir.'

'Smythe – where is he?'

'This way, sir.'

'You all right?' asked Merriman, noting a patch of blood on the officer's brow.'

'Fine, sir. Word just came up from Mr. Webster. I'm afraid we lost another from the fire.'

'I shall go and see the surgeon presently.'

'Damned bad luck with the mizzen, sir,' added Essex as they passed several crews adding yet more lines to hold down the long guns.

It was only then that Merriman really questioned himself. He had seen the bad weather approaching yet still risked close action. And while his ship and his men had performed well in defeating the pirates so efficiently, a significant price had been paid. For now, *Thunder* had a fair chance of clearing the coast. But if the wind increased and did not shift, their fortunes could rapidly change.

They were approaching the bow when they finally reached Lieutenant Smythe. It was not difficult to see what had caused the damage: the rear of a cannon had been blown out with such force that the iron had been torn and warped. Much of the wooden carriage had also been destroyed and the deck and roof were streaked by black scorch marks.

Second Lieutenant Smythe was lying against the hull, another crewman working away to his left. His uniform and his face had been singed by the blast and he had somehow lost a shoe. His hands were clasped in his lap, his blonde quiff obscuring his eyes. Kneeing beside him to his right was one of the surgeon's mates.

'Sir, I've tried to encourage him but he simply won't get up. Hands and face were a little burned by the flash but I don't think he's wounded anywhere.'

'Go and aid Mr. Webster. I'm sure he needs you.'

'I did also try myself, sir,' added Essex.

'Some of the gunports are still open,' said Merriman. 'See to it.'

Merriman had no doubt that the kind approach had already been tried with Smythe. He didn't have the time for kindness, nor did he believe it would work.

'Smythe!'

The pale eyes looked up at him. Where they had earlier sparkled with expectation, there was now only a lifeless glaze.

'Stand, sir, so that I may address you. *Now*, lieutenant!'

Gradually, Smythe began to move. He rubbed his hands together, drew his legs up and then slowly hauled himself to his feet. Finally, his unblinking eyes focused on the man in front of him.

'Do you know where you are?' asked Merriman, now keeping his voice down.

'Yes, sir.'

'Where are you, lieutenant?'

'Aboard *Thunder*. I meant to come and see you, captain. I am sorry. I...what was it?'

Merriman wasn't sure what he meant.

'What was it, sir? They...' Smythe touched his face as if doing so for the first time.

'Your skin was burned, lieutenant. Some powder went up.'

Smythe's vacant gaze shifted to the ruined gun. 'They were on fire. Rolling. Screaming. He took hold of me. He wouldn't let go. What happened? What happened?'

Merriman reached out and gripped his shoulder. 'I told you. We were engaged with the pirates. Some powder went up. Several men were killed.'

'He wouldn't let go.'

Turning, Merriman caught the eye of an old hand named Wheeler. Dropping a length of rope, the veteran sailor came over.

'Sir?'

'I believe Lieutenant Smythe should rest a little, Wheeler. Would you take him to the ward room for me.'

'Aye, cap'n.'

Wheeler gently placed his hand on Smythe's arm. 'This way, lieutenant.'

Eyes wide, Smythe turned to Wheeler, who gave an encouraging smile. 'To the ward room, sir. It'll be nice and quiet there.'

Once down on the orlop deck, Merriman hurried along to Mr. Webster's room. Here, young Adkins sat on a stool, nursing his injured leg. Another man was laid out on the floor, bandages covering much of his face. A second was on a table, where his leg was being stitched up by the surgeon.

Handing his needle and thread to one of his assistants, the Welshman crossed to the captain and the pair spoke by a bright lantern.

'Sir.'

'Mr. Webster, how are you faring?'

'The two burned men were brought here but they did not last long.'

'A mercy, I daresay?'

Webster nodded. 'The same goes for poor Calder.'

'And yourself? Never easy in a rough sea.'

'While I had plenty to concentrate on, it did not trouble me. Now that things are slowing down a little, I feel rather sick.'

'Understood. Get some air and some rest when you can. Well done.'

'Thank you, sir.'

Merriman had been in no doubt that he had an intelligent and conscientious physician aboard in Mr. Webster. He was relieved to now find that man was also courageous and stoic.

'Well then, Adkins, your first war wound.'

The midshipman looked up from the stool. The cut had been bandaged but the injury was evidently causing him pain.

'Yes, captain. It's not too bad. Am I needed on deck?'

'Not for the moment. Rest awhile. But someone will need to update the log fairly soon.'

'I heard the wind's shifted to the west, sir.'

'Quite so. But even without the mizzen, we're making good speed.'

With that, Merriman left the orlop, recovered his sou'wester and made his way back on deck. Even during the time he'd been below, conditions had worsened. The sailors completing the work on the quarterdeck and those manning the lines all now wore protective clothing. They held on to rails and stays as *Thunder* rode across the wind. The ship was pushed hard over now, the starboard side of the deck free of water, the larboard side inundated, despite the scuppers. Even the experienced Harris was having such difficulty with the wheel that a second man was assisting him.

The captain raised his hood and scrambled across to the larboard rail and First Lieutenant Shrigley.

Shrigley pushed back his own hood and nodded. 'Steady at forty knots I should say, sir. Main topgallant has torn but we managed to get the reefs in.'

Merriman looked up to see the shredded sail whipping around like a thing possessed. 'The topsails should really be down but then we lose even more power. The coast?'

'No nearer I should say, sir. I checked the chart – it falls away here to the east.'

'That won't save us.'

'No. Sir, it will likely get worse before it gets better, wouldn't you agree?'

'I would, Alfred.'

'Captain, perhaps you should get some food and rest while you can?'

Despite the circumstances, Merriman found himself smiling. 'By God, Alfred. You've come such a way from the lad who fell into that hold full of fish.'

'How many times, sir? I was pushed.'

'Of course you were.'

Relieved to see that both Master Henderson and Bosun Brockle were also on deck, Merriman scrambled back across the sloping timbers and went below once more.

He was not surprised to find the great cabin in some state of disarray. Peters and two other men were trying to raise one of the partitions but Merriman told them to desist and concentrate on tidying up. Several lockers had flown open, depositing papers, maps and navigational equipment.

'You'd like some coffee, sir, I expect?'

'I would, Peters, but we can have no open flames in this weather. One fire is enough for one day and we must set a good example. Complete your tidying then fetch me a tot of rum – a *large* tot.

'Aye aye, sir.'

On another occasion, there would have been something comic about watching the three men gather the objects as the cabin tipped this way and that. Merriman stationed himself at the rear, looking out at through the rain-lashed glass at the foaming, surging water below. He knew from experience that a heavy ship of the line could weather forty knots for some time. If it rose to fifty or sixty, the dangers increased exponentially, especially with no mizzen mast and on a lee shore. And yet, had he really expected to sail for months in the Atlantic without encountering a storm? It was a virtual certainty.

The wind seemed to ease for a time, which helped Peters and the others complete their work. Taking a deep breath, the attendant composed himself before finding the tin mug that Merriman used in such conditions and half-filling it with rum. While the men favoured a mix of three to one for their grog, Merriman took his straight; then again, he did consume a lot less. Enjoying the warming liquid as it slid down his throat, he then asked Peters what there was to eat.

'Some cold ham, sir. No bread left, I'm afraid. Biscuit, perhaps? A little dried apple?'

'That'll do nicely.'

Merriman had always found that the dry, powdery navy-issue biscuit was well-suited for conditions likely to make one sick.

After he had finished the rum, his little meal was served on a tin plate. While he was eating it, a wave struck the cabin windows with such ferocity that one pane of glass cracked.

'Damn and blast it!' declared Peters. 'We only had them replaced in January.'

'It appears that the Atlantic Ocean has little regard for our refurbishments, Peters. I suggest a board to cover it. Is my hammock up?'

'It is, sir. I thought you'd prefer it, given the sea state.'

'Very good.' Merriman handed Peters his plate and stood. 'Not sure I'll get much sleep but I should try.'

A few minutes later came a knock on the door.

'Enter!'

It was Second Lieutenant Harrison. The marine wore a sou'wester of his own and his expression was grave.

'Message from Lieutenant Shrigley, sir. Headland spotted to larboard. Close.'

By the time Merriman reached the door, Peters had his sou'wester ready.

Even in the darkness, the headland was visible: higher than the area surrounding it and ominously close. Merriman had just taken his turn with a spyglass and reckoned that Shrigley was about right: it was around three miles off the bow.

'Charts show there's a bay beyond, sir.'

'First we have to get past this,' said Merriman, lowering the telescope. 'Tom, can we not make another point to windward?'

'Sir, it's right on the beam,' answered the sailing master. 'We're close-hauled and the leeway's something awful. Without the mizzen she's out of sorts. I'm sorry.'

Shrigley spoke up. 'Sir, there are men volunteering to try a repair.'

'Are you jesting, Alfred? Why we'd lose half of them over the side.'

'They just wanted me to pass it on, sir.'

The wind was still up around forty knots and Merriman reckoned that *Thunder* was making five. He glanced back at the useless mizzen. With less sail up they had less speed; and less chance of clearing the headland.

As the three men stood against the rail, Essex and Hickey came up from the stern.

'We dropped the lead-line, sir. Hard to be sure in these conditions but we've at least fifteen fathoms.'

Merriman nodded an acknowledgment.

'No shoals marked in this area, sir,' said Shrigley. 'But the only map we have is old.'

Merriman forced himself not to dwell on what was now undeniably a mistake: to engage the pirates on a lee shore with an ill wind looming. He reckoned that the captain and men of the *Stalwart* would be grateful for the intervention but it was hardly worth risking *Thunder* and his seven hundred crewmen. He recalled the words of his first captain:

The sea makes fools of us all.

'Your volunteers, Alfred.'

'Sir?'

'We still have part of a mizzen. Let us see if they can raise a single course. Even that might make some difference.'

With a determined grin, the first lieutenant hurried away.

Merriman spent the next half-hour with Essex and Hickey at the rail. Tom Henderson and Bosun Brockle supervised the work on the mizzen and Merriman could hardly watch as men climbed the mutilated mast, dropping lines so that others could follow.

The wind continued to punish them, pushing them east, the only mercy being the full sails that might yet drag *Thunder* to safety.

'Stop that, lad!' snapped Merriman, annoyed by Hickey raising his spyglass every minute or so. 'We shall either pass by the headland or we shall not.'

The boy's reply was lost in the wind.

Merriman shook his head, the side of his hood plastered against his cheek by the wind. And only two minutes later, he raised his own telescope. The dark, curved outline of the headland was now midway between bow and beam, less than a mile distant, the *Thunder* no more than a half-mile off the coast. All he could make out were some vertical striations of pale rock and the spurts of white water at the cliff's base. Merriman felt a hollow form in his stomach as he thought of *Thunder* foundering on those cliffs. For all her weapons and her devices and her armoured hull, she would be sliced open by sheer rock as mercilessly as a rowing boat.

The minutes passed. Soon he could see the white markings and white water with the naked eye.

'By God, that was quick.'

He had just turned to find that the courageous sailors had jury-rigged a single large staysail, running the lines through blocks they had temporarily affixed to the stern. It was large as the usual mizzen top sail and set fair, the canvas full and barely trembling.

Merriman would never know if it made the difference but when *Thunder* finally drew level with the headland, it was still a good quarter-mile distant. Beyond it, the land fell away into a bay as Shrigley had promised.

Midshipman Hickey looked up, squinting into the rain, a broad grin on his face.

'We're clear aren't we, captain?'

'We're clear.'

Chapter Sixteen

Embayed

For the briefest of moments, it seemed that the *Thunder* might be set free. An hour after dawn, Merriman was roused from a restless sleep and came on deck to see some lighter sky to the west. Though the wind was still at thirty knots and a great swathe of dark cloud sat over the ship and the coast, the strip of pale sky seemed to offer hope. And when it reached them, the wind dropped off a little and became fluky and unpredictable for a time.

But *Thunder* was unable to make much of it and soon sea and ship were shadowed once again. The brief respite at least allowed the carpenters and riggers to improve their work on the mizzen in clear daylight. Merriman waited for his ship to pass another headland, revealing a long, shallow bay to their south. He heard from Lieutenant Essex that a lookout had earlier spotted the mouth of a river. It might have offered salvation but – upon examination – proved to be far too narrow for *Thunder* to risk.

Returning below to dress properly, Merriman passed his marine sentry, Glover.

'Morning, sir.'

'Morning, Glover.'

'Everyone is praying for a change in the wind, sir. Do you think it will come today?'

'We can only hope so. We're at least making good progress south.'

Five minutes later, as Peters put on his coat, there was a knock on the door.

'Come!'

Thunder was still pressed over and Tom Henderson had to hold the doorway as he passed inside.

'Sorry to disturb, sir. Wondered if I might have a word.'

'Of course, Tom.'

The sailing master closed the door behind him and came forward. 'If I might speak, freely, sir?'

Merriman had a suspicion of what was coming and it worried him more than anything else. As befitted his station, Tom Henderson was a mariner of great experience and peerless knowledge. Merriman could count the number of times he had come to his cabin with a request for a private audience on one hand.

'Leave us, would you, Peters?' he said, doing up his buttons.

'Aye, sir. Any breakfast?'

'Not at this moment. Tom, let us sit.'

Leaning into the slope, the pair made their way to the lockers and sat down. Henderson looked out of the nearest window.

'She's taking it well, sir.'

'She is. But you're not here to tell me what I already know. What is it?'

'We can't see the far end of this bay, sir. There's some beach but also plenty of rock. If there's not a change before the end of this day…'

'I know.'

'Sir, the mizzen. We've got one sail up but we desperately need more. There's not only the topmen will risk it. For the afterguard, the mizzen is *theirs*; they don't like to let the rest of the ship down. They're sure they can get the replacement spar up.'

'They might. But we were lucky not to lose anyone over the side last night. We both know we won't be that lucky again.'

'Agreed, sir but-'

'You're saying it's worth losing a few.'

Henderson sighed and leaned back. 'Not in so many words, sir. If not that, we should consider losing some weight.'

'You mean the guns?'

'No, sir, there are supplies that can go first. Ammunition perhaps. We'll need her a bit more nimble if we have to tack or wear sail. I...I've seen this before, sir. Cornwall. Ships stuck between headlands with an onshore-'

Henderson read his captain's expression and desisted. 'Well, that's enough from me. But the mizzen, sir – please do consider it.'

'I'll do that, Tom. Make sure you get some rest. I need you fighting fit.'

Merriman could not remember a worse day at sea. By noon, all agreed that the westerly had exceeded fifty knots. For every three hundred yards she moved south, *Thunder* was pushed a hundred east. Even worse, the powerful wind tore two more sails, only one of which could be repaired, and this at the cost of a topman who fell and broke his arm. There could be no question of attempting the mizzen repair: the wind was simply too fierce.

The rain at least held off in the middle of the day but there was no relief for those on deck. Every pair of eyes seemed fixated on the shore, which was now in alarmingly clear relief. There were a few sections of rock but most was either swamp or beach. Merriman heard some comment that this at least improved their chance of survival but he wasn't sure. Some might survive on boat and launch but the great ship would run aground and there were high waves crashing in the surf. Most likely she'd turn over.

From below came many reports of sickness. *Thunder* had been thrown this way and that for almost an entire day and night. At the request of the petty officers, Merriman allowed the men to take turns to come up and get some air. Lieutenant Cary was so ill that – according to Harrison – he was simply lying in his hammock, unable to drink even water. Merriman was immensely relieved to see Mister Webster in reasonable form, and still able to treat his patients. One of those was Lieutenant Smythe. Webster had given him a medicinal tonic that had apparently sent him into a deep sleep and Smythe had not left the wardroom.

As often occurred at sea, one man's sickness caused it in others, so that when Shrigley at last succumbed, Jones and Essex did so too. They gripped the rail, trying to maintain some semblance of dignity while vomiting.

'Weak stomachs, captain,' said Friar, the young topman. The bold youth seemed to be the only one aboard with any cheer left in him. 'Not proper sailors like you and me, sir!'

Merriman couldn't help smiling at his cheek. 'First voyage, isn't it, Friar?'

'It is sir.'

'You must be made for life at sea then.'

'I reckon so, sir. We'll get off this coast, won't we? Then we can hunt down the *Hercule* like we was meant to.'

'That is the idea.'

'Wish we could have a fire on. Cold duff's all right but it's much better warm.'

Before the cheerful lad could say anything else, Bosun Brockle came on to the quarterdeck with a report from the bilges.

'Hard to be sure with us over like this, sir, but water's holding steady at three feet.'

'Very good. Tell the lads on the pumps that there'll be a double tot for them if they can keep it that way until nightfall.'

Long before they reached the southern end of the bay, the inevitable conclusion was obvious: *Thunder* had no hope of clearing the southern headland. They had calculated the length of the bay to be twenty miles, its breadth at the widest point perhaps four. A mile short of the headland, during a brief lull when the wind dropped – and using the last of the daylight – Merriman seized the moment. The fo'c'sle men and waisters had been standing by for some time and the ship wore sail in a superb four minutes. Under direct supervision from Henderson and Brockle, the sailors on watch did a remarkable job, with no sense of panic; only ordered, energetic efficiency. And yet, by the time *Thunder* was heading north back across the bay, she had been pushed at least a half-mile towards the shore.

'Very good work,' said Merriman, gathered with Shrigley, Jones and Essex on the quarterdeck.

'We should be grateful for small mercies, I suppose,' said Essex. 'At least this bay is a long one.'

'Indeed,' said Jones.

'What do you think, sir?' asked Shrigley. 'We've enough room for one more turn, wouldn't you say?'

'I would. But no more.'

'What then? The anchors?'

'We will have no choice. Essex, I want the lead dropped at every bell. If it drops below ten fathoms, tell me.'

'Aye aye, sir.'

'Jones, ensure that everything below is orderly and that our hold weight is well distributed.'

'Aye aye, sir.'

'Shrigley, I ask you to personally check all four anchors, plus the cables and fittings. We will almost certainly depend on them.'

It was three in the morning when *Thunder* wore sail again, a mile short of the headland they had no chance of rounding. All agreed that – in the darkness, and with half a mizzen – five and a half minutes was a fine time. But the manoeuvre cost them dear. Merriman watched, his entire body tense, as the ship turned slowly, all the while being pressed back into the bay. By the time her sails filled and she headed south again, the breakers on the nearest beach were visible with the naked eye.

Knowing he would not sleep, Merriman remained on deck. The relentless wind and dangerous conditions kept the lookouts from the masts but two had been posted at the bow. Not long after the turn, they reported flaming torches visible on the shore. An hour later, Merriman and his officers could clearly see the lights themselves. Some seemed to be moving and following the *Thunder*'s progress.

'I hope those are merely interested observers,' remarked Shrigley between mouthfuls of food: the officers had been provided with some dried beef to keep them going.

It was now impossible to remain dry while on deck. As well as the rain, all the spray found its way to the larboard side and Merriman often found himself sloshing through water ankle-deep.

'Not wreckers, you mean?' said Essex, tearing off a strip of the tough beef with his teeth.

Merriman said nothing on the matter, though he knew it was another problem to add to a growing list.

'You two – what about Smythe? He should be back up on deck by now, fulfilling his duties.'

'We did try, sir, but he seems incapable of even dressing himself.'

'At the next opportunity, you will bring him up, whatever his condition. It is an appalling example to the men.'

'Yes, captain,' replied Shrigley.

* * *

An hour after dawn, the wind dropped below forty knots. Knowing he might not get another chance to make this decision, Merriman ordered that the topsails be furled and the courses reefed. Summoned by the bosun's whistle, the men sped out of the hatch and up the rigging. Despite the slightly easier conditions, with less sail they had less stability. Merriman wondered at the courage and agility of the topmen, dismayed to see that Friar was amongst them.

Later, he turned to examine what was now a crowd of natives upon the beach. Some sat in a group on a dune to the north, observing, while others walked along the sand, close to the booming surf. The strength of the wind was evident in the way it blasted at their hair and made it difficult for them to walk. Almost every face watched the *Thunder*. By Merriman's best estimate, his ship was no more than a mile and a quarter offshore.

The upper sails were stowed – at a cost. No less than five men were injured: three had fallen, two had been struck by a swinging yard.

Shrigley went to check on the men as they were carried below, then reported to Merriman. 'Two broken ankles, strained knee, broken ribs, bruised back.'

Though he didn't say so, the captain was relieved that the crucial operation hadn't resulted in any deaths.

'If we are to founder, it had best be on sand. We will presently turn into the wind and drop the heavy anchor. You will oversee it, Alfred.'

'Aye aye, sir.'

Thunder's main anchor weighed three tons, her second anchor two. Merriman knew now that the fate of his ship – and possibly every man aboard – would depend on those anchors and cables holding.

Three lead readings confirmed that they were in eighty feet of water. When he had confirmation from Shrigley and Jones that all were ready, Merriman ordered the helm to turn into the westerly and the main anchor was dropped. Even above the noise of the wind and the flapping courses, he could hear the great cable running out.

Merriman looked over the stern. The wind was pushing *Thunder* back and – though Harris was fighting it – the bow was beginning to come around to the north. Fortunately, word soon came back that the anchor had touched the bottom. Not long after that, Adkins arrived to confirm that the cable had been tied off on the riding bitts. Merriman wiped water out of his eyes and looked at the beach. They were too far from either headland to gauge their progress backward; all he could depend on was his instinct and feel for the ship. The result was that he knew the anchor had held before it was reported to him.

Though he hated the thought of having no sail at the ready, it was an impediment to the anchor holding and so the remaining courses were furled. Once that was done, the sailors stood waiting, all of them turning to look at the sea and the shore to confirm that the anchor was indeed set. The wind continued to howl and *Thunder* was being thrown up and down by the shorter, more regular waves found in shallower seas.

Shrigley hurried back to the quarterdeck. 'Slight crack in one of the bitts but otherwise all looks well, sir. Thank God the yard gave us that great hunk of iron from the *Repulse*. The last one was only two and a quarter tons.'

'Nevertheless, we cannot depend on it. Have the waisters lower the launch and prepare the second anchor. If we have a problem, they can deploy it swiftly.'

Shrigley appeared hesitant. 'Sir, perhaps we could wait for a break-'

'Dangerous, I know, Alfred. But not as dangerous as depending on a single anchor. Instruct the waisters to also rig the crane. All haste.'

'Aye aye, sir.'

'And give someone the job of finding something on land we can take a bearing on. We *must* know if we are dragging.'

Merriman could not stand another moment on deck. He was beginning to feel as if he had lived his entire life facing this gale on this ship and – realising that Smythe had still not appeared – he made immediately for the wardroom. Though fully dressed, the officer was sitting on a stool, staring blankly into space.

'Lieutenant.'

Smythe immediately stood and brushed his hair out of his eyes. 'Yes, sir.'

'You're needed up on deck. Report to Shrigley.'

'Sir.'

Merriman took a few steps but soon realised that Smythe hadn't moved an inch.

'*Now*, lieutenant.'

'Yes. Sir…how…how do I face them?'

It was evident to Merriman that Smythe had regained his senses. Now he clearly needed help to regain something else.

'You mean the men?'

Smythe nodded.

Merriman answered in the manner he thought most truthful and most helpful: 'You're afraid that word has spread. That they will know that your nerve failed you. That they will all look at you differently now. You are quite correct. However, other than those few aboard whose first voyage this is, the men will have seen similar reactions from *many* men and *many* officers. I hate to think what it was like to witness what you did. But the best way to win back respect is to get up on deck – show that you have the courage to carry on.'

'Yes, sir. Thank you. It's just that I…I…' Smythe let out a long sigh before continuing. 'I have always endeavoured to be a natural man of action, as my father and grandfather were before me. I think I knew that I wasn't and that is why I have always tried so hard. Too hard.'

Merriman reached out and gripped the younger man's shoulder. 'You have lost nothing but a few days. As your captain, I require only that you follow orders. Now – up on deck at once.'

The captain made sure that the troubled lieutenant did exactly that, then made his way to the great cabin. Though he didn't feel particularly hungry, he ordered Peters to prepare him a meal. The attendant took off his soaking sou'wester and helped his superior out of his sodden clothes.

'By God, sir, you should have come down sooner. You'll catch a chill.'

'The least of my worries, Peters,' replied Merriman, slumping down as the attendant removed his socks.

'Sorry there's no hot water, sir.'

'No matter.'

'I'll put some new clothes out in a moment. Please take this for now.' Peters retrieved a blanket and draped it over Merriman's shoulders. The captain put his head back against the cabin's side. As activity was now concentrated at the bow, he could hear nothing except the relentless blasting of the wind. He closed his eyes.

Dear Lord,
Of my many sins, one is my repeated failure to regularly address you or attend church. I don't suppose you will particularly concern yourself with me. However, there are almost seven hundred souls aboard this vessel and our mission is a noble one. If you must take us in battle, so be it, but please do not allow my ship and my men to die like this.

When he opened his eyes, Peters had already returned with the dry clothes. Merriman refused his offer of assistance with dressing, instead telling him that dinner – and a tot of rum – was more urgent.

Now that the shore was so close, and disaster so near, he allowed himself a moment's consideration of home. They could not know what he was facing yet the thought of Helen and the children brought him a smile. He would return to them. And he would return *Thunder* to England. Officers and men had fought so very hard; they had earned salvation.

After downing two biscuits, some dried sausage and some dried apple, Merriman sipped swiftly on his rum until he began to feel sleepy. He then took himself into his sleeping quarters and climbed into his hammock, pulling the blanket on top of him. With the ship rising and dipping, this was the best place to be and he soon drifted away.

When he was awoken, he could tell that darkness had fallen. Shrigley came in, accompanied by a sailor bearing a lantern.

'God, I have slept for too long. How are we faring, Alfred?'

'Barely three hours, sir. Please stay where you are. The main anchor is holding. Hickey has got bearings on a couple of dunes and is convinced that we're not dragging. Essex and myself concur. The midshipmen have taken it upon themselves to monitor our position.'

'Very good. And the second?'

'Crane is up, sir. Second anchor lashed to the deck beside it. Took us two hours – lots of bruises but somehow no broken bones. The launch is ready, just forward of it. We have the beams on the thwarts and slings tied on.'

'Well done, Alfred.'

'More torches on the shore, sir.'

'And the wind?'

'Steady on the nose at forty to forty-five.'

'By God, it is unrelenting. One of us two must stay on deck at all times. Can you manage another couple of hours?'

'Of course, sir. One other thing – Smythe seems a bit more like himself. Whatever you said to him must have worked.'

'Not me. Just a bit of fresh air.'

'It's certainly fresh, sir. I wonder if we'll ever get our clothes dry again.'

'We'll soon be flying south with the sun on our backs,' said Merriman. 'I've no doubt about it.'

'I'm sure you're right, sir.'

'Oh, Alfred, one thing before you go.'

'Sir?'

'Have a list drawn up of our best thirty oarsmen. Ensure they are well rested and well fed. I've a feeling we might need them before long.'

Chapter Seventeen

In The Water

Thunder was beginning to fall apart. By dawn, the wind had accelerated to an unrelenting blast in excess of fifty knots. Wave after rolling wave assaulted the African shore and the British ship, tossing her up and dragging her down. The galley had not lit a fire for two days, seasickness was rife and the persistent rain ensured that only the well-equipped officers had any dry clothes.

The main topgallant mast had come crashing down and the battered bowsprit seemed unlikely to last much longer. The temporary crane rigged for the second anchor had been disassembled and taken below. The two boats had become such liabilities that both were let out at the stern. Down below, numerous guns had shaken free of their lashings and one bulkhead had split clean down the middle from the constant strain. To his great credit, Peters offered Merriman breakfast that morning, even though he himself was very ill. In fact, the attendant told the captain that only he and a handful of others had not vomited at some point.

'Is there a prize?' quipped Merriman grimly as he donned his coat and sou'wester. The temperature was so low – and it seemed so long since they had seen the sun – that it felt more like November than May. He told Peters to go and rest, then headed up. The captain had completed a stint in the middle of the night then given way to Shrigley. Merriman could not recall a more miserable shift on deck; facing the elements head on and dreading the moment when *Thunder* was at last overcome and thrown onto the shore. The native wreckers had done them no favours; their torches could have provided a useful reference point had they not constantly moved. Merriman even wondered if they had done so on purpose.

Halfway up the steps, he almost collided with a pale-looking Adkins. 'Captain, I was just coming to fetch you. We think the main anchor might be dragging.'

Spitting curses under his breath, Merriman followed the youngster up on deck to find Shrigley, Henderson and Jones at the taffrail. Before he reached them, he decided that *Thunder* was indeed dragging her anchor; it was far easier to make such judgements with the perspective of time below.

The trio turned as he began dispensing orders. 'Shrigley, let out more cable and see if she'll catch again. Jones, get that crane back up. Essex, ready the launch crew – we'll get the second anchor out as soon as we can.'

Shrigley covered his face to shield it from the rain. 'Can we even use the boats, sir? They're jumping around like wild things.'

'They'll be steadier with plenty of men in them. Get to it!'

Despite the conditions, Bosun Brockle and his crew had done little else but prepare for this eventuality and the crane was up within a quarter-hour. With two dozen men on the rope, the anchor was lifted off the deck and the crane arm pushed over the side. Shouts and curses filled the air as Brockle and Henderson oversaw the delicate, dangerous operation. Even before the anchor was lowered, two men had almost been knocked overboard and another had turned his ankle.

Below, another two dozen men were in the launch, led by Lieutenant Jones. As the anchor entered the water behind the twenty-foot vessel, the men used boathooks and lines to manoeuvre it onto the weighted slings hanging beneath.

Seeing the marine officer, Harrison, nearby, Merriman issued him some instructions. 'Would you find some throwing lines for both sides and place your men by the rails? In case anyone is thrown from the boats.'

'Aye aye, sir.'

Merriman then made his way up to the bow. Here, Henderson was watching the great anchor cable, his fingers splayed upon it.

'Please tell me she's caught again.'

Henderson's grimace was a clear answer.

'Damn it!' Turning back, Merriman saw an unusual sight.

Close to the mainmast, a black-haired sailor was kneeling on the deck, moving some small objects around in his hands. He seemed to whisper something to himself then gestured to the sky. Merriman might have taken it for a performance but there was an air of utter conviction about the man. Despite the weather, he wore only a short sailor's jacket and seemed unperturbed by the lashing wind and rain.

One of the bosun's mates was standing by and he noted Merriman's interest.

'That there is Davey Solomon, sir. He's American, half-Indian, and he follows his father's religion. Usually keeps himself to himself but I suppose he's as anxious as the next man.'

Sick of the sou'wester hood, Merriman pushed it down and walked back along the starboard side. He watched with relief as Jones signalled to Brockle that the anchor was safely in the slings below the boat. The crane rope was detached so the only remaining line on the anchor was the cable, which was currently laid out along the deck. Jones had orders to take the anchor out two hundred feet and drop it. With a man stationed beside him to monitor their load, Jones took the rudder and ordered his oarsman to heave.

The waves were ten to fifteen feet in height and the boat was falling and rising with such force that some of those strokes barely touched the water. It was fortunate, thought Merriman, that their backs were to the oncoming spray. With a small crew, Brockle now ran the heavy cable along to the bow, where it was made off to an iron ring beside the bitts. Meanwhile, his men secured the arm of the crane.

Merriman headed back to the quarterdeck and took his first opportunity to look back at the coast. Even through the heavy rain, he could see several hundred men gathered on the beach, so close now that he could make out differences in size and garb.

Shrigley was already there. 'Captain, I've been watching the water. Hard to tell due to the swell but I think there's a bar behind us.'

'Sandbank?'

'Yes, sir. Hundred yards. Maybe less.'

'By Christ.' Merriman hurried over to the larboard side, where the last of the oarsmen were joining Essex in the boat. He was glad to see that a line had already been run from the vessel to the bow. He cupped his hands around his mouth to make himself clear.

'Lieutenant, neither anchor is set! You must do what you can to hold her!'

He knew – and surely Essex did too – that the boat's efforts could only make a minimal difference. And yet given the proximity of the bar, there was not much else he could do.

'Aye aye, sir!' yelled Essex. He was soon bellowing at his men and they too pulled away, despite the combination of wind and swell.

Merriman pointed at Shrigley. 'You watch that bar.'

Face lashed by the elements, he hurried across the deck and saw that the launch was pulling slowly away from the bow, dipping and rising as the men hauled. Gripping the rail, he made his way forward and was immediately addressed by Henderson.

'I thought she'd caught but still dragging, sir!'

Merriman addressed the bosun's mate manning the second anchor cable.

'How much is out?'

'Hundred fifty feet, sir.'

'Shorten it to hundred twenty.'

'Aye, sir.'

As the men went to work, Merriman looked back at the stern. Shrigley made no gesture but he now realised he could see the shorter chop of the water over the sand bar. He looked at the launch. As well as the anchor slung beneath, the men were pulling the heavy, sodden rope that ran up to the bow. They were barely fifty feet off the bow but they had to drop it now. One of the oarsmen alerted Jones to the captain's signal and the lieutenant ordered men to the slings to let the anchor drop. But in the rolling sea, this was no easy task.

Merriman felt a hand on his shoulder.

'Sir, we're close,' said Shrigley, who had appeared at the bow with remarkable haste. '*Very* close.'

'How long?'

'Minutes.'

But there was some hope. Essex and his boat were a good forty feet beyond the bow. Merriman and Shrigley stepped aside as a sailor made off their line on another ring, wisely getting out of the way as the rope snapped taught. This jolted the boat so strongly that several oarsmen slipped from their seats. But Essex's imprecations were thrown back on the wind to the watching officers. The sailors answered him and twelve oars dug deep.

'I do believe they are actually holding us,' said Henderson, gazing admiringly at his compatriots aboard the boats. 'They're doing it – bless 'em one and all.'

Merriman wasn't sure about that but he was grateful nonetheless.

'Back to the stern, Alfred – spread the word. If we strike the bar...'

'Aye, captain.'

'Sir, the second's away!' yelled Henderson.

Merriman watched as Jones and two others recovered the sling from under their stern, then turned his gaze to the cable, which the master was now also monitoring. If they had been in eighty feet of water earlier, that was surely much reduced now. The second anchor didn't have far to fall.

He then signalled Essex's boat and received an answering wave from the lieutenant. In order to ease the line, Essex turned the boat to port but he was caught out by a steep wave, the little vessel falling sideways down the far side of it. Oars fell into the water and the sailors' hands shot to thwarts and rails.

But one unfortunate found no grip. With a despairing grab at a compatriot, he fell into the foaming sea and disappeared.

'Man in the water!' yelled Merriman, running – and almost slipping – as he crossed to the larboard rail. The sailor emerged close to the bow high on another wave, eyes wide with fear, arms flailing. Even if he was a good swimmer, he had no chance of fighting the wind and waves and he was already being pulled towards shore.

Merriman ran down the side of his ship, leaping over several lines until he spied the marines stationed at the rear.

'Harrison, throw it out – as far as you can!'

The marine saw the man in the water and duly did as ordered, the rope uncoiling in the air as he cast it over the side. The line landed and lay on the surface. The sailor seemed so disorientated that he didn't see the rope until he struck it. The line bent as his weight took him on and then he had sense enough to grab it. Merriman snatched up the line ahead of Harrison and bellowed at the man.

'Just hold on! We'll pull you in!'

Only when he saw a nod of acknowledgement did Merriman began to heave on the slender line, with Harrison assisting. It didn't take long to bring the man up to the hull and another enterprising marine appeared with a rope ladder which he hooked to a bollard and hung over the side.

Knowing he couldn't afford to neglect his wider responsibilities, the captain now looked over the taffrail.

The turbulent water above the bar was quite apparent and *Thunder* was no more than a boat length from it.

Yet again, he made his way back to the bow, where he found Henderson smiling.

'Second's set, sir. Line's too steep for my liking but she's holding.'

Merriman was also relieved to see that both Essex and Jones had turned their vessels back towards the *Thunder* without further incident. Only then did he notice that the swell had lessened a little.

'Well, I'll be hanged!' uttered Tom Henderson. 'Main anchor's caught something too, sir. Might be thicker sand or a band of rock beneath us.'

'Thank God.'

Merriman checked both cables himself. He lacked Henderson's expertise but the gentle quivering upon both thick lines reassured him.

'Lighter sky to the west, sir,' said the sailing master. 'There's hope yet.'

And there it was: a band of pale grey separating the dark cloud from the horizon.

Once more, the captain and his officers maintained their vigil. The sailing master would not leave his post at the anchor cable, which suited Merriman well enough. He watched as Jones and Essex guided the boats back to *Thunder* and alongside. Merriman oversaw the disembarkation of the crews and recruited dozens of sailors to help the men up the nets.

'Every last sailor careful there! I don't want any more of you taking a dip!'

Many were clearly exhausted and had to be assisted over the rail, where they slumped down onto their backsides. Webster's two assistants had sensibly made preparations and handed out mugs of beer. Jones and Essex were last to come aboard and Merriman shook both their hands. 'A superb effort, gentlemen. Make sure you have every man's name for double grog today.'

Overhearing this, one of the oarsmen had strength enough to thank the captain and raise a cheer from his cohorts. Merriman ordered that the boats be let out from the stern once more.

He then noticed the unfortunate seaman who had fallen in. Out of his wet clothes and now wrapped in blankets, he was being examined by Webster and summoned the strength to salute his captain.

'I cannot swim, sir,' admitted the man, who Merriman recalled was named Trenton.

'You can now,' he countered, slapping the sailor on the shoulder.

'Mister Webster, have you dealt with many taken out of the water?'

'I have not, captain.'

'Watch him – or have him watched – for at least an hour. Sometimes they ingest more water than they realise. They seem in good spirits and deteriorate rapidly. They can drown on dry land. I've seen it before.'

'Very well, captain.'

On the quarterdeck, Merriman saw how alarmingly close they were to the churning water above the sandbar – no more than fifty feet. Lieutenant Smythe was there, gazing at the Africans on the beach. They were all gathered in one group now, watching intently.

'One is reminded of carrion circling above a dying man,' remarked Merriman.

Smythe turned around and nodded. 'Quite, sir.'

The captain noted the dull and dirty state of his jacket but was pleased to see him on deck and apparently in reasonable form.

'Should we chuck a ball or two their way, sir?' suggested Shrigley, who had just come up on deck.

'I don't think that will be necessary,' said Merriman. 'Don't tell me you slept through all that?'

'I'm ashamed to say I did, sir.'

'Do not admonish yourself, Alfred,' said Merriman with a grin. 'All went well – eventually.'

'Very good, sir.'

Merriman spotted the half-Indian man Davey Solomon, who was talking to some of the oarsmen and pointing to the west. Merriman looked that way too. Beyond the shadowed sea and the rolling waves, the line of lighter sky had widened and extended across the whole of the horizon.

'At last,' said Shrigley, holding out a flattened palm. 'The rain has stopped. Wind's dropping too.'

Though he had never noticed Davey Solomon before, Merriman spied him later below deck: the American was on his way down; part of a crew relieving those hard at work on the bilge pump. There was apparently now four feet of water and Brockle had turned his full attention to reducing it.

'Solomon, is it?'

Merriman was close to the hatch and gestured for the sailor to approach.

'Sir?'

Up close, Merriman could see more evidence of his origins in his dark eyes and thick, black hair.

'Earlier – on deck. Those objects, your…invocations. Some kind of religious ceremony, I gather?'

'Sorry, captain,' said the man, suddenly fearful. 'I should not have done it.'

'No need to apologise. I just wondered what exactly you were doing? I'm assuming it wasn't a prayer to the Lord?'

'Not exactly, captain. I…may I show you?'

'Please.'

Solomon reached into the pocket of his blue sailor's coat and retrieved a little leather bag. From it he took a circular piece of stone, divided into four quarters, with shapes and colours upon it.

'Some call this the sacred circle, for me it is the medicine wheel. The circle reflects the four seasons, the four ages of man and four animals: bear, buffalo, eagle and wolf. For a sailor, it also reflects the four directions of wind. Yellow is for the western wind and so I turned the wheel in that direction and asked for assistance.'

'I understand that your people do not have one god. Do you ask the spirits?'

'Some tribes favour spirits, sir, but not mine. We do believe in one god but that he created lesser gods that can influence the affairs of man.'

'What is your one god called?'

'Manitou. He is within every living thing and every part of the world. Men of the Bible believe the same thing.'

'We men of the Bible prayed and nothing changed.' Merriman gestured towards the sky. 'Perhaps Manitou is listening. Perhaps he watches over you.'

'I think we have different names but it is the same god, captain.' Solomon gave a curious smile. 'That is what I tell my mess-mates anyway. I find it helps keep the peace. I don't want to give them another reason to insult me.'

'It's bad?'

'Honestly, sir, I had it far worse on the American ships. The Yankees think us savages and they hate us. For the English, I am something... exotic.'

Solomon gestured towards the hatch. 'Sir, I should stay with my crew. May I be excused?'

'Of course.'

Above, the sky had broken up into clouds of every size and colour between black and white. The sea-state had changed too; the waves striking the coast were no more than five feet in height. And, perhaps most tellingly of all, the 'wreckers' on the shore had dispersed, with only a few hardy – or perhaps optimistic – souls still watching the British warship from the beach.

Shrigley came up beside Merriman. 'Sir, at last. The wind is down below twenty knots.'

'Still dead on the nose but it's calm enough to use the boats again. They can pull us off the shore and we'll go from there.'

Shrigley let out a long breath. 'Thank the Lord.'

'Or Manitou,' whispered Merriman.

'Sorry, sir?'

'Oh, nothing.'

Chapter Eighteen

Gentle Seas and Strong Spirits

By sundown, *Thunder* was three miles off the coast, having been towed alternately by the boat and the launch. The wind had died to nothing, meaning that raising the anchors and finally freeing themselves from the bay had been almost ridiculously easy. As midnight approached, the wind – still a westerly – rose a little and the ship was able to make a couple of knots to the south. During her long trek out from the coast, the carpenters had taken down the broken mizzen and were ready to raise the new spar the next day. Satisfied that all was well, Merriman retired to bed and ordered that only a minimal crew operate the ship during the night. As a sign to all that Lieutenant Smythe had recovered himself, Merriman placed him in charge, though he bolstered the quarterdeck with the reliable duo of midshipmen Hickey and Eades.

The following morning was like something from a dream. A strong sun beat down upon the ship, hot enough to melt the pitch between the deck timbers and cause more work for the sailors. During the night, the wind had veered to the north-west and doubled its strength. Those sails damaged during the battle and the storm were repaired and replaced and those mounted on mainmast and foremast were sufficient to propel *Thunder* southward at a stately three knots.

Before the repairs began in earnest, there was the matter of five dead crewmates. Merriman paid tribute to each individual as he had for Garland and the bodies were sent into the clear, blue water. After the readings and a respectable period of pious silence, he took the opportunity to address the entire ship's compliment.

'I stand before you a proud man. Proud of the unfortunate shipmates we lost but also each and every one of you. The last few days have tested *Thunder* and her crew but here we are: with a fair wind, ready to continue south and complete our task. Once our work is complete – and if the weather remains clement – this evening we shall take three hours for our leisure. There shall be double grog for all and you may enjoy yourself as you see fit. Cards, music, singing.' Merriman had earlier spotted the hapless sailor who had fallen from the launch. 'Trenton – perhaps another swim?'

'Not bloody likely, sir!'

Though the sailor received icy glares from some of the officers, Merriman chuckled at the response.

'Men, there is plenty of work for everyone. Go to your stations.'

Descending to the great cabin once the hatch was clear, Merriman was glad to find that Peters had put out his bed. He had only slept for a few hours and now the tiredness of so many difficult days struck him. He laid himself out, his chest speared by a golden ray of sun, and slept until woken by ringing at four bells of the morning watch.

Hauling himself to his feet, he felt a little less exhausted but still remarkably weary and heavy-legged. He was not surprised that he had slept through the cacophony of hammering and shouting from above. Peters must have heard him rise because his lined, lumpen face swiftly appeared.

'All right there, Captain Merriman, sir?'

'Fine thank you, Peters. Any reports from above?'

'All fair wind and sunshine, I gather, sir. We've got washing drying on every space – largely thanks to Mr. Webster. He insists that the men dry as much as they can why they have the opportunity. He believes that damp clothes cause ailments worse than coughs and colds.'

'And he is quite correct. Peters, the men are to be given some free time tonight. Ask cook what we still have in the way of treats and come back to me with our choices for dinner. The officers and the midshipmen will dine with me.'

'All of them, sir? We'll need an extra table and chairs for the young gentlemen.'

'You better go and find them then. Seven o'clock. And I'd like a basin of water – cold.'

Having refreshed himself, Merriman returned to the great cabin, pleased to see that his desk was back in position – at least until dinner. He sat down and opened the document passed to him at the Admiralty. It wasn't the first time he had examined the papers but – having checked the chart – he knew that they would soon be sailing into the midst of Captain Jourdan's main hunting grounds. As he read through the files, his old arm wound began to ache, so he located his faithful ball of rags. Merriman had often found that these old injuries flared up after a period of battle or danger; he supposed his body didn't have time for them when he was under duress.

Twelve of Jourdan's fourteen prizes had been taken between the territory of Benguela – which *Thunder* would pass that night – and the Cape of Good Hope. That didn't particularly narrow the search; it was a stretch of coast more than a thousand miles long. There were, however, more rivers and ports at the northern and southern ends, meaning more opportunities for *Hercule* to refit and resupply. Merriman was glad of the intelligence they had picked up from the Irish captain, which confirmed that the 'lone wolf' had struck again recently. Of the fourteen prizes, descriptions of the attacks were available for eight. As Newcombe had suggested at the Admiralty, there was no clear pattern other than a remarkable ingenuity and maritime skill.

Still squeezing the rag (despite the shooting pains it caused in his arm) Merriman nodded to himself, glad that his officers and crew had acquitted themselves well during the clash with the pirates and the ensuing crisis. He did not, however, have any wish to engage the French captain with half a mizzen, so he decided to go on deck and check on progress.

'By God, this ship looks like a laundry!'

Shrigley greeted him close to the hatch. He was wearing a sunhat, with his sleeves rolled up. The first lieutenant grimaced.

'I am sorry, sir. Every last man has wet garments and Mr. Webster was most insistent.'

Other than the area around the mizzen, where several dozen men were still hard at work, just about every stay, sheet and piece of available deck was covered by trousers, shirts, jackets or undergarments.

'I do hope there are no other vessels in sight?' asked Merriman, wishing he'd brought up his own sunhat.

'No, sir.'

'That's a relief. If word of this spectacle reached the Admiralty, I'd expect a court martial.'

Shrigley smiled.

'Now, what about this mizzen?'

'When the previous mast was struck, there was some damage to the fittings and housing, sir. That's pretty much repaired so now they're placing the new mast. There won't be time to secure it in daylight today but they can lash it in place, finish the job tomorrow. The day after, top and topgallant can go on.'

Merriman said nothing, causing Shrigley to frown and eventually speak.

'Sir?'

'Well, it's not slow but two more full days without the mizzen? Do we dare sail on, knowing the chances of encountering the *Hercule* have never been greater?'

'I see your point, sir.'

What Merriman did not say was that the last time he'd taken such a risk, he had almost lost his ship.

'Let us see the state of the weather tomorrow and go from there. If we were to heave to, I wonder if we might complete the work in one day?'

'I shall consult Brockle and Henderson, sir.'

'Very good.'

'Dinner at seven with me, Alfred. Full dress. All the officers and the midshipmen.'

'Aye aye, sir.'

At ten minutes after seven, the officers sat down in the great cabin. The slight delay had been caused by Peters and two assistants hastily dressing the additional table which the midshipmen would occupy. The four young trainees, the four lieutenants plus Merriman, Lieutenant Cary, Mister Webster, Purser Rolfe and Master Henderson were now all seated.

In light of his excellent efforts with the repairs, Henderson was invited to give the toast and he gave lusty tribute to the king and offered ruination to the French and their navy, which was met with a roar of approval. Merriman was relieved that the weather remained calm for this evening of relaxation. He had asked for volunteers for lookout duty; there were always a few men and officers aboard a ship who were less interested in group activities. On this particular occasion, all looked happy to be present for dinner except perhaps Lieutenant Smythe, who had barely looked up since arriving.

At the head of the table, his back rather close to the stern lockers, Merriman had Shrigley to his left and Henderson to his right. He now hailed the midshipmen, who were almost seated in the passageway.

'Mr. Chamier, I understand that we're to be treated to some entertainment later?'

'Yes, captain – just a few offerings we've been working on.'

'Very good.'

'At no cost to your studies, I trust,' said Essex sternly.

'Not at all, lieutenant,' countered the youngster.

'Very good indeed,' said Jones. 'For once, I am not responsible for the after-dinner activities.'

'After a few glasses, you'll go and get your violin yourself.'

'You think you know me so well, Alfred. But in fact, I am quite enigmatic.'

Shrigley laughed. 'I have shared the wardroom with you for five years, Philip. Even if you had a wife, I'd know you considerably better!'

Jones took the point in good humour.

'Did I see you taking a stroll around the deck just now, Mister Chamier?' asked Master Henderson.

'You did, sir,' answered the midshipman. 'Myself and Hickey, that is.'

'And what do you think of the entertainment above decks?' asked Shrigley.

Hickey grunted with amusement at this.

'Something to add?' prompted Lieutenant Jones.

'No, sir. It it's just that Chamier was a bit taken aback by some of the sailors' songs.'

'He's not the only one,' ventured the surgeon. 'I have attended all manner of patients in all manner of locales but seldom have I heard such filth.'

Shrigley, Jones and Cary all smothered smiles.

'Fortunately, you are not obliged to dine with them,' said Jones.

'You will get used to such songs, Mr. Webster,' said Merriman. 'And such language. It is an unfortunate fact of life that sailors do love to swear and sing in a...ribald style.'

'Quite so, captain,' said Cary, before turning towards Chamier. 'Just do not recite them in the presence of your mother.'

'There was some wrestling on the foredeck, Lieutenant Cary,' added the youngster. 'Some of your marines appear to be experts.'

'We practice unarmed combat when there's time, young man. A soldier must make a weapon of himself if he loses gun and blade.'

A great bowl of onion soup arrived then and the two servants began doling it out. At a nod from Merriman, Peters busied himself topping up the glasses. He gave less to the midshipmen, drawing frowns from Hickey and Eades.

'I gather you spoke to the half-Indian fellow, sir?' said Jones.

'I did indeed,' answered Merriman. 'And interesting it was too; to hear of his native beliefs.'

'I wonder if we are closer to America or England?' replied the lieutenant. 'Whoever he appealed to, it seemed to have some effect.'

'Coincidence,' said Lieutenant Essex. 'It is the Lord who freed us from the bay. He is master of all things.'

'Not me,' said Cary, after a long sip of wine. 'It is I who governs my life – as best I can anyway.'

Merriman had seen Essex with a Bible in his hands on several occasions. He was clearly a pious, serious character but Merriman could not find fault in his work.

'We are all entitled to our view,' said the purser quietly. 'To each his own.'

'Well said, Mister Rolfe,' stated Merriman.

'Very tasty,' said Lieutenant Smythe, his first contribution. 'Compliments to the cook, Peters.'

'Tasty indeed,' said Cary, putting down his spoon. 'But soup is never ever the same without bread. Do they make bread in Africa?'

'I believe so,' answered Merriman. 'Certainly in the north. I suppose it depends on what crops they farm.'

'We're passing another blank section on the map,' observed Midshipman Eades. 'Only the ports are denoted. Lieutenant Shrigley, perhaps we can sail back here one day and conduct a voyage of exploration? We could name a river or a mountain. Draw up a map that would be used by every captain and navigator that came after us.'

Shrigley aimed his glass at the youngster. 'I admire your ambition, Eades. If I return here as a captain-explorer, you shall be my navigator.'

'You two go ahead,' said Jones. 'I shall remain in London and follow the obituaries – awaiting news of two unfortunates who ended up in a crocodile's belly.'

Eades remained quiet as his three compatriots chuckled.

'Nothing ventured, nothing gained,' countered Shrigley.

The main dish was a spicy beef stew served with rice, which kept a lot better than most perishables. By the end of it, every last man was sweating, especially as all still wore their coats.

'Gentlemen,' said Merriman, feeling slightly dizzy as he stood, 'feel free to disrobe. It is exceptionally warm.'

By nine o'clock, he was feeling really quite drunk; no surprise given the number of bottles of port and wine the officers had imbibed. But the desired effect had been achieved; even the pious Essex, the ashamed Smythe and the reserved Webster had been drawn into the brotherly spirit and were now singing along with the others, led by Cary and Jones.

Shrigley joined in too when he returned. Merriman had been unable to fully relax and so sent his first lieutenant to check that all was well with the ship and that the lookouts had seen nothing to alarm them. Once the latest verse of 'The Sea Fight' had concluded, Shrigley leaned towards his captain.

'I'm tempted to say all is quiet, sir, but it's far from it. There were two different groups of musicians and merry-makers but now there's just one, assembled around the mainmast. One of the marines got carried away after an arm wrestle so Harrison sent him to the quarterdeck. Some drunkenness but Brockle's keeping an eye on it all.'

'Very good. I do believe he is the finest bosun I've sailed with.'

'Excellent man.'

An hour later, Merriman discovered that his vision was swimming so he decided it was time for the midshipmen to deliver their offering. Adkins and Eades went first, singing a shanty in unison, their young voices melding in a way that was pleasant to the ear and won praise from the musical Lieutenant Jones. After embarrassing himself with a loud belch, Hickey delivered a dozen japes and puns of varying quality but finished with his strongest material and earned a cheer. Then came the turn of Chamier, who seemed a tad unsteady on his feet but delivered a poem he had composed himself that afternoon:

> The westerly came and pushed us to the bay,
> *Thunder* fought the elements by night and day,
> The wind became a gale in a moment so quick,
> There was no man aboard who didn't feel sick.
>
> The gale became a storm and the anchors did drag,
> The oarsmen pulled hard and showed pride in their flag,
> Then the storm became a breeze and clear sky we did see,
> Up went a shout, for dear *Thunder* was free!

Despite his evident drunkenness, young Chamier's verse was delivered with such clarity and vigour that all gave a cheer. As he sat down, the lad received such a hefty clap on his back from Lieutenant Cary that he struck the table and knocked over several glasses. A tutting Peters descended to tidy the mess.

'A fine composition, Mr. Chamier!' declared Merriman.

It then became evident that Mr. Webster had broken his rule of 'one drink with dinner' by some distance. He leaned forward and waved to the second lieutenant. 'Mr. Jones, tell me, do you know "Men of Harlech"?'

'I know the name, Mr. Webster, but not the tune. However, if you sing a verse or too, I will likely pick it up.'

'He will at that,' said Essex. 'Talented musician.'

'You will, however, need to fetch your violin in order to play it, Mr. Jones.'

'Very true, captain. I shall return presently.'

'Some more air in here, Peters! Blazes, it's warm.'

With no more than a nod, the long-suffering attendant opened the remaining windows. Knowing that he should eat some more to mitigate the effects of wine and rum, Merriman then asked the attendant to give him more dessert – a heavy pudding infused with rum and fruit.

Looking along the table as he ate, he was pleased to see Smythe now engaged in conversation with Cary and Essex. He also noted the loud singing and tramping feet above, and hoped that the revelry was still of a tolerable nature.

He turned to Shrigley, who was leaning back in his chair, a glass of port in his hand.

'A pleasant evening, Alfred.'

'Very much so, sir. My father used to say that, eventually, one realises that there is nothing better than sharing a meal with friends and family. As I get older, I start to believe he was right.'

'Very wise. Friends we have here with us. To family.'

The pair raised their glasses.

Even in his addled state, Merriman saw Shrigley gaze at the floor for a moment, evidently lost in reflection.

By the time Merriman finished his second bowl of pudding, the others were asking about Jones. The wardroom was very close and yet he had still not returned.

'Go and find him, Adkins,' instructed Shrigley.

A clearly impatient Peters asked Merriman if he could began tidying up but the captain told him to wait. Two minutes later, Adkins appeared and informed them that Lieutenant Jones was now up on deck and playing with the other musicians aboard.

'I fear you may have to wait for your accompaniment,' Merriman told Webster as they filed out and made their way along to the hatch.

Once on deck, they found a crowd of at least two hundred men gathered around the foremast, singing a shanty which all knew well. In no time at all, the officers – Merriman included – were singing along. At one point, he looked out at the dark, silent ocean that surrounded them and was struck by the sheer, singular oddness of naval life.

When the song concluded, Bosun Brockle shouldered his way through the crowd to Merriman.

'All well and good, cap'n, but I reckon that's sufficient, don't you?'

'I do, Brockle.'

Shortly afterward, the bosun's whistle sounded and the revelry began to die down. There were a few sharp words for some who had overindulged but soon the men were tidying up and filing below.

'Oh dear,' said Shrigley, 'I fear we shall have to carry these two to bed.'

Slumped by the binnacle, dead to the world, mouths stained by wine, were Chamier and Adkins.

Chapter Nineteen

The Tangled Knot

Merriman watched forlornly as the two long guns were thrown over the side. One was the piece that had exploded and killed the crewmen, the second had suffered the misfire. In both cases, the iron was so misshapen as to be beyond saving. Shortly after they were cast into the deep, the crew began moving two of the deck guns. Though smaller, these would ensure that *Thunder* still had a full complement below.

Four days had passed since the night of revelry and Merriman was glad he had indulged officers and crew because the going was now hard. In the end, he had decided to continue south, despite the risk, and the new mizzen had now been erected.

The sun seemed to grow hotter with every passing day. Though all were told to be careful, a number of men were now suffering with heatstroke. And, despite Mr. Webster's protestations, Merriman had ordered that the scuttlebutt be removed; there simply wasn't sufficient water to allow the men to refresh themselves at will.

'Well?' asked the captain, sheltering under the canopy with Lieutenants Essex and Shrigley.

'We still have a third of our casks full but the quality of the water is not good, sir,' said Essex. 'We asked for new casks at Portsmouth but none were available. The result is slime. Mr. Webster declared it unfit for consumption but...'

'He can be overly fussy,' interjected Shrigley.

'That water will be adequate,' said Merriman. 'Didn't we collect some during the storms?'

'Several casks full, sir, but, well – we had other problems to contend with.'

'What about the beer?'

'More than half remains, sir,' answered Essex.

'All right. They won't like it but the men can drink beer for their second allotment of the day: we can't waste all that water for their grog. Cut back on washing and mess allotments also – until we can find a new supply. If all else fails, we will have to make our way up the Orange river, but that is still many hundreds of miles to the south. As far as I can tell from the charts, there are no major waterways before that, nor any islands where we might locate a spring. In the meantime, ensure that any rainwater is efficiently collected. What about the livestock?'

'Three pigs and two goats remaining, sir,' answered Essex swiftly. 'About a dozen hens, I believe, and cook wants to keep them alive for the eggs – at least for the moment.'

'All right, now what about yesterday?'

The gun drill had proceeded reasonably well in general but illuminated certain issues with timing and aim. The next hour was spent discussing them and what exactly should be done to improve performance. By the end of it, Merriman felt weary and in need of some time alone. He retired to the great cabin and was about to begin act four of Julius Caesar, when Jones knocked on his door.

'Sir, a fight in the spirit room. A man has been stabbed. I'm afraid I don't know any more yet.'

With a nod, Merriman placed his book on his desk then pulled on his coat and his boots. He followed Jones down three decks to the spirit room, where all four walls were lined by barrels, kegs and casks. The pair were met by many curious faces, prompting Jones to remind them all to get on with their work.

Outside the spirit room, a young sailor was lying against the wall, being attended to by Mr. Webster and his assistants. He was crying out as the physician examined the wound, which was in his right flank. Blood had already soaked his pale shirt and pooled on the floor below.

'How bad?' asked Merriman.

'Narrow but deep, sir, though it could have been worse – the implement is not designed to penetrate. We'll get him to my room and try to staunch the bleeding.'

'Very well.' Merriman turned around. 'Clear the way there!'

Before moving the man, Webster wrapped a bandage tight around his middle. The poor fellow was evidently trying not to betray his pain but tears were streaming down his face. As the four departed, Merriman entered the room to find a large man pinned against the wall by two marines. Sergeant Harrison was also present, armed with a cudgel.

'Captain. We were close by and heard the commotion. But by then the damage was done.'

Merriman was very surprised to see that the culprit was the veteran sailor and expert gun captain, Able Seaman Muir. The grey-haired Scot lowered his head in shame when Merriman turned his gaze upon him.

'Used this,' said Harrison, showing a metal rod with a rounded end. 'Barrel turner. Lucky for that lad it wasn't a bayonet.'

'I doubt he feels very lucky right now,' remarked Jones.

'Is it true, Muir?' demanded Merriman.

'Aye, sir. I did it.'

'Why for God's sake?'

Muir glanced up at Merriman for a moment but said nothing.

'Able Seaman Muir, I require and expect an answer.'

'Sorry, cap'n,' said the Scotsman, in barely a whisper.

Merriman turned to Harrison. 'Have him put in irons and confined.'

'Aye aye, sir.'

Sighing, Merriman departed with Jones. They encountered Shrigley at the hatch and Jones summarized for the first lieutenant.

'I can hardly credit it,' said Shrigley. 'The man's been at sea for three decades. What on Earth would make him do such a thing?'

'I intend to find that out. Jones, round up any witnesses plus those who work in the spirit room, Muir's mess-mates and his gun crew. The injured fellow too – what's his name?'

'Butcher, sir. I'll get onto that now.'

'Sir, sail sighted to the east,' added Shrigley. 'Probably too small to be a merchantman or a naval ship.'

'You don't sound sure.'

'The lookouts aren't sure, sir.'

'Can you lay an easterly course?'

'Yes, sir, just about.'

'Do so. Report to me when we have more information.'

Disturbed by this unexplained crime, Merriman returned to his cabin. Midday had passed and Peters offered him luncheon but Merriman found that he could not eat, nor return to reading. In fact, he suddenly felt so dispirited that he would have liked nothing more to step off the *Thunder* on to dry land. Such feelings were not alien to him and they often arrived at odd moments after many weeks at sea. He would dream of endless forests and mountains and plains; anywhere that he could walk and walk – in clear air without the scent of salt water.

His melancholic reverie was soon disturbed by Lieutenant Jones. Merriman invited him in and they sat by the windows.

'It seems Butcher is in a bad way. Mr. Webster thinks that the tool punctured his lung. He is struggling to breathe and his pulse is dangerously quick.'

'He could die then?'

'A possibility, sir, but Mr. Webster is hopeful.'

'And what did you learn about the incident?'

'At the time only Muir and Butcher were present in the spirit room. Butcher was there collecting a barrel of beer on the purser's orders. We have no witnesses. All I have spoken to contend that this act of violence is very much out of character, which I agree with. Some of Muir's gun crew are also his mess mates. There has apparently been some competition with Butcher's crew but that's true of many aboard: all would like to be as quick as Lightning. Most of those I questioned seemed to be truthful but two seemed to know more than they were letting on.'

'I see. Have those two sent to me and then I must speak again to Muir himself. Anything on that sail?'

'There's a little fog, sir, which makes identification difficult. She is close to the coast and not moving swiftly.'

'Given our location, we cannot afford to pass by any vessel we sight at this stage. Continue east, aim to intercept her.'

'We are less than ten miles from the coast, sir.'

'Alfred, we cannot sail on in fear of embayment for the rest of our lives.'

'Very good, sir. I'll have those men sent to you.'

'Subtly, if you please.'

Merriman already felt that this might be a difficult knot to untangle. Muir's silence on the matter was most odd and his culpability odder still. He was a popular, experienced veteran and his many friends aboard would all be anxious to understand what had happened and why. Butcher no doubt had his friends too and personal disputes could easily lead to broader enmities between messes, gun crews and watches. Merriman had seen it before. He also knew how quickly news travelled and had no doubt that the vast majority of those aboard already knew of the incident and that Muir was in irons. They would also follow every further development, be keen to hear the details and, above all, the captain's judgement on the matter. Merriman despised dealing with such incidents, especially if they culminated in him issuing a punishment, which seemed inevitable in this case.

The first man sent to the great cabin was named Trevelyan, a sailmaker's mate who was also another of the crack Lightning gun crew. Merriman told his marine sentry not to say a word and he himself put on his coat, despite the heat. The big soldier played his part well, striding in behind Trevelyan and directing him to the opposite side of Merriman's desk. The sailmaker's mate was a short but powerfully-built fellow and he held his cap in his hands.

'This business with Muir. What do you know of it?'

'Nothing, captain,' answered Trevelyan, in an accent that Merriman instantly recognised as that of a Cornishman.

'You weren't aware of any tension between him and Butcher?'

'No, sir.'

'You are on his gun crew. Are you his mess-mate too?'

'I am.'

'Then you spend an inordinate amount of time with the man. Any change in him of late? Mood? Behaviour?'

'Not that I saw, captain.'

'I am not aware of him ever using violence against another sailor. Are you?'

'No, sir. Sorry. Wish I could help.'

Like Jones, Merriman felt that the sailor had simply decided to say nothing and that was that.

'Trevelyan, as your captain I expect the truth from you. If I later find that you were not honest with me, there *will* be consequences.'

'Understood, sir.'

'All right. Dismissed.'

The second man was named Hopkins, an idler when not working with Muir's gun crew. A tall, slender man with tattooed hands, he immediately apologised for not being clean shaven. He appeared less assured than Trevelyan and Merriman decided on a different tack.

'You've known Muir a while, I suppose.'

'More than ten years, captain.'

'He has damn near killed a man. What do you know?'

After a long moment of consideration, Hopkins replied: 'Butcher has a big mouth, sir. Not that it justifies sticking him but he was always jealous of us – of Lightning's crew. He used to say things to Muir, to rile him, try to get him to make a mistake so that we weren't the best no more. Never did though.'

'And he's been doing that for some time?'

'He's been on the gun two aft of us since the Adriatic mission, sir. Of course, there's always a lot of joshing and insults, all part of good competition, but Butcher often went too far. He could be...personal.'

'I see. But Muir had heard it all before. What was different this time?'

'I wish I knew, sir.'

'Lieutenant Jones has questioned everyone who might know something. If we have no more information, there is little I can do for Muir. You do understand that? This is your last chance, Hopkins.'

Merriman in fact intended to be as thorough as possible with the investigation but Hopkins didn't need to know that.

'We could encounter the *Hercule* at any time,' he added. 'I will not allow this wretched affair to drag on. Any decision regarding punishment will be made with all haste.'

This caused a reaction that Hopkins could not hide. Closing his eyes for a moment – perhaps seeking divine assistance – the sailor let out a long sigh, anxiously rubbed the back of his neck and then spoke.

'Trevelyan clearly said nothing so I suppose it falls to me. He, Trevelyan that is, sir, went along to the spirit room a couple of nights ago. It was very late and I imagine he thought he might get a mug of grog out of Muir without being noticed. All was quiet there, only a single lantern alight and he...well...he saw Muir...embracing another fellow. Trevelyan made himself scarce but came back to the mess and told us. I didn't believe it but he said he knew what he saw. I told the others to keep it quiet but I wouldn't be surprised if word has spread. Butcher would have been the first to make the most of it.'

'I see. And, as far as you know, Muir is not of that persuasion?'

'Absolutely not, sir.'

'And has this other man been identified?'

'Trevelyan knew his face. Young topman named Childers. I don't know if word has reached him.'

'But this information was spread about the ship – common knowledge?'

'I didn't myself hear Butcher use it against Muir but it would not surprise me at all. Even a man so restrained as Muir-'

'All right, Hopkins. I appreciate your candour. Rest assured that your name will not be mentioned. If Trevelyan gives you any trouble, feel free to knock on my door.'

Merriman then had Peters send one of the servants to fetch the topman, Childers. The third of his witnesses was no more than twenty, an unassuming fellow with a mop of fair hair. He seemed both afraid and ashamed as he entered the great cabin. Once the sentry had left, he stood perfectly still, hands clasped in front of him.

'You know of this incident with Muir?'

'Yes, captain.'

'Anything else?'

'Only that rumours have been spread about him and me. Cruel rumours. Cruel and untrue.'

Childers almost hissed this last sentence and began wiping his face as tears fell freely from his eyes.

'You give me your word that no unnatural acts occurred?'

'Of course, sir. Of course. My word, my oath upon my family.

'You will be aware that the witness-'

'Trevelyan.'

'That the witness saw you embracing Muir. Do you deny it?'

Childers simply gazed at the deck.

'I will have an answer, young man.'

'I do not deny it.'

'A man might embrace another man for reasons of friendship – was it that?'

'Yes. No... Sir, have you spoken to Muir?'

'Not yet.'

'Captain, I beg you to do so. I am in a very difficult position. Only he can answer you. I just...I want this to be over. I have done *nothing* wrong. Nothing to be ashamed of.'

Merriman believed him; and he could see the great strain this situation had placed on the youngster.

'I will talk to Muir. And if you have spoken the truth, I will see to it that your reputation remains.'

Young Childers could barely get the words out. 'Very...very grateful, sir.'

On his way to the brig, Merriman called in on Mr. Webster. Butcher was still on his table, unconscious, his wounded side visible.

'Captain,' said the Welshman, rising from a chair. 'I gave him some laudanum for the pain. When he awakes, I will inspect the wound again and decide whether to sew him up. Punctured lungs can heal themselves over time but it is a slow process.'

'Please do your best, Mr. Webster. If this man dies, I will face an even more difficult situation.'

From there, Merriman journeyed down one deck and forward to the brig. There had as yet been no need to imprison any man and so Muir was sharing the small space with tubs of salted meat. When Merriman arrived, he found Cary and two privates on duty.

'Hasn't said a word, sir,' stated the marine captain.

'Leave me with him.'

'Of course, sir.'

At a nod from their commander, the two privates followed Cary out of the dingy space. The brig was secured by a heavy wooden door. As Merriman looked through the barred window, Muir stood up and saluted.

'Quite a mess, you've created for me, Muir. I would not have expected it from you. Tell me if what follows is correct: the details of what occurred in the spirit room with Childers aside, Trevelyan made his assumptions. Word spread and eventually reached Butcher. When he came to the spirit room earlier, he mocked you, you lost your head and stuck him with that barrel turner.'

'That's about right, sir. I ...I can't even remember deciding to do it. I wasn't thinking. Do you know how he is?'

'His life is in the balance.'

Inside the shadowy cell, Muir ran his fingers across his brow. The glow of the lantern outside was just sufficient to illuminate the lines on his aged face.

'Now, tell me what happened with Childers.'

Muir remained silent, and Merriman began to feel that their mutual silence was an explanation of its own.

'It is said that you embraced.'

Still Muir did not speak.

'You are not a young man, nor an ignorant one. If you do not tell me otherwise, there is only one reasonable conclusion I can draw. And in that case, you may not be facing only the charge of attempted murder.'

'Sir, I will tell you the truth but I must ask you to keep it between us.'

'You know I can give no such guarantee. Damn it, Muir, speak! Do you imagine that a captain of the king's navy has nothing else to do with his time?'

'He is my son.'

'What?'

'Ian Childers is my son. Conceived out of wedlock. I only learned of this just before we departed. His mother had kept it secret for twenty years but recently told him before informing me. I did not previously know of his existence but when he volunteered for *Thunder* to be near me, she sought me out. Sir, you must understand that I live in Portsmouth, as many men aboard do. If this becomes known aboard ship it will cause great damage to two families. I myself have four other children and if my wife...'

Muir leaned back against the cell wall and covered his eyes.

'So that's it,' said Merriman. 'Now the pieces of this puzzle fit.'

'I was in agony, sir. When the rumours spread, I did not know whether to tell the truth or not. If I did, there were consequences for so many; if I did not, both of us faced disgrace.'

'You were under great pressure. And, unfortunately for Butcher, he was there when you snapped.'

'It is no excuse, sir, I know. I must face justice for it.'

'Oh, you will, Muir. There is no escaping that. The truth must be known – if not for your sake's, then for Childers'.'

'But, sir, my family...'

'That is not my concern. My concern is this ship and her crew. The truth will be known and you will be punished and that will be the end of the matter.'

'I fear I will lose everything.'

'The truth will out, Muir. Such things have happened before and they shall happen again. You are still a member of this crew and a damn fine gun captain. And when this is done, you will return to your post. Understood?'

'Yes, sir.'

Merriman was in very great need of some fresh air. Once up on deck, he found that the coast was obscured by fog and that *Thunder* was still pursuing the mysterious vessel, which was apparently still visible to the lookouts. Merriman had Childers sent for, thinking it sensible that their conversation be observed by as many as possible.

'It is done,' he told the topman, who looked just as apprehensive as he had in the great cabin. 'The truth is out. I recognise that it may cause great damage when the pair of you are back home but that is for then. For now, at least, your reputation remains. I will ensure that all know the facts of this case.'

'For that I am grateful, captain. And my father?'

'I have not yet decided upon his fate.'

With that, Childers was dismissed.

Merriman was pleased to see that the final piece of work on the mizzen was almost complete; the topmast had been attached. Once Brockle had briefed him regarding this matter, Merriman withdrew to the stern with First Lieutenant Shrigley and related all that had transpired.

'You got there in the end, sir.'

'That liar Hopkins will get what's coming to him.' Merriman found himself tugging on his ear. 'But what shall I do with Muir? Is lashing even sufficient?'

'Twenty-four might do it, sir.'

'He's almost sixty years old, Alfred. Twenty-four might kill him.'

'And we need him, sir.'

'There is also that.'

Chapter Twenty

The Lash

The coastal fog grew thicker, meaning that the mysterious ship was never sighted again. Wary of shoals and the uncharted coast, Merriman ordered that *Thunder* stay clear of the fog banks; safe on the open sea. After two whole days, the fog dissipated and the land became clear once more. And a spectacular sight it was: great dunes of orange sand that ran almost to the water. First Lieutenant Shrigley remarked that it appeared just as he'd imagined the Zaara desert.

It was in mid-morning that another, much smaller mast and sail were spotted, hugging the coast and heading north using the same westerly that propelled *Thunder* southward. Before Merriman could give the order to investigate, the little vessel had already turned towards them. The reason for this soon became evident: the captain saw through his spyglass that the boat had raised an ensign. A man in the bow was waving frantically.

As they neared the boat, Jones pointed out a great number of dark creatures on the beach directly behind the small vessel. The officers had just decided that they were large seals when the animals scattered and hauled their heavy bodies towards the sea. It was Shrigley who spotted the cause for the mass exodus: a heavily-maned lion that came bounding down a dune, quickly followed by another. An unfortunate seal was caught feet from the waves and set upon by the two big cats.

'A dangerous locale', said the first lieutenant.

'Indeed,' replied Merriman. 'These men are very fortunate that the fog cleared. Given that flag, we must see if we can learn anything from them. We shall delay the punishment until this afternoon. Inform those concerned.'

'Aye aye, sir.'

Merriman had concluded that he had no choice other than to have Muir lashed; and that only twenty-four would do. There was no excuse for his actions and he would have to be punished and – as importantly – be seen to be punished. But crewmen had previously been given six or twelve lashes for comparatively minor infractions such as drunkenness and failing to appear for duty. Merriman knew how difficult the lashing would be for the veteran to bear but he could see no alternative. In truth, it was in his power to order as many lashes as he liked: there were after all cases of as many as seventy-two, though that was considered by most to be excessive and brutal.

Thankfully, Butcher's condition seemed to have improved. Webster seemed sure that the lung could repair itself and that the man had a fair chance of recovery. Merriman had taken soundings via the petty officers and established that his compatriots were anxious to know of the punishment to come. His decision had been made – and he considered it appropriate and fair – but the reaction of the crew was less predictable. All in all, it was a sordid, nasty affair that he wished he could avoid.

An hour after it was sighted, the boat came alongside. The man in the bow was so overcome by emotion that he failed three times to successfully throw a line. Of the two others with him, one was muttering prayers and the other was laughing as they tidied the sail they'd just lowered. Shrigley sent four men down the nets to help the trio up and then secure the boat. Once aboard *Thunder*, all three dropped to their knees and slurped down the mugs of water offered to them. Despite their condition, Merriman could see that they had not been adrift for very long. Their skin had not suffered, nor were they unusually thin. He gave them five minutes before addressing them.

'Well then, who do I have before me?'

The eldest of the three, who possessed a bushy, grey beard offered his hand. 'Bless you, captain. Bless you. My name is Sellers, bosun of the merchant vessel, *Elizabeth*. These two are Matthews and Gaskill, my two mates.'

'And where is the *Elizabeth*?' asked Merriman.

'Taken by a French ship-of-the-line,' snarled Sellers. 'We thought we were far enough north to be clear but the bastard popped up out of nowhere – excuse my language, sir.'

'The Lone Wolf, they call him.' added Gaskill.

'When was this?' asked Merriman.

'Four days ago,' said Sellers.

'Three,' said Matthews. 'Three. I marked each sunset with a notch.'

'Only three,' said Merriman, feeling a cold tremor ripple up his back. 'The *Hercule*. Captained by a man named Jourdan?'

'That's her,' said Sellers. 'Eighty-six guns.'

Merriman and Shrigley exchanged a glance. Their opponent possessed twelve more long guns.

'And accurate as I've ever seen,' added Sellers. 'Dropped cannonballs just ahead of our bow then struck us there and at the stern to make her point.'

'You here to sort her out then, cap'n?' asked Gaskill with a grin.

'Something like that. And when she departed?'

'Heading south,' said Sellers. 'Put a prize crew on *Elizabeth*.'

'And why were you three cast adrift?'

Sellers let out a long sigh. 'Temper got the better of me, sir. One of their officers struck our captain because he'd fought back. Our deck guns killed three of theirs. They got four of ours.' Sellers nodded towards his compatriots. 'These two stood up for me.' The sailor looked to the sky. 'By God I'm grateful I didn't lead them to their deaths.'

At that, Gaskill reached out and gripped his bosun by the shoulder.

Merriman turned to Shrigley. 'Rather reminiscent of our friend Mr. Trent on Sao Tome. They too were cast adrift.'

Sellers looked up at Merriman once more. 'Might I be so bold as to ask for a bit of food, sir? They gave us naught but a skin of water.'

'Of course. I presume you don't object to us abandoning the boat? It will be an encumbrance.'

'Not at all, sir, though I'd asked for the plate, if I may?'

'Very well. Smythe, see to it that these men are given a square meal and found somewhere to rest.'

Seemingly surprised to receive an order, the troubled officer came forward and quietly ushered the men below.

The young topmen, Friar, was one of the many watching and he issued an enthusiastic, 'Welcome aboard!' to the three sailors. As usual, his antics caused some mirth from his older compatriots. The watching Bosun Brockle instructed the men in the boat to remove the brass plate at the stern before casting it adrift.

Merriman caught Shrigley's eye. 'Once they've eaten, draw out every detail you can. And take notes for me.'

'Aye aye, sir.'

Merriman stepped closer to Shrigley. 'What about Smythe? Doesn't seem to be much improvement.'

Shrigley grimaced and answered in a low tone. 'I believe he's lost all confidence in himself, sir. Barely says a word, fulfils his duties only when prompted. Seems to hate being among the men. I have tried. We all have.'

'All right. When there's time, I shall talk to him. Let us return to our course and we shall have Muir brought out.'

With only a few hands left at crucial stations, the remainder of the crew was called aft to witness the punishment. A grating had already been put up against the mainmast: this was where Muir would receive his lashes. While the sailors gathered, most slow-moving and grim-faced, Merriman ran his eyes over them. He saw some of Muir's gun crew and messmates though Trevelyan had made himself scarce. Merriman had already dealt with him: he was to clean the heads for the remainder of the journey – the most hated duty aboard. He wondered if Childers was present but saw no trace of the unfortunate youth.

More obvious amongst the growing crowd were individuals he knew to be cohorts of Butcher, most notably a tall Irishman named Furlong. Word had reached Merriman that he had made veiled threats against Muir. The captain hoped that the upcoming punishment would satiate Furlong and his compatriots' thirst for revenge. If not – if they protested or tried to take matters into their own hands – they would suffer punishments of equal severity.

He looked on as Muir was brought up by Second Lieutenant Harrison and one of the marine sergeants. Muir was barefoot, wearing only trousers and shirt. Having spent several days in the brig, he blinked at the sunlight, which made him appear even older than his sixty-one years.

'Courage, Andrew,' came a cry from the crowd.

'Quiet there!' yelled Bosun Brockle, who was already at the grating with his four deputies. Like all who took the position, they knew what it entailed and on this day the duty fell to Bosun's Mate Collins.

Cary now joined Merriman, Shrigley, Jones, Smythe and Essex on the quarterdeck: all were in full uniform. Next to arrive were the midshipmen and it was young Adkins who handed the captain the Articles of War. As was his habit, Merriman made a quick appraisal of the sails and the sea to ensure that he – and the ensuing punishment – would not be interrupted. Mr. Webster was last to arrive and he stood next to Merriman, fulfilling his role as judge of whether a victim of the lash was able to continue.

'Able Seaman Andrew Muir has admitted his guilt in regards of a violent assault upon the person of Able Seaman John Butcher, which resulted in serious harm. This assault took place on May the Eighteenth at around half-past eleven.

It is likely that Butcher made a provocative comment towards Muir but that in no way mitigates this offense. However, Muir's actions were clearly not premeditated and so I do not consider this a case of attempted murder. Rather, it was an assault, which causes me to invoke both the twenty-second and thirty-sixth articles of war.'

Though he knew it by heart, Merriman now opened the book and read it.

'If any person in the fleet shall quarrel or fight with any other person in the fleet, or use reproachful or provoking speeches or gestures, tending to make any quarrel or disturbance, he shall, upon being convicted thereof, suffer such punishment as the offence shall deserve.'

Merriman took a breath. 'The thirty-sixth article covers those offences not stipulated elsewhere and this allows me to use whatever punishment I see fit. All those present should be aware that I have taken into account the previous good conduct of Able Seaman Muir and his many years of exceptional service. The punishment shall be twenty-four lashes. Seize him up.'

Now Brockle and his mates removed Muir's shirt and placed him, spreadeagled, upon the grating, tying him with yarn. Brockle took it upon himself to place a leather apron around Muir's waist, which was to protect the lower part of his back. Merriman knew for a fact that Brockle was a good friend of Muir but he showed no sign of favour.

While this went on, Merriman looked again at the crowd. If Muir's cohorts considered the punishment unfair, they didn't show it. As Merriman expected, Furlong and Butcher's friends were less happy. They were whispering and muttering, though none looked in the direction of the officers.

Bosun's mate Collins took the cat-o'-nine-tails from the bag. He then moved behind Muir, who remained steady upon the grating, though his fingers were trembling.

'Go ahead,' ordered Merriman.

Silence, he had found, was only really achieved on a warship during services, funerals and lashings. It was not a true silence, of course; the usual sounds of creaking timbers, groaning pulleys and the hiss of the sea remained.

Collins drew his fingers through the cat's tails then retracted his arm and unleashed his first blow. Muir emitted a slight grunt but made little further reaction as Collins struck again, again and again. Merriman noted that some of the crewmen purposefully looked away, as did young Chamier. He spied Friar too, dwarfed by the big men beside him, watching with hands clasped, for once his expression fearful and grave. Merriman felt an odd sense of shame that he immediately dismissed from his mind.

By the sixth lash, Muir's skin began to break up. Merriman always insisted that the bosun and his mates struck with approximately equal force and he could see that Collins was doing no more than duty required of him. At the tenth lash, Muir gave an odd shiver and his head went limp against the grate.

It seemed that Brockle perhaps wanted it all over with because he snatched up a nearby pail of water.

'Sir?'

'May I inspect him, captain?' said Mr. Webster.

'You may.'

Webster crossed the deck. By the time he reached Muir, the veteran seemed to have come around. The physician briefly looked him over and then stepped away with a nod to the captain.

Bosun Brockle in turn nodded to Collins, who set to his work again. The welts upon Muir's skin turned from lines of pink and purple to deep red as they began to bleed.

Webster had not moved far and was seen to momentarily close his eyes and clamp his lips together. This did not surprise Merriman at all. Like many ship's surgeons before him, he would simply have to become accustomed to the practice.

Muir continued to bear the punishment in near-silence but, before the fifteenth lash, he passed out once more. Mr. Webster took a mug from the pail and gently sloshed water on his face to rouse him. The Welshman cradled Muir's face and examined his eyes, then took his wrist to measure his pulse.

'Fakery!'

The predictable source of this accusation was Furlong and he received two immediate responses. One was from Lieutenant Cary, who immediately stalked across the deck, a hand on his sword-hilt.

'Close that mouth of yours, Furlong, or by God you'll take a few blows yourself!' This came from the usually even-tempered Lieutenant Jones, who now followed Cary across the deck and – like the marine – stationed himself by Butcher's supporters. Furlong turned his gaze on Cary but even the big Irishman didn't dare provoke the burly marine officer and he soon made the wise decision to look away.

Webster now walked back to Merriman, wiping sweat from his brow. 'His heart rate is not only very fast but irregular. A strong fellow but he is old. I suggest the punishment end, captain.'

When Merriman did not immediately respond, Webster continued: 'I'm afraid I must insist.'

'With respect Mr. Webster,' said Shrigley. 'You *cannot* insist.'

Merriman did not believe for a moment that Muir was faking but he also believed that Furlong was not the only one who considered the punishment lenient. He could hardly cut it short. Then again, if the flogging resulted in Muir's death, there would be damage to morale amongst his own.

'How many is that?'

'The fifteenth lash was not administered, captain,' answered Shrigley.

Merriman took a step forward. 'Collins, five more and that will be all.'

Furlong and his compatriots made their view plain but no one said anything.

And now every blow was difficult to watch, for Merriman feared that Webster might be proved right. Muir's back was a ragged mess of blood and ruined flesh but the man remained conscious until the final blow. To his credit, Webster showed no reaction but immediately took charge when Muir was let down. The veteran's friends and the surgeon's assistants then carried him below.

'Glad that's over, sir,' said Shrigley.

Merriman said nothing. He walked to the taffrail and looked down at the *Thunder*'s wake. He had seldom felt so low or so old.

Peters knew better than to offer his captain meat on the day of a flogging. But in fact, Merriman couldn't face anything and he occupied himself by ordering Smythe to the great cabin. The third lieutenant did his best to appear alert and energetic but Merriman relied on what he'd previously seen and the thoughts of his first lieutenant.

'Smythe, many days have now passed since the events that affected you. I have spoken to you twice about what you need to do and yet it seems that you haven't done it. I am told – and I observe – that you are not fulfilling your obligations or engaging with the men.'

Standing with his hands clasped behind him, Smythe hesitated before replying. 'I have tried, sir. It...I wonder if something has changed within or me or...is it simply that my true character has been revealed?'

'Forget this self-indulgent nonsense,' snapped Merriman, surprising himself. 'Let me make your situation plain, Matthew. I am already considering demoting you to fourth. God knows Essex is contributing far more than you at the moment. Beyond that, if you do not buck your ideas up, you will not remain on the books of the *Thunder* beyond the duration of this mission. Is that understood?'

'Yes, captain. Might I-'

'Dismissed.'

With a stiff salute, Smythe departed. Merriman spied Shrigley in the passageway and waved him inside. As the marine sentry closed the door, Merriman offered the first lieutenant a seat.

'I tried the carrot with the fellow but it is now time for the stick. If there's no improvement over the next few days, he'll drop down to fourth. I cannot imagine that he will be much help to us if and when we face the *Hercule*.' Merriman leaned forward on to his desk. 'Now, what have you learned from our castaways?'

Shrigley reached into his coat pocket and retrieved a pencil and a small notebook.

'Certainly some points of interest, sir. All three men answered my questions and they agree that the ship is in exceptional condition. All parts seem well maintained and fully manned. While the French crew took over the *Elizabeth*, there was some communication between the sailors. One fellow – a Dutchman who spoke English – seemed quite proud of himself. He had occupied a lowly position on one of our merchantmen but, when it was taken, was offered a better position on the *Hercule*. The numerous prize crews have indeed denuded the original complement somewhat and these places have been taken by volunteers from the seized ships. Apparently, there is so much coin and gold aboard that they have sufficient to offer these sailors an excellent wage. This fellow said he'd gone from utter depression to utter joy in a single day.'

'I suppose we shouldn't be surprised. And other than what they have physically seized, there will be an enormous payout when they eventually return home. Sixteen ships taken now. Why even the cabin boys will have heavy pockets. Was anything said about the size of the crew?'

'No, sir.' Shrigley consulted his notes. 'As I said, it did appear fully manned but no figures were mentioned, nor could Sellers and the others make much of an estimate during their brief time aboard.'

'Presumably they were set adrift before the *Elizabeth* departed to the north?'

'They were. Sellers was laughing about it. This Dutchman who had been boasting suddenly found out he was to join the prize crew. Apparently, he'd let it slip to his new masters that he'd served with an infantry regiment as a young man. His smile faded when a musket was thrust into his hand.'

'So, Jourdan put some of his sailors on the *Elizabeth* in place of marines?'

'It seems so. Er...' Shrigley consulted his notes again. 'A dozen went aboard the *Elizabeth* and perhaps another dozen were seen on the *Hercule*.'

'That fellow Trent told us that marines were put aboard the Rochester, did he not?'

'He did indeed, sir.'

'What would you say, Alfred? If one has the men, how many marines for a prize crew?'

'I would say somewhere between three and eight, sir. It depends on the size of the vessel, the crew, their attitude to being taken, likelihood of mutiny and so on.'

'Let us say a minimum of three, then – for sixteen ships. Jourdan might have lost fifty soldiers.'

'True, sir. But I suppose his original complement may have been bolstered – from other naval vessels or the French colonies.'

'Possible, I agree. And yet now he's converting sailors to marines. Interesting.'

Chapter Twenty-One

Out Of The Sun

That night, the wind veered to the north. White cloud covered the entirety of the sky as *Thunder* rolled along in a following sea. Though there were some accompanying difficulties, her speed remained between five and seven knots throughout the day. Merriman had planned another gun drill – he particularly wanted to test Smythe and Muir's leaderless crew – but the ship was made unsteady by the waves; and he felt he had to make the most of the wind. *Thunder* was approximately six miles off the coast and it was from that direction that the ship appeared.

Merriman was on deck at the time, checking the final repairs to the damaged bowsprit. It seemed that the land behind the vessel had obscured their view because it was less than four miles away when sighted, heading offshore in a westerly direction. Within a quarter-hour, the lookouts, Jones and Shrigley (who had ventured up the cross trees) all agreed: the ship to the south was a three-masted vessel of a size equivalent to *Thunder*. Ten minutes later, two hawk-eyed lookouts concurred that they could make out a splash of red at her stern and horizontal lines upon her hull.

'My gut tells me it's her,' said Tom Henderson, who had remained at the bow.

Merriman nodded and lowered his own spyglass. In truth, his eyes could not make out what the lookouts had but he too felt that this was their target.

Soon came another call from above. 'Bearing away.'

A minute later: 'Heading south.'

'A swift decision,' said Henderson.

'We have the weather,' replied Merriman. 'A *sound* decision.'

For the remainder of the day, *Thunder* pursued what they assumed to be the *Hercule* down the African coast. The ships seemed to be virtually matched in terms of speed and they got no closer than three miles. Wary of running into a trap, at sundown Merriman ordered that sail be shortened to slow the ship. After all he'd read about the French captain's surprises and tricks, he even considered heaving to and not moving until the daylight.

He remained on deck beyond sundown and had to force both Shrigley and Jones to rest in order to take over from him later. By midnight, the wind had dropped below ten knots and *Thunder* was making barely three. In a way, Merriman was glad of it; the gentle breeze and the calm seas made it easier for his lookouts to scan the ocean around them. As a precaution, he ordered that the bow and stern lights be put out and that only half-shuttered lanterns were permitted on deck. This was far from ideal for the sailors moving around but the wind was constant and there were only a few dozen manning the yards and rigging.

It was a strange, eerie vigil. The solid cloud of earlier in the day had broken up and when the sky was clear above, the light of a near-full moon played on the surface. Merriman found himself pacing the deck, sometimes accompanied by one of the midshipmen, sometimes alone, always with his spyglass in his hand. During his early circuits of the ship, older hands would speak to him, asking if he thought the *Hercule* had slowed down too; if the French ship was hunting them; if the captain would attack at night. Merriman was too preoccupied to say much and soon the men left him alone.

He and Eades were on the larboard side, close to the bow, when the midshipman suddenly cried, 'There!' and pointed into the darkness.

'What do you see?' asked Merriman.

'A light, sir. At least I think so.'

The moon was at that moment obscured by cloud and the area before them utterly dark: it could not have been moonlight upon a wave. Eades was young but experienced and Merriman knew he would not have mistaken a cresting wave for a light. Not wishing to shout, he called over a nearby sailor and sent him up the mast to alert the lookouts. While waiting, Eades kept pointing at his sighting and the pair continued to scour the black depths of ocean and sky.

'There. Yes.'

It was three points off the bow, in the direction of the coast. Judging the distance was exceptionally difficult but Merriman did not think it was very close. Two minutes later, the sailor came down from the cross trees.

'He sees it, captain. Hard to say but two or three miles, he reckons.'

'We have spotted native fishing vessels out at night, sir,' offered Eades. 'Someone said that certain types of fish are easier to catch then – especially when it's calm.'

'That's true.' Merriman leaned on to the rail. 'We shall monitor – see if it moves. Eades, find a servant and have some coffee sent up.'

By the time the coffee arrived ten minutes later, Merriman had concluded that the light was not moving. A second enquiry to the lookout eighty feet above confirmed this opinion.

'Probably just drifting,' he said. Lifting the cup to his lips, he was dismayed to find the coffee rather weak.

'Peters didn't make that.'

'No, captain. It was Daniels. Sorry.'

'Not your fault.'

The midshipman cleared his throat, then took out his spyglass and checked the light again. 'Sir, I must say I don't like all this waiting.'

Merriman wasn't particularly in the mood for conversation but he always felt some sympathy for the youngsters aboard at difficult times.

'Nor I.'

'Lieutenant Jones says that he hates waiting for close action more than the action itself.'

'That rather depends on the nature of the action.'

Merriman couldn't help concluding that the well-matched vessels would inflict considerable damage on each other, whatever the outcome.

'I remember what you told us in the Adriatic, sir,' added Eades. 'That one never knows what a day aboard a ship-of-the-line will bring. It's best to expect anything and be grateful if you lie in your hammock at the end of the day, safe and well.'

'Is that what I said? We never do know, Eades. Perhaps the *Hercule* is still heading south, bound for the cape at speed.'

'How far will we follow her, captain?'

'As far as we have to.'

Though Shrigley came on deck at two o'clock in the morning to relieve him, Merriman found he did not wish to leave. He and the first lieutenant stationed themselves at the bow. Shortly afterward, all on deck heard a very odd noise from behind the ship: a, hissing, bubbling sound that drew the two officers to the stern. Essex and Adkins were already at the taffrail, studying the water to larboard.

Then came a great thumping slap not unlike the report of a gun.

An alarmed Adkins asked, 'Will we beat to quarters?'

'I don't think so, young man,' said Shrigley, pointing directly astern. All of them watched as the whale rolled over, exposing a pale part of its body before slapping its tail once more and then disappearing beneath the water.

Adkins laughed. 'What a relief.'

'At least we didn't hit it,' said Essex.

'Might have woken it up,' said Shrigley. 'I believe they sleep at night, sometimes on the surface.'

'Speaking of sleep, I suppose I should retire.'

'Yes, sir,' said Shrigley. 'Rest assured I shall alert you to any sighting.'

'Very good.'

Once below, Merriman was on his way to the cabin when he encountered Mr. Webster.

'You're up late.'

'Yes, captain. Your attendants possess the most reliable source of hot water on the ship. We need it to clean Butcher's wound. There are early signs of suppuration.'

'I see. And how is Muir faring?'

'Recovering, I think. His pulse has settled down and would you believe that he instructed me on the best treatment for his wounds?'

'He has seen a good many lashings in his time.'

'But never received one before this.'

'Is that right? You did well, Mr. Webster. I know it's not easy for a physician.'

'I thought I was prepared for it, captain, but I realise it is one of those experiences one cannot really prepare for.'

'You may well be right. I presume you have not placed them together?'

'No, sir. Certainly not now that Butcher is conscious.'

'We will have to bring them together at some point but not yet. I thank you for all you are doing, Mr. Webster – you have shown yourself to be most conscientious. Do get some sleep when your work is done.'

'Yes, sir. I hope you get some rest.'

Merriman made his way to his bed. Some instinct about the coming hours told him not to undress fully so he laid out in trousers and shirt and refreshed himself by pouring some beer from the jug Peters had left out for him. Like most of the liquid aboard, it was beginning to sour but Merriman had tasted far worse and he emptied the mug.

He turned down the lantern hanging from a hook beside his bed and closed his eyes. Merriman soon drifted off but was awoken by the change of watch at four o'clock. He slipped back into a fitful sleep, waking to be momentarily convinced that he was aboard the *Conflict*. Later, he woke again, this time sure that he was aboard the *Lord Stevenage*. Lastly came a dream of a laughably simple but horribly powerful nature. He was striding across a landscape of grassy hills, unaware of either origin or destination. He glanced back regularly at a sea of faces; his officers and men; Muir, Garland, Friar, Adkins, old compatriots, dead friends. Every time he looked over his shoulder there were fewer of them, until finally he was alone.

The *Hercule* came out of the dawn sun. That sun was so low and so bright that she was not sighted until within three miles. Reaching across the northerly wind, her bow was aimed straight at *Thunder*.

The first Merriman knew of it was the marine's drum that snapped him out of his awful dream. By the time he had his bearings, Peters was there, placing his boots by his bed and grabbing his coat.

'Three miles, you say?'

'Yes, sir. To the east. Looks like the Frenchman.'

In only a few seconds, Merriman had pulled on his shoes. He stood and allowed Peters to help him into his jacket then set about his buttons. The veteran was standing by the door with his hat by time he had finished buttoning and tightening his belt.

'You won't want your sword yet, sir?'

'Bring it up a little later, Peters.'

'Best of luck, sir. He'll not have encountered the likes of you before.'

'Time will tell.'

Out in the passageway, Merriman encountered Essex and Jones.

'Shall we go to the gun decks, sir?' asked Essex, his face flushed.

'Shall we turn towards him, captain,' asked Jones. 'I wasn't sure if-'

'Calm yourselves, gentlemen. Follow me up to the quarterdeck. I trust that Shrigley and Smythe are already there?'

'They are, sir,' said Jones, pressing himself backward to let Merriman pass. The captain paused to allow some sailors up the steps and then followed. He donned his hat and took a quick look around. Two dozen men were now raising the nets. Master Henderson was at his usual station by the wheel and Harris was on the helm. Merriman looked up at the sails and saw that all was well. He made his way to the quarterdeck, where Shrigley and Smythe were now putting their hats on.

'Fifteen knots of wind, Tom?' asked Merriman as he passed him.

'About that, sir. Moving between north-east and east-north- east the last hour or so.'

'Thank you.'

Reaching the quarterdeck, Merriman turned to the south-east. He could see the *Hercule*, dark hull and pale sails clear on the sunlit water.

'What's our speed?'

'Five knots, sir.'

'She'll be doing something similar. Half an hour then. Let us first put the boats into the water. Then we shall turn towards her while we're still a little upwind. That makes the larboard guns most likely to fire first but we shall see. Alfred, please see that all is well down there, then return to me. The rest of you, below please and to your stations. Ah, one more thing, the langridge – one ready for each gun.'

Because it was fired at very short range, they had not drilled using the canister shot but Merriman intended to make use of it, should the opportunity arise.

The three lieutenants made for the hatch.

'East, sir?' asked Henderson.

'East, Tom.'

With that, the master began doling out orders and soon the boat and the launch were lowered into the water. As this was done, men came up carrying the few remaining chickens, the three pigs and the two goats. They would be placed in the boat to keep them out of the way. Merriman noted young Friar, standing with his fellow topmen and ready to move. He almost wished he could put the lad and young Chamier in the boat too.

As the sailors began to prepare for the turn into the wind, Merriman made his way along the larboard side, sailors moving out of his path. He considered the situation. Rather clever of Jourdan to abandon the coast to make use of the sun but it hadn't brought him a great advantage. In fact, Merriman could have turned and remained upwind: but such manoeuvring could last all day. His men were well drilled and those on duty were fresh. Beyond all that, he – and those under his command – had waited long enough. They had located their prey; the time to resolve this long-awaited clash had arrived.

Returning to the quarterdeck, Merriman was greeted by Peters. Removing his coat, the captain watched the men put the finishing touches to the netting as Peters hung the sword belt over his left hip.

'Comfortable, sir?'

Merriman nodded, then gripped the black scabbard and ran the dirk in and out a couple of times to ensure it would not stick if required. Peters returned his hat, took a brief look at the approaching French ship, then headed below. On his way, he passed John Webster. The surgeon made straight for the rail and clamped his hands upon it. Merriman approached.

'Are you all right, Mr. Webster?'

'Yes, captain. Just getting some air while I can.'

'Ready down below?'

'As we can be, yes.'

'You are in pretty much the safest part of the ship. In the middle, low down.'

'It is not my welfare that concerns me.' Webster wrung his hands. 'I do hope the battle is not too terrible.'

The Welshman drew in several draughts of air and then returned below. Merriman could hardly blame him; surely his attitude to war was the logical view. Only among fighting men, would the prospect of battle be seen as anything other than cruel and insane.

Hand on his sword pommel, Merriman looked around to ensure that all the deck gun crews were in place. Like many of those not currently occupied by a task, they were watching the *Hercule* as the two warships cut across the calm, gleaming sea towards each other. From the stern, came an odd cacophony of noise from the penned pigs, goats and chickens as the boats were let out.

Shrigley came up, hat in his hand. Just behind him was Lieutenant Cary.

'Guns ready, sir. Canister shot put out too.'

'Very good. Ah, Cary, I was about to send for you.'

'Captain.'

'My intention is to hold your marines back until we need you. If we get within musket range, I suggest twenty men at the most be deployed. I do not want the French to know of your existence until you lead sixty redcoats onboard.'

Cary's eyes shone. 'Very good, sir. Straight for the quarterdeck?'

'Precisely.'

'I'll send Harrison up with nineteen others at your order. The rest I shall ready by the hatches. May we use grenades, sir?'

'Certainly.'

With a salute, Cary departed. Flanked by Shrigley and Henderson, Merriman made his way to his customary position behind the wheel.

'He's not moved an inch, captain,' remarked Harris. 'Straight at us.'

'Mile or so now,' said Shrigley.

'About that,' agreed Henderson.

Bosun Brockle had been at the bow but now made his way aft, issuing orders either verbally or with a finger. He encountered some object that he didn't like the look of and threw it over the side. He spoke to the fo'c'sle men and the waisters and then the afterguard, all poised and ready for his next order.

'Seems this fellow does not want to waste time on manoeuvring,' he said.

The warships closed. A shrieking gull flapped past the taffrail. Shrigley made some adjustments to his sword. The wheel squeaked as Harris moved it in order to put the vessels bow to bow. Henderson cleared his throat.

'Half a mile,' said Shrigley after a time. We must be closing at ten knots. Five minutes or so.'

Merriman looked up to check that Adkins was in position by the hatch, ready to receive and pass on orders to the gun decks. Eades was at the binnacle with Hickey and Chamier.

'We must get a measure of him,' said Merriman. 'Keep us at least a hundred yards apart, Harris.'

'Aye aye, sir.'

'Adkins! Tell the larboard side to ready themselves. Range one hundred yards.'

After a nod, the young man's head disappeared as he raced down the steps. Close to the mainmast, one of the waisters left his fellows, walked to the rail and vomited over the starboard side. Merriman had seen this numerous times before and was not surprised when two more followed.

'Slow her down, sir?' enquired Henderson.

Merriman shook his head. For the first exchange, his main aim was to gauge the quality of his opponent's gunnery, hopefully without sustaining too much damage to his own ship. Slowing down would likely result in more damage to both vessels.

'And afterward, sir?'

'If he attempts an immediate turn, we match him. Eades, come here!'

The midshipman hurried over.

'You have a single task, young man. Watch the *Hercule* for me. Any change – let me know immediately.'

'Aye aye, sir.'

'Alfred, below if you please now. You will give the order to the larboard battery.'

'Aye aye, sir.'

'Three hundred yards,' said Henderson. 'Nose down again. He doesn't want to get too close either.'

Merriman got his first sight of the sailors aboard the *Hercule*: a fo'c'sle crew hauling on a line. He could see the ports and the long guns, the tricolour on the mainmast and the larger flag billowing out behind the stern. It was an immaculately-maintained standard, the red and blue vivid and bright.

'Two hundred yards', said Henderson.

As far as Merriman could tell, only *Hercule*'s courses had been furled; as with *Thunder,* the lower sails were not used during close action. The ships would pass at a speed of around ten knots. Despite the close range, it was a stiff test for the accuracy of their fire.

Their weapons primed, the deck gun crews readied themselves. At Bosun Brockle's order, all the unoccupied sailors knelt down and took cover.

Merriman did not want any delay in communication. He knew Shrigley would be crouched over by the forward gunport on the larboard side. The first officer was more than capable of timing the first shot to ensure an accurate broadside.

'More like one hundred fifty, isn't it, Tom?'

'It is, sir.'

'Adkins – the first lieutenant is to fire at will. Range one hundred and fifty yards.'

With a nod, the midshipmen descended the hatch once more and his order was swiftly passed on.

'Come on then,' breathed Henderson. 'Let's see what you've got.'

Chapter Twenty-Two

Close Action

The *Hercule*'s guns opened up a fraction earlier than *Thunder*'s. Crouching down behind the wheel, Merriman looked up at the rigging but was in fact more focused on what he could hear. Just as Shrigley gave the order, the first enemy balls struck and the sound of tearing sail cut through the cacophony. Then came more solid impacts and wreckage fell from the foremast, causing the fo'c'sle crew to scatter.

Shot hit the mainmast and a piece of timber was blasted downwards with great force before slamming into the capstan. Despite the damage, Merriman could feel the timbers below trembling from the power of his own ship's guns.

The next impact was a terrible smash to larboard. The very air around Merriman's head seemed to shimmer and swirl and he abruptly found himself lying on his back beside Tom Henderson. The frowning sailing master had a hand to his left ear.

'By god, I do believe it passed right between us.'

His words sounded muted and dull and Merriman realised his own hearing had been affected. Turning to larboard, he saw a round hole in the side of the ship: it was must have been a twenty-eight pounder to penetrate the thick timbers of *Thunder*'s hull. Henderson was by now on his knees and the two men helped each other up.

Merriman watched the stern of his ship pass the stern of his enemy. He saw a knot of officers there and was gratified to see some damage inflicted upon the French ship: a couple of torn sails and two shattered gun ports that would now be rendered unusable. His survey was interrupted by an awful sight to his left: a crewman from the quarterdeck guns had been hit. His bloodied, broken arm dragged along the deck as a compatriot hauled him towards the hatch.

Turning towards the bow, Merriman saw Brockle hurrying forward. He was dismayed to also note a good deal of wreckage caught in the nets below the foremast.

'We've lost the royal there, sir,' said Henderson.

Considering the range, Merriman was not too disheartened: until Shrigley came up from below. Emerging from a cloud of smoke, eyes red, he limped over to the captain.

'You all right?'

'Nothing, sir. I fell. At least six shots straight into the main deck, two into the upper deck. Four guns out of commission.'

'Four?'

Shrigley grimaced and looked over Merriman's shoulder at the *Hercule*. 'Did we damage her at all?'

'A couple of ports smashed. Not much done to the rigging.'

'Sir, sails flapping. Looks like she's preparing to come about.'

Merriman turned to see that the keen-eyed Eades was quite correct. 'Tom, we must match her.'

'Yes, sir.' Henderson began his orders with, 'Hands to the braces!'

'Casualties?'

'Two dozen at least,' answered Shrigley. 'Five serious – they're on their way to Webster. I'm afraid I've had to relieve Smythe. He is simply not communicating.'

Merriman smacked a fist into an open palm but there was no time to dwell on the matter. 'Looks like there will be a second exchange. This time to starboard. We did quite well.'

'He did better,' said Shrigley with a grimace.

'They've been out here for months. And with no shortage of practice.'

'I'll get down to the starboard battery, sir,' said Shrigley before limping away.

'We've lost the fore royal and topgallant, captain,' stated Brockle, returning from the bow. A couple of injuries from falling bits but all walking wounded.'

Merriman nodded and realised that his hearing was returning to normal. As the tacking sequence unfolded, he watched the *Hercule* with Eades. So far, it seemed that the sail handling was as good as her gunnery. He resisted the temptation to inform Brockle and Henderson that the French ship was quicker; that would only make things worse.

But soon *Thunder* was through the wind too, and the sailors were hauling the lines in and making adjustments. Once again, the warships faced each other, now picking up speed.

Henderson returned to the wheel. 'Sorry we couldn't do better for you, captain.'

'No matter, Tom. Adkins! Have Lieutenant Harrison and his marines join us on deck.'

In a flash, the twenty redcoats came charging up the steps, Harrison in the lead, musket in hand.

'The officers, sir?'

'No. I know the range is long but aim for the gun ports closest to the bow. Fire as early as you can. Let's see if we can put them off a little.'

'Aye aye, sir.'

Though the splashes of colour would have been easily visible to the French, Harrison did take the precaution of leading his men down the starboard side and temporarily gathering them behind the capstan and mizzenmast.

The ships were bow to bow once more but soon the *Hercule* turned a point to the south.

'That range suited him well enough, I reckon,' said Henderson. 'It will be the same again.'

'Looks that way,' said Merriman. Though concerned about the damage a second volley from the French vessel would cause, a repetition actually suited his wider purposes well enough.

'Adkins, to Lieutenant Shrigley at the starboard battery. Range one hundred and fifty yards. Distance to enemy three hundred. He is again to fire at will.'

Merriman let out a long breath. 'Harris, come up a bit. Keep at one fifty for the gunners.'

Henderson spoke up: 'Sir, foretopsail needs-'

'Leave it. Too late. No need to expose the men.'

Now Harrison deployed his marines. Muskets already primed, they steadily crossed the deck and knelt on one knee by the starboard rail. At the lieutenant's order they aimed at the *Hercule*'s bow. One of the muskets misfired and a marine had to drop his weapon but the others continued unperturbed. Merriman reckoned they'd be lucky to make any real impact but he wanted to give the French captain something to think about; and he wanted him to see the marines.

Once they had fired, Harrison waved his men down and Merriman also took cover with Henderson, scabbard scraping the deck as he did so. He guessed that the warships were closing at around eight knots and in seconds the dual barrages began.

A piercing scream went up from ahead of him. Between the blasts of the long guns, Merriman heard a crack from above. A spinning yard fell through several lines and seemed certain to strike the waisters crouching below the mainmast. But the protective netting did its job, slowing the timber so that the quick-footed sailors had time to dive clear. Seconds later, Harris uttered a bitter oath. Merriman saw that two of the wheel's rounded handles had been blown clean off.

The screaming man ran aft, one hand clamped over a bleeding eye. Clearly maddened by the pain, he slipped and fell. Bosun Brockle tried to help but he somehow got himself to the hatch and slid down past a horrified Midshipman Adkins. Merriman could see several more injured sailors being dragged aft by their fellows. The *Thunder* and the *Hercule* unleashed their final volleys and then he at last straightened up.

He could see Jourdan. The French captain stood with his bicorne hat in place, spyglass in one hand, regarding the *Thunder* with a studied curiosity. Around him, two of his officers were pointing at the British ship. Another was leaning over the side, looking down at the larboard side. One port had been destroyed and the long gun was hanging down, almost touching the water. Other than that, Merriman could see no significant damage.

'Quarterdeck guns – aim for the rudder,' said Merriman. 'Fire at will.'

The two crews seemed surprised by the order but they followed it swiftly enough. By the time they fired, the *Hercule* was at least three hundred yards distant and the balls struck the water some distance behind the stern. It was a rather desperate attempt and Merriman hoped the French would view it as such.

Vaguely aware of injured men being carried towards the hatch, Merriman forced himself not to look at them but instead at Midshipman Adkins.

'From Lieutenant Shrigley, sir. Two dozen more wounded below. Heavy damage to the main deck near the bow. Four guns out there, three more on the upper deck. Lightning's gone, sir.'

Merriman just nodded. He saw that Henderson was holding a rag against Harris's bleeding chin.

'Can you carry on?'

'Of course, sir,' replied the helmsman.

'Tom, I'm going below. She's yours.'

'Sir. If he tacks?'

'Notify me. But don't turn until I give the order.'

Descending past the upper gun deck, Merriman had to step over more wounded sailors. The smoke had by then cleared enough for him to see that there were yet more injured still ahead. The crews did not notice him: they were too busy moving wreckage and ensuring that they were ready for the next volley. Those whose guns had been damaged beyond repair were aiding their fellows. Lieutenant Essex seemed to have matters under control. There was no sign of Lieutenant Smythe.

On the main deck, the situation was similar. One poor fellow was screaming for his mother, held down by one of Webster's assistants, his face a mask of blood. Two dozen sailors were heaving on one of the thirty-eight pounders, which had been blown into the middle of the deck. Shrigley emerged out of the smoke, his face coated with black dust.

'Sir?'

'We're not going to win this at range. I will give you as long as I can before we exchange again. First, I want a full battery to larboard, even if you have to move guns across. How long?'

'With more men – ten minutes.'

'You'll get them. Second, load them all with langridge. Third, set them to fire horizontally, directly into the ports. Fourth, once they're ready, keep the men on this deck to a minimum. When the guns are in position, loaded and primed, every spare man is to head up on deck with a cutlass.'

Shrigley absorbed all this with creditable speed. 'You mean to close with him, sir?'

'It's our only chance.'

Only as he departed, did Merriman realize that it was his second lieutenant leading the efforts with the damaged gun. Jones had a rope in both hands and was bellowing at the men to heave at it. Merriman had only time clap him on his shoulder and from there he called out for the armourer, Mr. Stones.

While he waited for him to arrive, Merriman was relieved to see Lieutenant Cary.

'Your orders, sir?'

'I am going to try and get in close. Send hooks and ladders up for Harrison. If I'm successful, we must keep the ships together and board as quickly as possible. Lob some grenades and then take your boarding party across. Lieutenant, they will keep blasting away at us. Speed is the key.'

'Understood. I'll fetch the equipment.'

'Get your men up ahead of mine. They'll be coming behind you from the main deck.'

While the two had been talking, the armourer arrived.

'Ah, there you are, Stones. Boxes of cutlasses by the doors on main and upper deck. Also, you know who is handy with a blade. Arrange the best of them so that they follow the marines aboard the *Hercule*. Swift fellows with stout hearts.'

'Does that include me, sir? I should like to lead them.'

'Very good.'

As he made his way up the steps, Merriman passed Peters, who was using a pail and a cloth to clean away blood. Adkins was back in place at the top step and gazing so intently at the red water within the pail that he hardly seemed to notice Merriman.

'Keep your eyes on deck, lad,' advised the captain on his way past.

'He's turning now, captain' said Eades.

Merriman looked out over the taffrail. The ships were approximately a mile apart and the *Hercule* was indeed turning back towards *Thunder*.

'We shall wait a moment. Come up two points, Harris. We must stay to windward of her.'

While Merriman had learned something of his French foe during his journey south, he thought it unlikely that the enemy captain knew anything of him at all: another of the few points in his favour. He could not, however, wait too long to spring his surprise – that might raise suspicions aboard *Hercule*.

He made a few calculations, waited another minute, then told Henderson to put *Thunder* through the wind. Second Lieutenant Harrison and his men had been given the grappling hooks and were now arranging themselves along the larboard rail.

Seeing this, Bosun Brockle – whose shirt was smeared with several bloodstains – hurried back to the wheel. The helmsman Harris now had a bandage wrapped around his chin to staunch his wound.

'Sir, you mean to board? How will we get close enough?'

'We seem to have settled into a pattern. If we repeat it, *Hercule* will prevail. Her guns are more accurate and she has more of them. It is simply a matter of time.'

'But captain, boarding is a last resort, we are still in good fighting shape. Perhaps the next exchange-'

'We are firing only one more volley, Brockle. Canister shot. From point-blank range. Our only advantage lies with our marines.'

'Sir, it is hardly nautical-'

'You forget yourself, bosun!' snapped Merriman.

Brockle swallowed anxiously and straightened up. 'Quite right, sir. My apologies.'

Merriman waved Henderson over. 'Tom, we must get alongside. Assuming we can stay to windward, I will wait until the last moment and aim to strike him about the beam. That should slow both vessels and give us a chance of securing ourselves to her. I'll need maximum speed before that. She might bear away but that will mean exposing her stern. We shall blast away with our canister shot and then I'm having the gundecks cleared. I'll need every man on deck and boarding.'

'Sir, if they can still bring their guns to bear, they can just keep firing. Even if we prevail on the *Hercule*, there might be nothing left of *Thunder*.'

'That is a risk we have to take. Now, give the orders. Maximum speed and as much of it as you can give me when I turn into her. Get to it.'

Brockle hurried away. Tom Henderson looked down at the deck and remained silent. Other than Alfred Shrigley, there was no other man aboard whose opinion Merriman valued enough to indulge at this point.

'If you have something to say, master – say it.'

'I'll get to it, captain.'

'Very good.'

Despite their obedience, as the crew began the turn through the wind, Merriman questioned himself. It certainly was a risk but a calculated one. Now was not the time to doubt himself.

'By God, Harris, you're bleeding all over the place. Allow me.'

'Obliged, sir.'

While the helmsman retied his bandage, Merriman took over the wheel. *Thunder* had already gone through the wind. The foresails had backed and now the crew were hurriedly luffing the main and the mizzen. Keeping the wheel hard over, Merriman looked east towards the *Hercule*, which was coming on again with sails set fair. There seemed to be a calm, irrepressible nature to this man Jourdan and his ship; presumably a result of his long run of success. Merriman could only hope that his overconfidence might work against him.

His eye was drawn to the men in red crouching by the larboard rail. As well as the grappling hooks, they were also equipped with several ladders. And while half were armed with hatchets, others had long boarding pikes. Merriman was pleased to see these preparations but suddenly realised they were woefully undermanned.

'Eades, round up three dozen men from the deck crews and send them to assist the marines. They are to help them with the ladders and hooks. Any hook that sticks is to be hauled in and secured. And tell Harrison that he is not to board yet. His sole occupation is to keep the ships together.'

'Aye aye, sir,' As the midshipman hurried away, Merriman saw Lieutenant Cary peering out from the hatch. To his great credit, the courageous marine appeared to be one of the calmest aboard and Merriman was grateful for it. Much would depend on him.

With the mizzen and mainsails now in position, *Thunder* began to pick up speed again. The *Hercule* was perhaps five hundred yards away. Henderson was bellowing at his crews to get every fraction of speed. Those recruited by Eades slid down next to the marines and listened to Harrison and one of the sergeants.

Rather reluctantly, Merriman ceded the wheel to Harris. He was relieved to see that the French ship was repeating the earlier routine. Except something was different: something had changed; and by the time he noticed it, Merriman could do nothing about it.

The *Hercule* had not yet fired her bow chasers and now he saw there were six of them. Smoke issued from the barrels and they were not small barrels: eighteen-pounders at least. Two cannonballs missed the mark, hissing away to the north, but four found their target.

It was a superb piece of raking fire and the effects were predictably terrible. Cries went up as the balls tore their way through the ship, downing men at foremast and main. The binnacle exploded in a shower of wood. Poor Hickey staggered away, his young face contorted by agony.

Again forcing himself to ignore the horrors before him, Merriman saw that at least those at the side had not been affected; the marines were ready.

The *Hercule* was less than two hundred yards away, half that to the south. Merriman reckoned *Thunder* was doing four knots. He hoped it was enough.

'Mr. Henderson, prepare to ease sheets. Harris, prepare to turn into her. On my mark.'

Chapter Twenty-Three

Blade and Ball

At a silent signal from Henderson, the sailors let out their sheets. By that point, Merriman had already nodded to Harris and the helmsman had turned the wheel. This evidently caused some confusion aboard *Hercule* because the bow momentarily swung north towards *Thunder* before resuming its previous course. The French guns roared but were now aiming at a smaller target. Merriman heard at least two impacts on the hull but this was soon forgotten as *Thunder* – picking up speed with the wind behind her – suddenly bore down on the French vessel.

'Come to larboard!' he ordered. 'Right at the beam.'

On the *Hercule*, wide-eyed sailors threw themselves away from the rail as the *Thunder* loomed.

'Back to starboard!'

Harris barely had time to carry this order out but the result was that the ships collided at an angle of forty-five degrees. *Thunder*'s bowsprit shattered noisily and then the bow smashed into *Hercule*'s side. Merriman held onto the remains of the binnacle as the juddering impact sent sailors flying on both sides. The collision slowed both ships and now *Thunder* scraped along *Hercule*'s hull, the stunned crews suddenly face to face.

Back on the quarterdeck, the French officers were shouting orders in what sounded to Merriman like panicked fashion; not that he could blame them. He had never witnessed such a radical, unorthodox manoeuvre, let along carried one out. He was about to order Harrison to launch his hooks but the marine was already up and ready. Five lines sailed through the air and three snagged in the rigging.

French sailors closed on them immediately but the marines immediately hauled them in. Five more grappling hooks flew across the gap and soon the vessels were side by side, bow to stern.

'Adkins, now!'

The midshipman nodded and relayed the order. Though he knew the shot wouldn't reach the deck and much would strike the hull, Merriman also knew that the French gunners would be reloading and that some of the canister shot would get through the ports. The guns fired in short order and the sounds from the *Hercule*'s gun deck told Merriman that the langridge had done its job. However, once the French had reloaded, they would take their turn. Right now, his men were leaving the gun decks and he hoped to keep casualties down. He had to take the vessel and force a surrender before those guns did too much damage to *Thunder*.

'Sir, look out!' Bosun Brockle grabbed Merriman by the arm and dragged him to starboard. It was just as well because the high rigging of the two ships had clashed, causing several yards to come free and fall to the deck. In the event, the debris was caught by the nets and Merriman was actually glad of the entanglement; he was not solely reliant on the marines and their hooks to keep the vessels together.

He looked up to see that the French were fighting back. Dozens of their marines and sailors had swarmed to their larboard rail. Many were hacking at the grappling lines and one officer was lining up men with muskets raised.

'To cover, sir!' shouted Brockle. He, Merriman, Harris, Henderson and Eades ran to the larboard rail and crouched down. On the way there, Merriman spotted dozens of sailors protecting themselves in similar fashion. Nearby, one of the deck guns discharged towards the quarterdeck, scattering the French officers. Immediately after it came a volley from the enemy muskets and cries went up from a few marines.

'Captain?'

His left shoulder against the hull, Merriman looked over to see Cary's face at the hatch. He then looked forward and saw that – despite the musket fire – Harrison's men were now trying to put ladders across. Even if they failed, the ships were close enough for the marines to climb aboard.

With a nod, Merriman waved towards the French ship. Cary bounded up the steps and across the deck, his men spreading out around him. They did not rush and many calmly raised their own muskets as they approached the rail. In their wake were six redcoats holding grenades, the fuses already alight. Merriman's view was obscured by all the others lined up against the rail but he saw two of the grenades thrown onto the French ship and heard the detonations.

What followed was one of the worst sights he had witnessed. One marine with a grenade was struck by musket fire and sent sprawling onto his back. The explosive went off by his side and launched his body into the air. The only mercy could have been that he died instantly.

Another barrage from the French muskets was answered by Cary's men. Looking over Henderson's head, through the puffs of smoke, Merriman saw several then drop their guns and take axes or pikes as they made for the *Hercule*. He was about to get up to gain a better view of the overall situation when the French long guns blasted into *Thunder*'s hull. The shots were near-simultaneous and the impacts caused the whole ship to shudder. Though the men should have by now vacated the gun decks, many screams went up. Merriman grimaced but he knew he should have expected it; the heavy balls would go right through the sides even of the armoured warships.

Raising his head above the rail, he saw redcoats swarming onto the *Hercule*, just forward of her mainmast. In places, the grenades had made a gap in the defensive ranks and they were able to land before being attacked.

Elsewhere, the French were ready for them and several were sent reeling back, wounded. Two fell between the ships.

Merriman felt a hand on his arm. Shrigley was there, damp hair plastered to his brow. 'Sir, the sailors?' He pointed to the hatch, where the armourer, Stones, was waiting with his warband.

'Not yet. No need for them to expose themselves unless Cary makes a breakthrough.'

Everything now depended on the lieutenant and his marines.

'Come,' said Merriman, leading Shrigley along the larboard rail. As they passed one of the deck guns, enemy fire struck a sailor who staggered backwards. Merriman managed to break his fall and lowered him to the deck. Fortunately, it was only a glancing blow but the sailor's brow was bleeding profusely. Shaking some of that blood from his hand, Merriman took a handkerchief from his coat and pressed it to the wound.

'Much obliged, cap'n,' said the man, blinking as blood ran down into his eyes.

Moments after they reached the main mass of the marines, four grenades detonated in quick succession. Coughing as he entered a cloud of smoke, Merriman watched Cary climb onto one of the ladders and dance nimbly across on to the *Hercule*, his cutlass at the ready.

'With me, men!'

Cary's well-drilled and loyal marines needed no second invitation and followed him onto the section of deck cleared by the grenades. Merriman was pleased to see that – though outnumbered – most of those they fought were sailors, not marines. He also noted that some of the Frenchmen were armed with knives or boathooks: they had been caught utterly unawares by the ramming manoeuvre.

Merriman turned to see poor Adkins lying on his front, halfway between him and the hatch, eyes fixed on the captain.

'Send the men up!' he shouted, soon having to repeat himself due to another blast from a carronade.

Though not as swift as the marines, Mr. Stones and his sailors swarmed onto the deck.

Merriman got up on one knee and quickly surveyed the situation. Another dozen marines were across and their slashing blades had allowed them to form a bridgehead of sorts. Some of the retreating Frenchmen stumbled back over bloodied bodies: presumably victims of the grenades. Further aft, two officers were directing marines and soldiers to form a line, presumably to prevent the attackers reaching the main hatch and the quarterdeck. Other sailors had formed small groups targeting the lines that were holding the ships together. Where they couldn't pull the grappling hooks out, they were slicing the ropes with hatchets.

Merriman addressed the nearest redcoats, many of whom had crouched down to reload. One of them was Sheldon, the big marine who'd gone ashore with him in Portugal.

'We must keep those lines on. Aim at any man trying to cut a line. Sheldon – see that it's done.'

'Aye, sir.'

Merriman and Shrigley moved forward again and saw that the 'bridgehead' had been widened. The ever-reliable Bosun Brockle had taken it upon himself to secure one of the ladders while his subordinate Collins did the same on the French ship. A second wave of marines began to cross.

But then came another volley from below. Merriman uttered a bitter oath as the *Hercule*'s cannons sent yet more balls into *Thunder*. Amidst the shrieks and splintering wood, Lieutenant Jones suddenly appeared. Something must have happened to his sword belt because he was holding the scabbard in his hands.

'Sir, we must get to their captain or their guns. Half cannot be brought to bear but the others are aimed straight at us. We have significant damage to both gun decks and a fire close to the bow. Some powder went up. Essex has taken charge there. How are we faring?'

'Cary's across. But we must push on. Alfred, stay here.'

'Sir, where are you going?' demanded the first lieutenant.

'Across with the men.'

'Sir, please let me. You can stay with *Thunder*.'

'You have your orders,' said the captain, handing Shrigley his hat. 'Jones, with me.'

Merriman did not make this decision for himself but for his ship and crew. Though some were new to this vessel, many were not and they had proved themselves capable and loyal. He knew from experience that the sight of their captain joining the fight would oblige every man to do his best and follow his footsteps.

That didn't mean he felt no apprehension as he and Jones skirted the line of marines. He found himself face to face with the big Irishman, Furlong, who made way and helped Merriman up on to the ladder. Knowing he was vulnerable, he tiptoed across, glimpsing dark water below before dropping onto the deck of the *Hercule*.

A cheer went up from the men on the *Thunder* as he drew his blade.

Unfortunately for Jones, the *Hercule*'s larboard battery then fired once more. As the balls tore into the ship, she was rocked and Jones slipped from the ladder.

'Sir!'

Merriman was closest to him but could only reach despairingly for Jones as he overbalanced to his right and fell from the ladder. Merriman heard him strike something solid and then the water but had no chance to help further. A man ahead of him stumbled backwards and knocked Merriman on to the rail.

'A line! Quickly!' This came from Furlong who – while others continued to cross the ladder – was looking downward.

'We have control forward of the mast!' shouted someone. The men surrounding Merriman were a mix of sailors and marines but they now took five precious steps to his right, towards the *Hercule*'s stern. This opened up more space and Harrison now led the remaining marines across, some swinging via ropes onto the French ship.

A redcoat only yards from Merriman was struck by musket fire in the chest. He collapsed to his knees, wheezing and reaching for the wound. Only when others pointed upward did the captain see the French sharpshooters perched on the mizzen. Second Lieutenant Harrison hailed those behind him with muskets and told them to target the French marines. Some were still reloading; biting cartridges open, putting powder into pan or barrel, ramming cartridge and paper home with the rod.

Amidst the shouts, cries and sounds of fighting, Merriman could not gain a clear sight of Lieutenant Cary. He was desperate to push the men on; to capitalize swiftly on their surprise assault. Even though they had had perhaps a hundred men on the *Hercule*, they were still outnumbered and had to retain the initiative.

Keeping his sword low to avoid striking his own men, he bellowed: 'Aft! Press them back! Push on to the stern!'

This drew a roar from those around him. He saw the mix of red and blue coats ahead of him take another few steps forward. Following his men, he had to step over numerous bodies and several badly injured Frenchmen. Brushing away pangs of conscience, Merriman walked on, hearing the increasingly loud clang of swords up ahead.

Then came another volley from the long guns below. At least some of the cannons must have been angled upward because two blew straight through *Thunder*'s deck, one ripping through the capstan and another smashing into the mainmast. At least five men were struck by murderous shards of wood and fell.

Despite this, Merriman was relieved to see more men lining up to follow on to the *Hercule*. Yet he was beginning to worry that he might not have a ship worthy of sailing when this battle concluded.

'Onward! Find the officers. Find the captain.'

By the time the press of advancing British sailors and marines passed the mainmast, Merriman had caught up with Cary and Harrison. Now advancing across the whole width of the boat, the attackers broke into smaller groups to face the defenders. A volley of musket fire downed at least six men in front of Merriman's position. He helped one poor fellow lurch out of the fray while Harrison dragged another clear.

Merriman then looked up to see Cary trading blows with a French officer and a burly sailor with a great scimitar more worthy of a Moorish raider. As he stepped towards them, Harrison grabbed his arm and tried to take his place.

'Captain, sir – please.'

'Unhand me, lieutenant!'

Shrugging him off, Merriman came up beside Cary, who had just deflected a blow from the great scimitar. Also present was a young French officer who drove his blade at Merriman. With Cary beside him and another marine to his left, Merriman had no room to manoeuvre. He could only parry and managed to cut the Frenchman's blade harmlessly away. However, the crafty fellow raised his other hand: and it was holding a pistol. Merriman tried to bring his blade back to deter him but Cary's shoulder blocked his arm.

The pistol came higher, the barrel aimed squarely at Merriman's chest. A torn golden epaulette hanging from his shoulder, the Frenchman gave a sly smile. Merriman could only wait for the flash: wait for death.

Then, from his right, a slash of gleaming metal. The tip of the sword sliced into the Frenchman's face and blood filled the air. Screaming, he dropped the pistol and spun away.

When he saw blonde hair dancing on the head of his saviour, Merriman realised it was Lieutenant Smythe. The disgraced officer now seemed a man possessed. Jaw set, knuckles white on his sword hilt he addressed the burly sailor, neatly dodging a lusty hack from the scimitar before elegantly jabbing his blade into the Frenchman's heart. A clubbing blow from Cary's pommel knocked the unfortunate defender to the deck.

Merriman watched as the silent Smythe fought on, hacking his way forward and creating space in his wake. Cary and two more marines rushed past Merriman, more redcoats with them.

Soon they were close to the main hatch, where the French had formed a solid line. Musket fire downed several attackers and then it became a bloody melee across the width of the *Hercule*. Merriman turned and rallied the men, urging them forward. He was surprised that there'd been no surrender, having seen many a defending captain give up once his fate was sealed. He had boarded the French vessel and it was clear that the battle was only going one way. This continued killing was senseless and he could have cried when he heard yet more blasts from below.

Suddenly, Cary appeared from the press. His disfigured nose leaking blood, the marine captain waved more men into the line.

'By God, will we have to seize the tricolour out of this bastard's dead hands? I saw him – standing behind them, urging his men on. We have his ship.'

'Not yet, I'm afraid.'

As they spoke, Merriman caught sight of the appalling scene behind them. The middle section of the *Hercule* was a scene more befitting a battlefield. The blood-soaked planks were covered with at least fifty fallen men, some so close that they lay on top of each other. Many were still alive and calling for help. Merriman looked across at *Thunder* and saw that a few unarmed sailors were still there. Shrigley wasn't present but one of the bosun's mates was.

'Collins! Gather those men and help these wounded. If they can be moved, get them down to Mr. Webster.'

Merriman had no doubt that the surgeon was already dealing with dozens of casualties but he had already lost enough men today; they had to do what they could for those with a fighting chance. He was greatly moved to see young Chamier eagerly join Collins' group.

'There, sir!' Cary pointed to the *Hercule*'s starboard side and the near end of the quarterdeck. Here were fewer of both sides and a clearer path to the stern.

'Please wait here a moment, captain.'

As Cary hurried aft, Merriman felt a pulse of pain and looked down. Upon his hand was a narrow cut. He had no idea how he had sustained it and wiped the blood away on his coat.

'Are you all right, sir?'

The deep Irish brogue could only have come from Furlong, who towered over Merriman, a pike in his hand.

The captain nodded just as Cary returned. With him were Harrison, a veteran sergeant named Beck and Lieutenant Smythe. Breathing hard, Smythe's blue eyes looked about him but seemed to take nothing in. His coat had been torn in three places and his neck was slick with sweat and blood.

'We take the captain or die trying,' said Cary. 'With me.'

Merriman wished to stay close to him but was overtaken by Smythe and Harrison. As they crossed the deck, then moved aft along the starboard rail, avoiding yet more dead and wounded, he at last caught sight of his nemesis. Up on the quarterdeck, Jourdan was making no attempt to hide himself. He stood tall with his hat in his hand, his other hand a fist as he roared at the men fighting ahead of him.

'I'm tempted to take up a musket,' remarked Beck.

'No,' said Merriman. This seemed an affront to honour but Jourdan had seemingly forgotten the concept in his determination to retain his vessel. Above all, Merriman just wanted this deadly clash over; and if that meant killing Jourdan himself, he was willing. But it would be with a blade.

The courageous Lieutenant Cary was of a different breed to most embroiled in the battle for the *Hercule*. With no apparent care for his own welfare, he shouted at his men to clear the way and slashed and jabbed at the defenders himself. Smythe seemed to have become another man entirely and the two of them advanced with incredible speed, aided by Furlong and Beck, who used pikes to jab at those who threatened the swordsmen. The pair cut down at least eight defenders who simply could not match their aggression and lethal skill.

But their advance ended at the quarterdeck. Here was a line of French marines fortified by resourceful sailors using boathooks as lances to keep the attackers at bay. Behind them were two more officers and then Jourdan himself, who ranged up and down the line, slapping his men on the shoulders and shouting in their ears. Merriman would have demanded that he end the slaughter if he thought he would have heard him.

The captain had seen men overtaken by a fighting zeal before but none of those experiences prepared him for what he saw next. Lieutenant Smythe sliced off the tip of a boathook aimed at his head, grabbed it with his spare hand and pulled the French defender towards him. His blade went into the big sailor's ribs and the unfortunate collapsed to the deck. Before he landed, Smythe had pulled his blade clear and launched himself at his next target.

Cary parried a strike from one of the officers and then cut him across the cheek. But this French officer – a slender fellow with a craggy face beyond his years – was his equal. With no regard for the blood pouring down his face, he aimed a perfect thrust at Cary's chest. The blade pierced the marine's skin and sent him backwards into Merriman.

Dropping his own blade momentarily, Merriman helped him to the ground.

'I'm fine,' said Cary, though he clearly wasn't.

'Let me help, sir.' A British sailor dragged Cary to the rail.

When Merriman looked up again, Smythe was entering the fray once more. He threw his sword arm like a punch, the pommel catching an officer in the face. The next man in his path was sliced across the neck and went down with both hands at his wound. Judging by his uniform, this was a senior officer and it was the sight of his demise that dragged Jourdan into the fight. Casting his hat aside, the French captain drew his blade and leaped at Smythe, spitting oaths.

The two drew back their arms and swung simultaneously. The blades clashed and sparks illuminated the air. Still apparently in the grip of a bloodlust, Smythe aimed a kick at the captain who evaded it neatly and centred his blade. Before Smythe could compose himself and strike again, the elegant Jourdan darted forward and stuck the blade into his chest. The lieutenant flailed uselessly at Jourdan with his spare hand then watched as the bloodied blade was retracted. Wheezing, head bowed, he dropped his sword.

Enraged by this, Merriman tried to advance but was blocked by Furlong and Beck. The French captain never saw the pike that skewered him under the armpit. When the big Irishman withdrew the weapon, Jourdan fell to his knees, gouts of blood already flowing onto the deck beneath him. The French officers nearby looked on, aghast, as their captain fell. Jourdan slumped back against the legs of a nearby sailor. He raised his hand. 'Bats-toi!'

So he wanted them to fight on. Exhausted and desperate to aid Smythe, Merriman locked eyes with another officer of his age. 'Monsieur, s'il vous plaît, arrêtez ça! Arrêtez, s'il vous plaît!

The officer looked down, watching as Jourdan fell back, clearly dead or close to it. As other officers went to the captain, this man gave a simple nod. He dropped his sword and raised both hands.

'Arrêt! Le capitaine est mort.'

The Frenchman waited and watched. First, those closest to him ceased fighting and then word spread. In less than a minute, not a single clash continued.

The officer shouldered his way through the French and the British, reversed his sword and offered it to Merriman. 'Surrender. We surrender.'

'Thank you. I accept.'

The officer continued issuing orders in French and his men laid down their arms.

'Men, keep your weapons but lower them,' shouted Merriman. 'The battle is over. Help the injured. If they can move, take them back to the *Thunder*.'

'Not sure we can, sir,' said Sergeant Beck, who was looking at their ship. A thick tower of black smoke was rising from the starboard side. *Thunder* was on fire.

Chapter Twenty-Four

Aftermath

'Clear the way there!'

Getting down to the site of the blaze was his first challenge. Merriman was loathe to leave the febrile situation aboard the *Hercule* but the French officers – one of whom spoke good English – assured him that their men would put up no further resistance. They were in fact more concerned by Captain Jourdan, who was surely breathing his last.

Thunder's lower decks and passageways were crowded with wounded men. Any that could move Shrigley ordered to go up on deck. He and Merriman clambered down to the orlop deck and found thick black smoke issuing from below, the acrid smell of pitch everywhere. A familiar face emerged as they approached the spirit room. Bosun Brockle had a handkerchief over his mouth but spluttered before speaking.

'A ball came through and set light to some of the alcohol. Flames have taken hold and spread to the side. We've got the fire out this side but it's burned right through. Sorry, sir, we were all too occupied to realise how bad-'

'No matter, Brockle. We'll deal with it from outside.'

'I hope we can, sir.'

Now coughing badly themselves, the two officers made their way back up on deck. The line of injured waiting to be seen by Mr. Webster and his assistants stretched all the way to the stern. Shrigley had already alerted the captain to two other points on the hull where *Thunder* had been holed below the waterline. He had despatched Adkins to inspect them but for now the fire was the priority. Reaching the starboard rail, they looked down and saw orange flames below billowing smoke. The blackened hull was depositing burning timbers into the water, causing it to boil and fizz.

Master Henderson was busily setting up a line of pails but Merriman could see that they might not be able to extinguish the fire in this manner.

'Alfred, find me a dozen men!'

'Aye aye, sir.'

Merriman ran to the stern and collared the youngest of the midshipmen, who was standing alone, face ashen.

'Chamier, help me pull in the boats.'

A nearby trio of sailors came to assist and soon they had the boats at the starboard quarter. The men climbed down and moved the animals into the launch so that the smaller boat was clear.

'Henderson – give each man a pail.'

Once this was done, Merriman ordered them to put out a net so that those Shrigley rounded up could climb down into the boat. Once eight men were down, he instructed them to fill their pails with seawater and address the fire.

'Tom, you're in charge here.'

'Sir.'

Merriman cast a look across at the *Hercule* and was relieved to see that the ceasefire had held. On more than one occasion, he had seen individuals unable to stop themselves; battling on after a surrender had been agreed. Even so, he needed to return to the French ship as swiftly as possible.

It was then that a rather bedraggled looking Lieutenant Jones appeared.

'Jones!' Merriman felt simultaneously ashamed that he had forgotten him and elated to see him alive.

'Are you all right?'

'Fine, thank you, sir. Banged my head on the way down but that cold water kept me awake. I swam around to the nets and climbed up. Feeling a bit dizzy though.'

'Find a seat somewhere and rest.'

'Yes, sir.'

Adkins arrived with a report from the bow. 'Captain, it's not a large hole but two feet below the water. Pouring in. I've only got a few men, sir.'

'And the other hole is on the beam, correct?'

'Yes, sir,' said Shrigley. 'I'll get more men for the bow and we'll get these holes patched.'

'Good.'

'Sir, we have other problems. The bowsprit has gone and the foremast was hit twice. I don't think it will even bear the weight of sails.'

'Understood. You stay here – make sure that fire's put out.'

'Yes, captain. Are you heading back to the *Hercule*? Would you like this?'

Shrigley collected Merriman's hat from the binnacle and handed it to him. The two ships had now been lashed together and so Merriman could simply step across onto the French vessel. Once his hat was on, he buttoned his coat and wiped off several bloodstains.

As he strode towards the quarterdeck, he passed innumerable fallen French sailors. Dozens were covered with hammocks. These did not cover the whole of their bodies and Merriman saw that many were disfigured with awful wounds caused by blades and shrapnel from the grenades.

Those of his men that could be moved were now back on the *Thunder*. Several who were unlikely to last very long were on the foredeck of the *Hercule* and he intended to go and see them presently.

As he picked his way through the French wounded and those assisting them, he did not lock eyes with the men. It wasn't that he feared their anger; it was the shame of being responsible for injury and death. War or no war, it was he who had ordered and led the attack. At least he was the victor.

When he reached the knot of officers gathered around Jourdan, the grey-haired lieutenant was gently placing a coat over the captain.

Merriman removed his hat. One of the officers turned to him and unleashed a vitriolic assault in his own language. The grey-haired man grabbed him by his collar and dragged him away. Another, younger officer addressed Merriman.

'Capitaine, *Hercule* is yours. Shall we lower our colours?'

'We need not do that now. Let us both first deal with our injured and proceed from there. Your name, sir?'

'Barbier, Second Lieutenant. It will be Cape Colony, I suppose?'

'Probably. I will send a crew over to collect your arms and disable your long guns. I'm sure you understand?'

'Of course.'

Merriman looked towards the hatch. 'You have a surgeon?'

'Two. And we need them.'

Barbier was paler than most of the Frenchmen Merriman had met. His wavy hair was a light brown and he had freckles upon his cheeks. He let out a long breath and gazed towards the coast.

'It is strange, no? For we French and British to fight to the death so far from home.'

'There is nothing so strange as war, lieutenant.'

Barbier looked down at Jourdan's body. 'The capitaine was the best I have served with.'

'A fine commander,' said Merriman. 'I just wished he had surrendered sooner. More men would have lived.'

'The capitaine hated you British more than any man I have met.'

'Is it true that he lost three brothers in war?'

His expression grim, Barbier nodded.

'Then I cannot entirely blame him for hating us.'

Barbier shook his head resignedly and rubbed his eyes. 'It was a bold manoeuvre and a fine assault, capitaine. Your marines made the difference. And who was this man? He fought like a lion.'

Barbier gestured to his right and the dead officer lying on his side, blonde hair obscuring his eyes.

'His name was Smythe.'

Seeing the fallen lieutenant prompted Merriman to have all the remaining British dead taken back to *Thunder*. He found himself carrying Smythe along with Eades and Chamier, who admitted he was desperate to see the French ship. Once they had crossed onto *Thunder*'s foredeck, they laid Smythe down. Merriman pushed his hair from his eyes and carefully closed them. Chamier turned away and was soon sobbing. Eades put a hand on his friend's shoulder and spoke to the captain.

'It was so strange, sir. When the marines boarded, he came up on deck and just stood there, watching. Lieutenant Shrigley shouted at him that we needed every sword. He said nothing but drew his blade and crossed to join the assault. I heard that he fought well.'

'With exceptional courage.'

'His nerve must have returned, sir. When we needed him, he fought with us.'

'Yes. And the record will show it.'

Just then, one of the topmen approached. 'Excuse me, cap'n, have you seen Friar?'

'No. Why? Don't tell me he joined the assault.'

'We don't think so, sir, but we can't find a trace of him.'

'Keep looking.'

Realising he had neglected to visit the injured still on the *Hercule*, Merriman returned there alone. Most were far beyond help but he spoke to all those still conscious.

'Hold fast, sailor. You did well. You're with friends. Rest easy.'

These were words he'd said many times to dying men. He felt it was a captain's obligation to make their last moments better if he could. One of them was Trevelyan, the tight-lipped messmate of Muir. He was lying against a piled-up sail, his waist and groin wrapped with blood-soaked bandages. His face was so pale that it was almost blue. He gripped the captain's hand when it was offered.

'Sorry, sir. About-'

'Forget that, sailor. Save your strength. I'll have some strong wine sent across. Lay back.'

The sailor's whole body shuddered with pain and he emitted an awful groan.

'I'll stay with him, sir,' said a nearby sailor.

As he returned to the *Thunder*, Merriman passed Sergeant Washington of the marines. Washington was accompanied by a dozen redcoats and had been tasked with collecting the weaponry.

'Captain, you heard about Lieutenant Harrison?'

'No.'

'A slash to the neck. He's gone.'

'By God. I thought he'd made it through. Where is Cary?'

'Down with the surgeon, I believe, being stitched up. Mr. Webster said he was lucky – blade didn't go in far.'

'Good. And your casualties in total?'

'Twenty-three dead, sir. Thirteen seriously injured and a few walking wounded.'

'That many?' Merriman turned to the gathered marines. 'Well done to every last one of you. Washington, please stay calm on there. They have lost as many as we have or more. Deal only with Lieutenant Barbier – he speaks good English and is a cooperative fellow.'

'Yes, sir. And what of their treasure?'

'Neither vessel is going anywhere for now. We shall appraise that later.'

'Aye aye, captain.'

Once at the stern, Merriman was relieved to hear that the fire was out. Bosun Brockle was now down in what remained of the spirit room, surveying the damage. Eades reported that crews were working on the other damaged sections. Encountering a group of men sitting at the quarterdeck, Merriman yelled at them, ordering one to collect the medicinal wine for the mortally wounded. The others he assigned to the crews pulling the broken bowsprit aboard and those assessing the damage to the foremast.

He was about to head below when Lieutenant Cary came up. Wincing with every step, the marine wore his red coat over bare skin and his entire midriff was bandaged.

'Should you be on your feet?'

'I'm all right, sir.'

'I told Washington to act with restraint but collecting the weapons might be a flashpoint. Perhaps if you supervise.'

'Of course. I'll round up anyone who can hold a musket. Show of strength and all that.'

'Sorry about Harrison. He did very well.'

Emotion flashed across the marine's face and he gritted his teeth, dispelling it in an instant.

'Fine man. Damned fine man.' Cary glanced over at the *Hercule*. 'Smythe...by Christ I wouldn't believe it if I hadn't seen it with my own eyes. Sir, you should get that seen to.'

Merriman had just raised his hand to look at the wound. It ran from the middle knuckle to his wrist. It was not too deep but was still bleeding and evidently in need of stitching.

'I suppose I should'

As Cary departed for the *Hercule*, Merriman took himself below and into the great cabin. Given the damage elsewhere, it had fared reasonably well, though a ball – a twenty-eight pounder by the look of it – had torn through both side walls. A couple of the windows were smashed but most were intact. Peters was there, brushing up debris.

'There you are, sir. What a relief to see you well. Hell of a battle by the sounds of it.'

'It was at that, Peters. A stiff drink, if you please, and then you can stitch me up – I don't want to bother Mr. Webster.'

Merriman slumped down in a chair. On the desk close by was his pocket watch. To his amazement, he found that it was not yet midday. He felt as if he'd lived at least seven days since dawn. He closed his eyes and saw images he knew he'd never forget; Cary and Smythe leading the charge, Captain Jourdan driving his men on, Jones falling from the ladder, Smythe's lifeless body among the French dead. Merriman opened his eyes as Peters handed him a generous tot of rum.

The attendant was also holding a little tin containing a medical kit. He knelt in front of Merriman and first cleaned out the wound. Merriman was embarrassed to see that both his hands were shaking.

'Sorry, Peters.'

'Not at all, sir. If I had taken part in that assault, I would be a gibbering wreck. Has it occurred to you that you might be getting a little old for sword work?'

'There's no doubt about that but the men need to see me with them.'

'And what if we'd lost you, sir? Where would we be then?'

'Just stitch, man.'

Peters lacked the skill of a physician but did the job swiftly enough. A part of Merriman wanted to drink another tot and stay in the great cabin but he knew there was another man aboard who would need his support.

He was relieved to see a little more order in the passageways, though there was still a line of men waiting to see Mr. Webster. The surgeon was now carrying out his work in the cockpit, where there was better light. The men bore their pain with great courage and Merriman stopped for a quick word with those most badly hurt.

He also encountered Hickey, who seemed to be treating himself. Sitting with a lantern between his legs, breeches pulled down to his knees, the midshipmen was removing the splinters embedded in his thighs. None seemed too large and he was boldly pulling them out with a pair of pliers. Hickey was so intently focused on his work that he didn't notice his captain and Merriman elected to leave him to it.

When he at last reached the physician, Webster was leaning over a man's leg. Below the tourniquet was a huge spike of wood, which the Welshman was having difficulty in removing.

Merriman did not wish to interrupt him but eventually one of Webster's assistants cleared his throat and nodded towards the captain. Webster turned. Across his chin was a bloody smear and his eyes were those of a man who longed to be somewhere else entirely.

'Sorry to disturb you, John. Is there anything you need?'

'Another pair of skilled hands but I daresay the French surgeon is occupied with his own men.'

'I suppose so. Thank you for all you are doing. I know every man here appreciates it.'

With a hesitant nod, the Welshman turned back to his patient and picked up a slender scalpel.

Up on deck, Lieutenant Cary was standing at the larboard rail, talking to Sergeant Washington and the French officer, Barbier. Cary turned as Merriman approached.

'Captain, there are a huge number of muskets and bladed weapons. As we are taking charge of the ship, might it be easier to store them in the armoury? Lieutenant Barbier here has the key.'

'We've already had a look, sir,' said Sergeant Washington with a grin. 'They've got two full sacks of silver and gold coins and some other booty. And she's a fine, fine ship. What a price she'll fetch.'

'Use the armoury then,' said Merriman. 'Are they cooperating?'

'By and large, sir,' said Cary. 'One voluble fellow didn't like being told where to go but the lieutenant here has been most helpful in keeping tempers down. Those not assigned to the wounded and dead we have gathered on the upper gun deck. They've all been checked for weapons.'

Barbier spoke up: 'Capitaine, I intend to carry out a brief service for the dead. The bodies must be disposed of before the weather strikes.'

Merriman could not recall the last time he had looked beyond the two ships.

Barbier nodded to the north. The distant sky was blanketed by dark grey cloud.

Chapter Twenty-Five

The Relentless Sea

This longest of days seemed without end. By three o'clock, the tethered ships were in a rolling sea, clashing noisily together, despite half a dozen lashings with three-inch rope. The only remaining blue sky was far to the south and a light rain had begun to fall. An even more ominous sign were the flights of seabirds flapping to the south or towards the coast. Poor Mr. Webster was forced to place his patients on the floor of the cockpit and his terrible work was made even harder. On both vessels, the dead had been placed in their hammocks and lined up on deck.

There was one piece of good news: the hole at the bow had been successfully sealed. But the hole at the beam and the section damaged by fire had not been repaired when the bad weather arrived. Water continued to slosh in and the overall depth within the ship's bilges had surpassed five feet.

Merriman was now crouched at the top of a stairway, looking down at Bosun Brockle, who was leading a crew of two dozen, desperately trying to fix sheets and pegs across the ragged gap left by the fire. It was at least six feet wide, the bottom just above the waterline. The lateral movement of the ship made their work virtually impossible as they laboured amidst many floating kegs. It was so dark that they had four men holding lanterns and another three mounted on hooks. Merriman didn't need the bosun to tell him that the water was rising; it had gone up several inches in the few minutes he'd been there. He'd come from the starboard side, where Henderson was having a similar problem, though the ingress of water wasn't so extreme. The bilge pumps were all fully manned but they could not keep pace.

'Keep me advised, Bosun.'

'Aye, captain.'

Though Brockle hadn't said so, Merriman could tell from his tone that he shared his view; if this weather persisted and they could not seal the hole, *Thunder* would struggle to survive.

With the fate of the ship in the balance, there were certain matters that had to be attended to. The main issue was the dead. Excepting those upon the *Hercule*, the work crews and the seriously injured, the remainder of the ship's complement hastily gathered on deck. Merriman completed the usual formalities and – even in these dire circumstances – read out the names of every fallen sailor and marine. In total, this amounted to sixty-one souls. There was no time for the usual ceremony, the bodies had to be simply cast over the side, while the crew looked on in silence.

They stood in the increasingly heavy rain, hands clasped, heads bowed. Merriman glanced over at the *Hercule* momentarily and saw several officers looking on through the gloom. Cary had earlier informed him that the French ship had lost no less than one hundred and four souls.

Despite his injury, the marine captain insisted on helping to bear his fallen second-in-command and commending him to the deep. The midshipmen took it upon themselves to bear Lieutenant Smythe.

When it was done, Merriman turned away and was met by the sight of a short youth staring at him from beneath a hooded cloak.

'Friar!'

'Hello, captain,' said the young topman.

'You're alive.'

'Suppose I am.'

He was accompanied by another, older topman who offered an explanation: 'I sent the lad down to fetch a spike, sir. When we struck the *Hercule* he was thrown into a wall and banged his head. Only woke up an hour ago. Quite a lump on his noggin but I we reckon he'll be all right.'

Friar, however, looked rather depressed and gazed longingly at the French vessel. 'I can't believe I missed all the action, sir.'

'I for one am glad you did.'

With an affectionate touch on the lad's head, Merriman returned aft. Down in the cockpit, Webster was still labouring under an awning hastily arranged by two carpenter's mates.

'Captain Merriman, sir!'

This came from Sergeant Washington, who was standing at the larboard rail. Two more marines were with him and – opposite them on the *Hercule* – were Lieutenant Barbier and another French officer. The rolling of the ships was now even more pronounced and Merriman almost slid on the slick deck as he neared them.

'Capitaine, we cannot remain together with the weather getting worse like this. It is dangerous for both vessels. Also, can I have permission to feed the men before darkness falls? Many are weary and-'

'No, lieutenant,' said Merriman, angry that his former opponent was trying to force him into decisions.

'Stand by – I will let you know on both counts.'

With a tight-lipped nod, Barbier withdrew.

'I think it's about time we exchanged our colours for theirs, sergeant,' said Merriman, 'please see to it.'

Cary – being assisted by Adkins and Chamier – arrived in time to hear this.

'Lieutenant, I want every last marine on duty. Adkins, speak to Stones and have fifty more men sent across. If we have to separate the ships, some aboard might see it as an opportunity to take advantage.'

'Don't worry, sir,' said Washington. 'We've got them all contained on the gun decks and all the cannons have been rendered inoperable.'

'I know, sergeant, but we cannot be too careful.'

As Washington and Cary departed, Merriman took himself up to the bow. Due to the weather and the many other demands upon the crew, repairs to the bowsprit and foremast had been abandoned. Three lengths of shattered wood lay across the deck, now rolling around from side to side. Merriman didn't have the energy to do anything about them. He shielded his eyes from the rain and looked over the bow to the north. Though there were at least two hours of light left, it felt like evening.

He trudged aft, until he reached the busy cockpit. He encountered Shrigley and Jones and the three officers headed down to the orlop once more. Henderson reported eight feet of water in the well and they found Brockle now ordering his men out of the spirit room. The bosun was last to leave, the water at his chest until he hauled himself up the ladder. He looked up at the officers and simply shook his head.

Around them, exhausted, drenched men lined the passageway.

'Excellent effort,' said Shrigley as the officers departed. None of them said anything more until Merriman led them to the great cabin.

'By god, Jones, you're still shaking.' He poured a tot of rum from the bottle and handed it to his second lieutenant.

As Jones drank, Merriman drew in a long breath before speaking. 'With hours of daylight and a calm sea, we might have had a chance. I cannot see the weather improving and in truth we should have already cast off from the *Hercule*. Do you see any other alternative?'

'I do not, sir,' said Shrigley, his eyes cast downward.

'I'm afraid not, captain,' added Jones.

Merriman was still holding the bottle of rum. He turned and threw it against the wall.

He debated not allowing the men back to their quarters because it would add time they didn't have. But Shrigley swiftly established a good system: the lieutenants would send the men in groups to fetch their belongings (only what could be carried in a wrapped-up hammock; no chests were allowed for the crew) and then report on deck.

While awaiting the first of them, Merriman crossed to the rail and called Barbier and the other French officers over to inform them that he was abandoning his ship. They did not seem overly surprised; *Thunder* was now listing badly to starboard. The lines holding the ships together were under great strain and Merriman was no longer sure that the *Thunder* would last until nightfall. The very thought seemed unfathomable but he had lost ships before; his main concern now was getting his men aboard the *Hercule*. One small mercy was the weather, which had at least not worsened: the rain was now no more than a drizzle.

Merriman asked Barbier to go down and select enough sailors to begin preparing the *Hercule*'s mainsails. Though there had been no time to carry out any repairs to the French ship, the officer seemed sure that she would make way, despite the enormous load. Merriman intended to supplement this group with his own men, who would soon have to sail this ship. Before the lieutenant departed, he introduced another officer named Montcalme, the grey-haired fellow who had halted the fighting after Jourdan's demise. His English was not as good as the younger man but he put himself at Merriman's disposal.

'Monsieur, we have to find a way of fitting all my men aboard. Is it possible to place all of your crew on the main deck?'

'We may have to use some of the hold but yes, I think so.'

'Your injured?'

'In the sick bay and cockpit.'

'May we use the wardroom and the great cabin for ours?'

'You don't have to *ask* me, capitaine.' Montcalme pointed to the ensign that now flew at the stern of the vessel.

'I prefer to.'

'This is an odd situation for us all,' said the Frenchman.

'It is at that. Once we are underway, I will ensure that everyone is fed and watered.'

Merriman returned to the *Thunder* and found that the first of the sailors were ready to depart. Also present was Lieutenant Essex, who'd taken charge of assembling crucial supplies. He now directed the men to take some of this cargo – and their hammocks – across to the *Hercule*.

One of Mr. Webster's orderlies was also present, supervising a crew bringing up those injured sailors that could be moved.

'Captain, Mr. Webster asked to see you. There are two men we can do nothing for.'

'Understood.'

Merriman climbed down into the cockpit. Webster was hunched over beneath a lantern, concluding an amputation. His poor patient emitted agonised grunts, a wooden rod clamped between his teeth. Webster was engaged in a very delicate procedure: tying off the severed arteries in the exposed stump with silk. Once this was done, he left another orderly to finish off and put a hand to his brow, clearly exhausted.

'Mr. Webster, I'm told there are two men we cannot move.'

With a nod, the surgeon led Merriman to the rear of the cockpit where the two men lay, both covered with blankets. 'Thankfully, Ryde is unconscious. Middleton is in and out. Ah.'

The second sailor raised his hand and tried to speak but he could produce no sound. Webster took his hand and reached for a nearby flask. Merriman raised Middleton's head while Webster administered the wine, its strength made evident by its odour.

'They both have several open wounds. Difficult procedures – an hour or more. I do not have time, correct?'

'I'm sorry. You're *certain* they cannot be moved?'

'Not without killing them. The ship *will* founder?'

'Yes.'

'I have enough laudanum left. They are already weak.'

'If you think that's for the best.'

Webster nodded again. He had not yet looked Merriman in the eye.

'How long to port? We are headed for land, aren't we?'

'We are. As soon as possible.'

'I'm glad it's dark now,' said Webster, looking up into the rain and gloom. 'I want this day to end.'

By the time he reached the great cabin, *Thunder* was listing at an angle of at least twenty degrees. Merriman had delayed going there until all the injured had been taken on deck. Two of the lines holding the ships together had already frayed and new ones tied. But the *Hercule* was now being dragged upward.

Peters had already placed most of his valuables and clothing in two sea chests. The attendant currently had Merriman's two other swords hanging from his shoulders.

'I took only the *best* wine, sir.'

Merriman nodded. 'Got all the charts?'

'Sir.'

As he stared at the wine cooler Helen had brought him, the heavy desk slid across the floor and crashed into the starboard wall. Outside, the water was alarmingly close.

'Peters, I seem to have lost my hat. Do you have the spare?'

The attendant nipped into the sleeping quarters and returned with it.

'Thank you.'

'One chest had already gone up, sir. Just this one now.'

'And your gear?'

'Up on deck, sir.'

'Come then.'

With Merriman at one end and Peters at the other, they hauled the heavy chest out into the cockpit. Only the officers and a few others remained. Mr. Webster had left. The laudanum had been administered and thankfully both Ryde and Middleton were unconscious.

A big marine helped Peters with the chest and Merriman came up behind them. He was relieved to see that almost all the dunnage had been transferred onto the *Hercule*. The injured were now being carried below.

Moments later, Shrigley, Jones and Essex arrived, having searched the ship for stragglers.

'That's it, sir,' said Jones. 'No one left below.'

'Water's at the lower gundeck to starboard,' added Shrigley. 'Won't be long now.'

'All right then, gentlemen, it's time.' Hand on the larboard rail to steady him, Merriman watched his officers leave. He knelt down for a moment and laid his hand on the rain-soaked timbers of the deck.

Sorry, old girl. I failed you.

With the ship groaning beneath him, he put on his hat then used a stay to climb up onto the rail. Shrigley helped him across and they joined the other officers close to the wheel.

Using hatchets earlier employed in the battle, Brockle and Henderson cut the lines holding the ships together. This was a job for experienced men and they stayed well clear when the last lines were torn apart by the sheer weight. *Thunder* sank down to starboard and every available hand used long oars and boathooks to push the ships apart.

While Barbier and his crewmen readied the sails, Merriman and his officers gathered on the quarterdeck. He saw that the ensign was already flying but this did not feel like his ship. His ship was lost and the sheer waste of material, weaponry and treasure caused him to clench his fists so hard that his nails bit into his flesh.

Thunder's weakened foremast gave way with a sharp snap before crashing into the water. The list became ever more pronounced until the main and mizzen lay at forty-five degrees.

'Capitaine, shall we set the sails?' asked Barbier.

Merriman nodded. 'Bosun, you shall take the helm.'

'Aye aye, sir.'

At Barbier's order, a French sailor made way and Brockle gripped the wheel.

As the sails fell and the lines were brought in, the bosun turned the *Hercule* away from the wind. At first it seemed that the heavily-laden vessel would not make way. But the sails filled, lines were made off and the French warship began to pick up speed.

Merriman's last sight of *Thunder* was of the mainmast tipping into the sea. He and his officers remained at the stern in silence, Shrigley occasionally peering back into the gloom with his spyglass. After several minutes, he spoke:

'That's it. She's gone.'

It was Jones that broke the ensuing silence. 'At least our merchantmen will be safer now, sir. We did fulfil our mission.'

'You'll forgive me, lieutenant, if I cannot summon much pride in that at the moment. I have lost a ship of the line. We all know the consequences.'

Shrigley spoke up. 'Sir, the Admiralty may well take into account your -'

'No, Alfred,' said Merriman. 'There will be a court martial. And it is no more than I deserve.'

THE END

HMS *Thunder*

There have been several ships names HMS *Thunder* that belonged to The Royal Navy. Most were bomb ships designed for shore bombardment and coastal attacks.

They were typically armed with mortars located amidships that fired large explosive shells or bombs with a high arcing trajectory onto land targets. For self-defence they also had a few laterally mounted cannon.

As is common when a ship is lost, sold, or broken up; the name is re-used. This happened from the late 17th century with the earliest wooden hulled ships until the mid-19th century with an ironclad floating battery and even later with a minesweeper with the Royal Canadian Navy.

What we do not have are records that show a fully rigged, third-rate ship of the line named HMS *Thunder*.

There were, however, HMS *Thunderer* and HMS *Hercules*, both 74-gun, third rate ships of the line. A model thought to be of either ship sits in the National Maritime Museum in Greenwich.

These are the closest match in name and description, and, most likely the inspiration for our Captain Merriman's ship HMS *Thunder* as depicted by Roger Burnage in Book Seven 'The Threat in the Adriatic'.

This graphic illustration on the following page is by Marine Artist Colin M Baxter. It was commissioned for this book to help readers (and the author) understand the sails and rigging a bit easier. If you look closely, you can also see captain Merriman and officers standing on the quarterdeck.

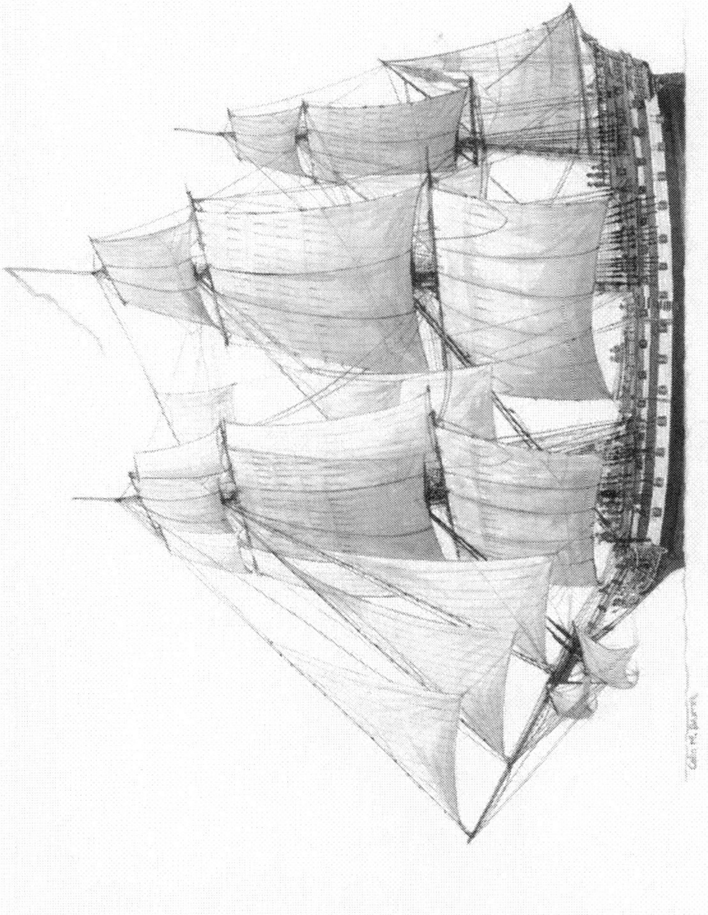

Author Biography

Robin Burnage

Robin Burnage is a first-time author taking on the challenge of continuing his late father's series "The Merriman Chronicles". His debut novel "The Threat In The Atlantic" picks up the story of Captain James Merriman on his return from his mission in the Adriatic in 1810.

Previously a property professional (for which he does actually have recognised qualifications), sailing and travelling always had a greater pull than accounting and spreadsheets.

He sold his business in 2012, bought a yacht and headed off on a five-year adventure as a full time liveaboard sailor. He also then travelled through Europe in an old Land Rover and then a motorhome before settling back in bricks and mortar.

He currently lives in Wales overlooking sand dunes and the Irish Sea. As always, he is dreaming of his next adventure.

More information about The Merriman Chronicles is available online.

Follow the Author on Amazon

Get notified when a new book is released!

Desktop, Mobile & Tablet:

Search for the author, click the author's name on any of the book pages to jump to the Amazon author page, click the follow button at the bottom.

Kindle eReader and Kindle Apps:

The follow button is normally after the last page of the book.

Please consider leaving a review or rating.

It really does help.

For more background information, book details and announcements of upcoming novels, check the website at:

www.merriman-chronicles.com

You can also follow us on social media:-

https://twitter.com/Merriman1792

https://www.facebook.com/MerrimanChronicles

Printed by Amazon Italia Logistica S.r.l.
Torrazza Piemonte (TO), Italy